THE
Monster
MONROE

RICHARD PIRES

Pires Farm Media

Pires Farm Media

ISBN: 978-0-578-13292-1

Library of Congress Control Number: 2013920512

PRINTED IN THE UNITED STATES OF AMERICA

Prologue

The romantics like to say war erupts overnight. They always like to say the world was asleep and awoke when evil began its reign. It's never really like that. It just happens and when the dust settles and the bodies are collected, the cry goes out and most will answer if, for anything, revenge. It's what I did in the winter of 1941. When the Japs bombed Pearl Harbor there was no other choice for me and no more choice for this country. We couldn't hide behind the isolationist diatribe anymore. Poland came and went, we didn't care. But this time it was our bloodshed. The fire came for us. Our time came to strike. It would take men to answer the call. To fight. To die. Raise a salute to duty and honor. Enlist to fight for your country. I answered the call.

That's when the nightmares started.

I dreamed about the world I knew. A child's view of the reality of it. No one really remembers that time. It gets lost in the shuffle of adulthood. A momentary lapse that slips into decades, then death. Nothing about it makes you feel better, pining for the past that is half remembered. Trying to piece events together with a blindfold on. You drop to its call, even if you don't want to. Rapture of a different nature. No God, but an event equally spiritual. The past can come into you without hesitation, locking the good sense you develop through years of trial and error into the back of your psyche. What you have left are the memories of events best left alone. Yet they always find you. They always haunt. It keeps you from letting go. It keeps you from moving forward. But sometimes these memories we hold back keep secrets, keep promises, keep truth. A promise is the worst to forget. A promise is what I forgot.

The nightmare was always the same: bloody hands slipping through mine. A deformed man crying over me as I lay on a sofa, beaten. Tears hitting my face from above. No clear vocals, no sounds. Just a beating heart, mine I think. Never sure though. For years, I dismissed it. It couldn't have been a memory because I would have remembered an event like that. The vision was so clear, yet lost in the haze of wake. Nothing would bring the image back once my eyes were open and I would forget within minutes of morning sun regardless. Then, I heard a name in the darkness.

Monroe.

The name on my lips as he walked away as the makeshift bandage around my head seeped with blood. The one they called the monster. His face mangled and world lost to the trenches of Wilson's War. I remember the promise. To tell his story so he could live. But I didn't have it. A promise lost in memory recalled in a dream, which floated away when I awoke. How could I have forgotten? He walked away from me in subconscious recollection only to dissipate in reality. But this time, as if there was reason, his name became clear. It became real, not a fantasy in the fog of dreamscapes. The promise returns as the child I was slips in and out of consciousness. A promise I can't remember, yet know I agreed to. A promise to a man ready to die; unable to deliver his story to the one person who needed to hear it.

Monroe.

An image flooded my head: red string wrapped around yellowed pages. Typed words on cheap paper. A work left to his daughter. Monroe's daughter, a woman I never met nor knew. Finding her is another issue I didn't except to have. The promise keeps me shackled to Monroe. I must find the words he wrote. I must deliver them to her. Home was the only place they could be, at least, I prayed it to be so.

My mother jumped at the chance to let me in the house. She was buzzing with a sense of duty, broom in hand, other around a glass of water for me. Never one to sit down and rest, she rushed to embrace me with both items firmly placed in her grip. The lines in her face seemed to disappear as she smiled. I felt like I was thirteen all over again even if the house was not where I grew up. Time slips so fast when you don't pay attention. All the small moments flooded me in my memory. I almost teared up as my mother held me.

"It's about time you come home."

I held her tight; the enlistment papers in my pocket weighed me down. I couldn't tell her what I had done. It was not the time for that.

"Are you hungry? I have some leftover roast in the icebox." My mother never waited for an answer; she was already preparing me a plate with about three pounds of beef layered with gravy that was heating up on the stove. "Bread?"

"No, thanks, Mom. I was down to look for something. An old stack of papers."

"I don't know, Steven. I threw away most of your things when you went to college."

"Everything?"

"I put anything that looked important in a trunk. It's in the attic, I think."

"You think?"

"I told your dad to put it up there. He may have thrown it out as to get out of lugging it up the stairs. It was heavy, and you know how his back is."

This was all I needed. A man's attempt at connecting with the daughter he never saw grow up lost due to an aging man's battle with arthritis. My mother stared at me with a mouthful of roast beef.

"I am sure it's up there. Look." She lifted the plate of roast beef under my nose. "Come on, eat."

I had no choice but to eat after that last-ditch effort. My duty was being tested, but no duty is more important than to please one's mother. And so I sat, my eyes looking above to the attic as I cut my roast beef and chewed. My mother couldn't have been happier. It was pretty good.

When I was a child, attics were frightening places. Nightmares of ghouls and ghosts kept me up at nights when noises cracked from them. Usually it was a rat or the house settling. But now I was faced with another nightmare: doubt. It had to be here. I could not get to the beginning of this tale without his words to guide me. To help me remember what happened when I was young. Everything was in order, surprisingly. My mother seemed to take her knack of cleaning to the next level. Crates were stacked along the eaves in proper order with labels etched on the side detailing the contents. I never saw college libraries inventories this nice. I got over the ridiculously clean attic to discover the trunk.

I hesitated to open it, afraid of the memories hiding inside. I didn't remember most of my youth. I blocked it. I remember the stories created by kids about Monroe. He was a shut-in, a local urban legend. Kids used to dare each other to knock on his door or throw a rock in his window to see if he would run out into daylight. Later these stories would become more sinister. The monster who killed Reverend Thomas and his wife in the night. The monster who kidnapped Sammy and took his eyes out of his head. The monster who ate the souls of children lost in the woods. So many names given. Many of them lost to time, like the victims of any horror. No one remembers the names or what was taken. They can only remember the one who did it.

Oh my God. I forgot Billy. My friend who never saw his fourteenth birthday. My friend I forgot in the subsequent years of growing up. I should never have forgotten him, yet I did. I never wanted to. It just happened. His face returned to me in that moment, bringing tears to my eyes. My past came alive just by opening this trunk. How does an inanimate object animate the ghosts of the past? How was I able to finally grasp the lost days of childhood which were not so long ago? If I went deeper would it hurt me more? Was I a fool for taking this burden for a man long dead? I didn't know any answers to these rhetorical questions. It just helped to ask the air around me. Of course it would not answer, but maybe if I had an ear out, there would be a murmur. But in the silence only one name seemed to ring out.

Monroe.

The deformed creature who lived at the end of the street in the biggest home in town. Long burnt down from the mob who came looking for him. They called him the Monster because it was fitting to his appearance. But he was not a monster. He was alone. Allowing him to be a perfect scapegoat for true evil. An evil that almost killed me. An evil that most forgot existed. I was guilty of it too. Memory is what we choose it to be. I can remember the smell of summer but not the heat. I can recall the taste of the first girl I ever kissed but not if she was pretty. I remember the blood in my mouth but not who gave it to me. We bury the past because we dare not look at it. Too many painful moments to bear, too many mistakes to accept. I know why Monroe wrote the memoir—so he could remember it with all its scars. And there it stood on the bottom of the trunk: a stack of yellow pages held together with red string from Walter Mitty's general store.

Chill tremors erupted over my body as I brought it up to the light. The ink still black as ever, the pages numbered in the corner with Monroe's awkward handwriting. A slight creak of wood erupted over the stillness from the winter breeze. My fantasies of ghouls and ghosts flashed before me, but this time they belonged to the past. The summer of 1928, when I was thirteen. The summer I forgot, until now.

I untied the string and found the first page, typed to Monroe's daughter:

For my daughter, these words are for you and no other. I have been forced into the darkness of the home you took your first steps in. I walk over them again and again to be able to re-live that moment. It makes me cry to remember but I need to do it. I have never been able to see your face fully. It only exists in fragments—moments of happiness brought on by a goofy face or watching you sleeping quietly in your crib. I write this for you to know me because Mother would tell you I died in the war. From a certain point of view, she was right. In reading my words don't feel animosity toward your mother or me. Time has allowed me to reflect, forcing me to write my life out objectively. So ignore the crossed-out phrases of subjectivity. It's just the ramblings of a drunk; the sober reflections hurt worse. I need to tell you about my life or as much of it as I can remember, simply due to the old axiom: A man's legacy is through his children. A small piece of immortality that makes living worth the damned effort. So in my vain attempts at trying to reconnect with you I give you these memoirs in order to be with you once more. Hopefully this is not a posthumous gift, only a grace period. I hope I can see your face again, and I hope your green eyes are as brilliant as I remember them. I am left with the constant hope of

waiting for you to return a glance in my direction
and smile. I love you, daughter. I love you.

The silence I was fearing ceased as his voice was conjured out of the recesses of my mind. His soft, raspy tone with hints of phlegm from all the cigar smoking and bourbon drinking. My memory was flooding back to me as I sat in the dimly lit attic with Monroe's life in my hands. I began to see the old sights of town long lost to progress, my friends long lost in the throes of life, the smells of a summer long lost to me. All the memories of those days were hitting me.

And I couldn't stop crying.

Chapter 1

My bike squealed to a halt as I hit the brakes. Marvin, my overweight friend with awful cotton shorts, slowly caught up with me and Billy, the much leaner and more athletic of the three of us, who was always racing up and down the street just to show off. Marvin skidded to a halt, leaving a black streak. His smile came to an end as he came into contact with the old Victorian two-story home, Monroe's house. Boarded top windows, busted porch floorboards, and dead brown grass with overgrown weeds shooting through the flower boxes along the front leading up the walkway to an offbeat white fence with paint chipping away from the years of neglect. The wet winters from years past had beaten the hell out of most of the rest, forcing all those who gave it a glance to look the other way. The neighborhood called it the Monroe House. It could've been confused with the House of Usher, standing like a monolith, broadcasting nightmarish images to anyone stupid enough to gaze at it. Gothic horror novels had nothing on this piece of architecture.

"You ever see the crazy who lives there?" I asked with squinted eyes, trying to peek through the windows.

"I hear he only comes out at night. People say his face is all deformed." Billy proudly relayed the best part of the gossip mongering.

"He has to wear a mask to hide it," Marvin followed. "Well, at least that's what my dad tells me. I've never stayed to watch him come out." Marvin took out a candy bar from under his sweaty shorts. "Perhaps we should wait." He passed the candy to me, and I took a large bite.

"Where does your dad come up with this shit?" It always felt good to curse with nougat and chocolate in your teeth.

"My dad told me the same thing," Billy said, grabbing the candy bar.

I was far from impressed with this gossipy intelligence. "Billy, your dad's been trying to make moonshine for the last three months. And Marvin, your dad's been drinking it."

"My mom says he's close," Billy said, smiling.

"It must be nice having parents who don't care about the law." I felt it was important to be a moral beacon in a system of ambivalence, which never worked.

"Everyone knows Billy's dad couldn't find his ass with two hands let alone run moonshine." Marvin ripped the rest of the candy bar from Billy's grimy hands. He took the rest of it in his mouth quickly.

"I'm just glad he invests in the stock market; no way that will bite him in the ass."

I turned my attention to the house, hoping we could view in full daylight the beast within the chipping walls.

"You think he'll come out?" I asked.

"Nah. Usually leaves the house on Fridays. A car picks him, or it, up, then heads into the city," Billy said, licking the caramel from his fingers.

Marvin threw the candy wrapper on the ground. "Yeah, for morphine." He squinted at the house. "Or maybe it's just a gin mill all the adults go to."

"I like that idea," Billy retorted, putting his feet to the pedals.

"Maybe we should wait and see if a flapper comes out," I suggested, hoping they didn't all bike off yet.

"Ah, my dad's magazines have enough of them. I'll just look at that." Marvin pedaled off with Billy.

"You guys have no imagination!"

"That's all I got!" Marvin shouted with a big smile.

"See you at church tomorrow!" Billy screamed back, riding off with Marvin, forcing me to stay behind alone, watching the house. Maybe this would be the day he came out. But nothing stirred.

"Nuts to this."

As I drove away I felt eyes watching me from the second-story window. I never turned around. But I knew he was watching, and that made me pedal faster towards home.

One could easily drive through our town in a blink of an eye if one drove a Ford, but in 1928 there weren't much cars kicking up dust. It was a quiet New England world within the borders of New York state about two days' drive from the city. I say drive but you could easily take the train for $2.50 a trip. There was a station not twenty minutes away.

Walter Mitty's General Store was on the corner of Baker and Tanner, the best store in town since it was the only store in town. If one wanted a corned beef sandwich or a piece of taffy, you could come here and be damned to find anything better. Walter was also the local contractor and real estate broker to everyone. He had done jobs all over and employed most of the men in town. He was also Monroe's only real friend left after the war. The sad fact was Monroe and Walter were the only two to come back from the Great War. The church kept most of those memorial bricks in the rose garden wall where most people passed by, never giving them a glance. Who wanted to remember that anyways? Most people just forgot what happened and moved on— a talent this town had plenty of. The church in the fork of Buckingham and River Road had a large tower rising high enough to block out the sun at high noon. Its bells would ring every Sunday to rustle up the devotees of Christ into the hot and uncomfortable pews. We also had an awful choir, with the ten heaviest women in town screaming like banished sirens. Unlike the beauties of Greek myth, these women were so bad, a man would be forced to throw himself onto the rocks headfirst so that his ears would fill with blood. Who were we to judge them, you might ask? We had to listen to them sing, so we had all the right.

My house was on 1st Street, along with many other two-story homes with simple colors. Most of the original owners left after the war, as most of the original townsfolk couldn't live in an ideal, small town where simplicity ruled. They all moved out of state or simply passed away, allowing their relatives living in tenant buildings a chance at small-town living. As you can imagine, most of them jumped at the chance to own a home even if it was drenched with so much memory of death, a result of Wilson's War. But that changed as time went on, and most people by the end of 1922 forgot about it completely. It wasn't even brought up in school because too many people on the school board rejected the idea of teaching children about what happened, who was involved, and what it was all about.

My mother was putting laundry on the front lawn line. In the summer the wind always came up better in the front than the back, so most of the women on my street had lines up. Every now and then there would be dozens of white sheets blowing in the wind, prompting one to rush along them and into an underground tunnel of softness. I can safely say most children in the neighborhood dirtied more sheets that way.

"You're late," Mother told me as she put up the last piece of clothing on the line. Her brown hair in a bun, the housework dress she had on displayed fresh stains from my baby sister Katie's aversion to stewed carrots and peas.

"It was Marvin's fault, he had those shorts on again. Can't ride fast with them on." It was the best excuse I could give at the last minute.

"What his mother dresses him in is not my concern. You're my concern. Now get inside and set the table before your father gets home."

"I'm here, I'm here. The adventures of dining may begin."

"Mashed potatoes are very adventurous. You can make shapes out of them. So belt up and wash your dirty little hands."

Dinner at my house was always a momentous occasion. Every night at about six o'clock, we would sit and discuss our day as much as possible. This being summer, most of the talk was about doing nothing at all, which roused a frown from my father. He was pushing me to work because I had just turned thirteen. My mother always shifted it back toward the idea of childhood and reckless abandonment. *You're only a boy once* was what she often retorted to my father as if she were a lawyer pleading my case, and that was usually where it ended.

At the dinner table, my younger sister Katie had her hair cut at an angle. Being three gave her leeway, though the botched beauty was incredibly distracting as I put the plates on the table.

"Dad's going to notice."

My mother brought out the fine glasses from the hutch standing in the corner. "It's not that bad. Next time she'll stay out of the honey."

"What did you cut her hair with? The hedge trimmers?"

"She sat still."

The front door opened, unleashing a gale of wind through the house. "That smells pretty good," my father exclaimed from the foyer. He placed his lunch pail on the table as he turned the corner, catching my sister's haircut immediately. "What happened to Katie? Did she get in the honey again?"

"I told you," I said, setting the table.

"The chicken!" Mother retreated from the raised eyebrow of Father.

He gazed at the wreck that was Katie's hair. "She's getting better. If you were cross-eyed." He kissed Katie's head and rubbed mine. "That's why I go to Floyd's. He may be seventy-two and talk too much and smell like dried horse hide, but he can cut hair."

"Costs a nickel too." Mother's voice shot out from behind the closed kitchen door.

"That's for the brandy," Father whispered to us with a smile. Prohibition was still going on strong, mind you. "Helps, especially when his shaky hands hold a razor to your throat. But, he's still got it. Smoothest shave in the state."

Mother came through the door with chicken sizzling on the plate. "I wish you wouldn't talk about drinking with the children. Sets a bad example. And stay away from Floyd's shaky hands."

We always forgot she had keen hearing, especially behind closed doors. But I insisted on bringing up an important point. "Mom, it's a crap law and probably will be repealed any day now." My father was the first to hit me over the head, quickly followed by my mother's dainty whack.

"What? *Dad* broke the law." I pointed with one hand and rubbed my head with the other.

"I never do it in the public eye," Father said, ripping off the chicken leg.

Mother hit his hand, forcing him to drop the leg. "Do as we say, not as we do. The benefit will be to you." Mother would always use rhymes to get a point across. She suspected we would remember it better. She was right—those damn words would stick in your head, especially when you were getting into trouble. Maybe that's why all the holy men spoke in parables and riddles, so it would stick. But then again one could argue a parable or riddle provided one a loophole strategy just in case you did get in trouble. I think most holy men went to law school.

"Law is law, little man. And why were you late? And don't

blame Marvin's shorts," Father said, grabbing a forkful of mashed potatoes.

Mother hit his hand with the spoon. "Say prayers first."

"Marvin, Billy, and me were looking at the Monroe House." I came clean with the truth. Both my parents had a shared roll of the eyes.

"I wish you would leave that poor man alone. It's bad enough everyone else gossips about him, let alone having three kids gawk out in front of his home," Mother said, swallowing down her chicken. She was in a rush to scold.

"I think it's time we went to Walter about a job," Father suggested to my utter dismay.

"Work? But I wanted to go swimming, ride my bike, fly a kite— anything that would make being a kid worthwhile." This pleading never worked on my father.

"You're thirteen, time to grow up. You're lucky Walter handles paint jobs and home repair when he could've been a miner. I'll talk to him at the parade tomorrow." My father always used that miner line. I never understood it because I knew he never saw a mine in his life, let alone worked in one.

"Parade!" my sister yelled, flicking a morsel of mashed potato toward me.

"After church," my mother reminded us, picking up the mashed potato projectile and wadding it into her napkin.

"Why?" I asked with a mouthful of chicken.

"Yeah, why?" Father repeated with a mouthful of chicken.

"Parade is reward. We're very blessed. The least we can do to thank God is give an hour of our time. I don't think that's too much to ask."

"It is if you have to listen to Reverend Thomas and the off-key choir," I added and quickly lowered my head to take the light slap from my mother's hand.

"Don't be disrespectful, son. Your mother is right, church is an obligation, on key be damned." My father got a laugh from Mother and me. Katie could only yawn.

"We still didn't say prayer." Mother shook her head, watching all of us eat.

Chapter 2

As I sat at the dinner table lamenting the concept of a summer job, Monroe was sitting at the typewriter. His house was dank, smelling of mildew. Mold was growing where the leaks fell from the roof. It was a miracle Monroe didn't die of exposure. Monroe would ascertain he was dead already, so it didn't matter. He was alone. He was in hell and his home was a physical manifestation of its broad strokes. A decayed reminder of what used to exist stripped of all color and light. An array of crates littered open spaces as if Monroe was in a perpetual state of moving. Where was a question never answered. He suspected one day it would happen. Either forced out or—by miraculous intervention—allowed to go back to his family. He wasn't a delusional fool, the reason he drank more. A miracle had to save him. And after the war, Monroe had stopped believing in them.

Monroe maintained his weekly ritual with the typewriter while drunk. Often he was drunk regardless, but when he was forced to look into the past, whiskey, bourbon, and wine was the only spectrum he could view it through. The deformity was out in the open at night; no need for the bag in his own home. No one was around. No one had set foot in this house other than Walter for almost a decade. Out in the open, even with the mold, was a welcomed relief. The summer heat made the bag hiding his features unbearable. Sweat would soak through the cotton of his mask and the thick air would grow much more humid. He tried to fall asleep or pass out with it on. Asphyxiation would be a welcomed release. It would be quiet. It would be clean. But Monroe couldn't sleep with the bag on comfortably, tossing and turning, never able to relax and let go. And his daughter's face always came to him. Then hope would return, the thoughts of suicide disappeared, and the self-hate returned in waves. Hope was the worst thing Monroe had in his heart. Yet it lingered like the mold.

The first time I saw your mother my heart fell out of my chest. Her hair was pulled back and she wore a white shirt tight around her midsection, giving off a hint of what was underneath. I was in love the moment I gazed at her from my father's field. She had been picking strawberries for a summer job. My mother had hired her in an attempt to pique my interest. The woman knew what she was doing. The first time I approached her, she had a mouthful of freshly picked fruit, and she spit it out, thinking I was coming to scold her. I laughed as she soiled her white shirt with red spit.

"That's okay, you know. My father never shows anger toward someone enjoying what he planted," I assured her, extending my handkerchief. "My name's Monroe. Yours?"

"Elizabeth," she informed me with another bite of strawberry. She was coy at first, and I could tell she was also intrigued by me, but don't ask me why. I still have a hard time understanding it myself. Maybe it was the heat or the rush of sugar to her head, but your mother stumbled over her basket planted at her feet. She laughed out loud at her clumsiness, making me laugh with her. Your mother had this throaty laugh that always made people turn around when she lost it at any moment of levity. I yanked her up off the ground with both our fingers entwined long enough to feel some kind of electricity. Never before had I felt a sting of joy so profound. This went beyond simple want. This was more than just a feeling of attraction. It was love, the only explanation for a feeling so perfect, like a jolt of pleasure from your head to your feet that cooled you from the hot sun and warmed you in the dead of winter. Love was the only noun to sum up the first moment between your mother and I.

"Thank you, Monroe. I didn't think I was this tired," she said to me as she gained her balance. "You'll forgive my clumsiness?"

"I will if you would permit me to ask you to dinner." I was bold and to the point. I didn't want to lose her to a weakness of self-doubt, which always crept up inside me when I stared down a beautiful woman.

"You can ask all you want, but the point of any question is an answer. What would be the best answer to quicken the forgiveness?" She was quick, always quicker than me.

"The obvious one: A simple yes would permit me to forgive you for stealing from mine and my parents' livelihood."

"Two strawberries barely equal a person's livelihood, let alone three. But you are a handsome pauper due to my theft, so may I say yes to your question?" She smiled so brightly it pains me to remember it.

"That would be the right answer. And due to my sudden destitution, I cannot offer much more than a basket of chicken, biscuits, and corn. Hardly a meal for a woman of such fine resolve, but I hope you'll accept."

"I will. You know me so well, and we barely just met. I suspect a good summer ahead." She walked away, never turning her head to see if I was looking. She didn't have to. I watched her walk all the way back to the edge of the field to the road back to town. I was in love. Finally after all the years of hoping and praying for an angel, one fell to Earth.

The first date was dinner and dancing. Obvious way to go since there wasn't much else to do in 1911. She was the only woman I knew of who made fun of the populace as much as I did. Her laugh was incredible, her hair was down around her shoulders, her eyes were hazel, and her hands soft even after ten hours of picking. We danced for about an hour and decided to leave the rest of the dance floor to the old-timers clinging to their last steps. Your mother and I stayed in the alley sharing a bottle of beer. Though one bottle was far from enough. By the end of that first night we went through thirteen bottles and about three packs of smokes. By midnight, when the dizziness was starting to take precedence, we stumbled to the barn near the ranch, and far enough away from the house to be comfortable. I watched her swig another bottle with nary a gag.

"Goddamn, you keep up better than most of my friends," I told her, wiping beer off her chin.

"Your friends aren't to be admired, I've seen

them. More than likely they'd be screwing chickens now." She laughed. The beer had gotten to her. "But don't let that deter you from enjoying their company."

That moment I kissed her deep and hard. She and I held our breath for a good minute and a half. We came up for air and then went right back to it.

"Wait, wait," she stopped me. "This can only keep going one way. I don't want you to think I do this all the time. I just like you a lot, that's all."

"Shut up." I put my hands on her breasts and squeezed. Like I told you before, there wasn't much to do in 1911. Let's just say that was the best night of my life. I asked her to marry me three weeks later and she said yes.

On the porch, three teenagers used a paintbrush to write "FREAK" on Monroe's front door. They giggled as they spilled most of the red paint onto the porch floor, putting their cigarette butts out on the rail along its side. Their beer bottles rolled down the wooden steps, spilling all over the walkway, clanking along the way.

"Shit. Those aren't cheap," one of the boys exclaimed as the precious beer fell to a wasted life. He laughed, reading over the slogan, and forgot the pang of loss. "I love it."

"No one's going to buy that we did it though," another declared as he lit another match for his smoke.

"They will," the painter of the group responded, giving his elegant calligraphy one more coat.

Monroe awakened from his time in the past with a scowl, getting out of his chair, slamming his hands down, making a loud boom in response to the thud of the paint can. Most teens knew the story about Monroe. His deformity was legend even before the end of summer. Everyone attempted to goad him out, be it knocking on the door obnoxiously or getting as close to the windows as humanly possible for a peek. No one ever came as close as these guys were about to.

Within an instant the door opened wide. Monroe's massive build filled the frame. "Get the hell off my property," he growled. His deformed face was covered in the twilight, but the teenagers were able to make out most of it. They screamed and rushed off, spilling the red paint, which mixed with the spilt beer, creating a slippery getaway for the teens. Monroe slammed the door shut behind him.

"No one is ever going to believe us now!" one of them shouted while trying to gain balance.

"Did you see its face?" another said, kicking one of the bottles against the steps and breaking it. "Like a goddamned monster." He laughed the way they all laughed.

Monroe could hear it as they ran off down the street. The faces of the pier crowd flashed over him. Their drunken cat calls and spittle flying out of their yellow teeth from bellowing laughter. His anger rose. He clenched his fist while stifling a tear and hating the weakness self-loathing brought. It caused a swell of ferocity. He punched his wall, breaking the plaster and wood. Monroe's fist throbbed with pain.

"You stupid bastard," he replied to his action, heading into the kitchen, knowing there were two bottles of whiskey left under the sink.

Most summers were spent like this. Sudden thumps against the wood or an occasional scream of panic as the door swung open, allowing the perpetrator a free look at the carnival pier main attraction. The screams of horror were often followed by the howls of laughter. It pained him to be the butt of jokes. To be regulated as town gossip made him especially angry, since half the town was built from the dirt up by him and Walter. No one remembered Monroe helping to pick out colors for their homes or giving them their first job. They saw what came back from the Front. A broken monster in a broken home.

He dwelled on the laughter. Sitting in the dark with a bottle of Canadian whiskey, he cried. It was all he ever did now. Drink, cry. Drink, cry. An unending cycle that allowed the hours to pass. He prayed for his heart to give up, but it continued to pump. He prayed for death, but life lingered. Small things in the grand scheme of it all. One broken man's life offered up to the altar of whatever is beyond. Monroe never got an answer. He just got the darkness of his home and the echo of laughing fools.

Chapter 3

C hurch service was always an event in my small town. Hundreds of Christians would gather, wearing their best clothes no matter the heat, snow, or rain nature produced to impede the gathering hordes from congregating. We would have preferred to stay home if the weather demanded it. But Mother was a stickler for divine acceptance. An hour in the rain, heat, or snow was a small price to pay for breathing air and eating food. Granted, one should be thankful, but not in the 103-degree heat with humidity soaking our underwear. The Almighty created this weather, so he should know firsthand what a bitch it was. My father and I were cursed with wool pants and tight cotton shirts, cutting off our blood circulation from the head down. Sunday was not a quest for spiritual enlightenment, but a course in pain dressing for God.

"There better be a robe policy in heaven," my father said, adjusting the collar.

"Don't worry, I saw the pictures in the missile, and we're good."

"We're about to enter the house of God in three seconds, so the both of you belt up!" Mother scolded, pulling Katie up further as she slipped through her fingers.

Father and I closed our mouths as we passed through the shabby doors, then headed straight down the aisle where on either side, rows of pews greeted and prepared us for the hour of discomfort. I noticed right away that the windows were sealed closed, not allowing a single trace of breeze to interrupt the sharing of goodwill and brotherly love. This was how it always ended up: hot clothes, hot air, and popped eardrums from the choir. Looking back, I truly miss it. Simplicity you cannot find anymore. A place that exists in memory that you really can't share with anyone who wasn't there. Seems to be the way most memories go, but maybe that's a good thing. The choir opened their mouths and belted "Hosanna in the Highest." I still can't hear certain frequencies because of them.

At the altar, standing high above us, was Reverend Thomas. He was a middle-aged man with a graying beard, short, well-trimmed hair, and a lazy eye. Watching it droop was always a problem with most of us young boys. We would always get a slap to the back of the head from our parents, who, like us, were too busy staring at it also. He would begin the service with a prayer for his wife, for the town's children, for the town, and then for the church—standard dialogue for the masses gathered. Anyone of us could recite it word for word, which we often did, exaggerating the lazy eye by about a thousand percent. Billy was the best at this. His lazy eye would droop lower than physically possible, almost to the point where he had all white in his eye. He would also drool more too—an addition to his shtick that always killed.

By now, the choir was beginning to sing their chants of glass-shattering love for Christ. We tried to sing along, realizing the futility of keeping key with a random smattering of sounds. Soon the horror was over and Reverend Thomas came back up to the podium with a new man at his side. A handsome man with dark eyes, dark hair, and a slim build, he was the antithesis of the reverend in every way. You could hear the single women murmur behind us. He had a Valentino sensibility not lost on the women and especially noticeable to the men. Thankfully he was a brother, and any thought of sexual misconduct went out the window. But that didn't stop the women from continuing to gape.

Reverend Thomas smiled at his wife down in the choir pit. She was a portly one, with large ankles that merged with her calves. "Ladies, you do us a fine service. In closing today, I want to let everyone know about our new brother joining us today. His name is Phillip from New York. He is a new, young servant of God looking to get away from big-city life. So I want you all to give a Christian welcome to Brother Phillip."

Brother Phillip waved to the crowd, and his smile beamed through to the hearts of every woman still sexually active.

"He will be on the church float later today, so everybody in town can get a better look at him," Reverend Thomas informed us with a pat on Brother Phillip's back.

My mother whispered into my father's ear, "God knew what he was doing when he made that boy."

Father smiled. "I was young and childless once too."

The annual Fourth of July parade often occurred two days before, simply because the town had a fireworks display the night of the fourth, and oftentimes, working a parade, then running off to a fireworks show is hell on the knees. Especially since most of the town leaders in charge of festivities were all over sixty, one could forgive them for jumping the gun a bit. Nevertheless, they put on quite a spectacle, with dozens of vendors from many counties gathered to sell us wonderfully fatty foods: caramel apples, hot dogs, popcorn, taffy, chocolate-covered peanuts, nuts, or any other damned thing. Every meat you could think of was available too: chicken, steak, lamb chops, and pork all found on sticks in every direction. Soon the town would be redolent of gastric emissions of the like none had smelled since.

Mother let Katie down from her grasp for a moment to buy popcorn at a vendor. Katie, already tired from service, began to sniffle, and then her lip quivered. Before she could begin the patent toddler bawling, Mother swept down and lifted her up. A sixth sense that still amazes me when it comes to mothers. "Pay the man, Steven," she ordered my father, checking out the chicken on sticks turning over open flame.

"Of course, dear, that's what I'm here for," he said lovingly, dropping two pennies into the steel box attached to the cart.

"You see? Church was far from unpleasant. With our obligation done, we can have some fun." My mother rhymed to drive the point home.

"You need to write those down," I told her, with my hands digging through the popcorn bag.

"No one cares. It's not like it's hard." She blushed at the compliment.

"Here, let me try one," Father interjected, yanking the popcorn from my grasp. "Out today there is no rain. Church clothes at home, I'd rather say Shalom. See, you do it much better than any of us." My father threw his hand down, nailing little Dougie Miller in the face.

"Steven!" Mother exclaimed as she masterfully kept Katie in one arm and used her other arm to console Dougie Miller, who was still in a state of shock.

"Oh, sorry little guy."

The boy held his hand to the welt growing on his forehead. He took off like a flash to his mother, Cheryl, a redhead with soft features. In looking at her you would expect a fast wind to blow her away. "That'll teach the kid to run from his mother."

"You need to pay attention."

"The little shit came out of nowhere."

"A man with a gut should look out for a runt." Mother smiled.

"You've had better ones."

Cheryl inspected Dougie's face and rolled her fingers through his hair, calming the approaching cry. Sammy Miller, her ten-year-old son, came up to her with two hot dogs.

"Sammy, stay with your brother for a minute. Make sure he doesn't run off again." She took the hot dogs from his hand, but Sammy was never one to stick around his mother. He jetted off to the other side of the street with two other boys. "Damn that kid. Always running around, not paying attention. Too much trouble can come from that."

Beyond the wooden fence separating the alley from the street of Walter Mitty's General Store walked Monroe with a burlap bag over his head, concealing his deformity. A telegram tight in his grip as he constantly checked over his shoulder in case a lone pedestrian came along. The July heat baked his head. He felt the sweat drip, eyes stinging. Sounds of the crowd cheering make him feel less nervous as it meant no one was around to see him make his entrance.

Walter stood at the side door, his arms folded. "Glad to see you make it out this year." He noticed the telegram at once. He never mentioned the futility of sending them. All he could do was smile and nod but always knowing the response:

```
Cease your telegrams. Stop. I don't want her to
see you. Stop. We moved on. Stop.
```

Messages from the past Monroe could never understand. His tenacity was legendary though. He thought eventually they would grow tired of the telegrams, forcing them out here to tell him to his face to cease. That never happened.

"I need to show my respects to the veterans somehow." Monroe gave a stilted salute to Walter. They both hid their memories of those days deep. One could understand their need to do so. Hell was not something anyone liked to recall. "And I have this." He handed Walter the telegram. "A useless gesture, but need to have something to do."

"I always send them, Monroe." He accepted it, like always. "I have the top floor storage windows open. I got a fan for you and a big pitcher of lemonade."

"Thank you, Walter. Such gestures demand reciprocity. I'm going to need a painter."

"Actually, all my guys are working the McHenry Mansion job, but I can find somebody. When do you need it?"

"Within the next few days when I'll be at the cabin. Just have anybody come out to repair the front. I'll pay in advance." Monroe headed up the stairwell leading to the attic.

"Your money's no good here, Monroe. I'll figure something out."

Walter watched Monroe stagger up the stairwell. He was drunk again. Hell, there wasn't a time when he wasn't. Walter was never one to judge anyone, least of all Monroe. They had been friends for decades. He was there for the good and the worst. The worst lingered. Walter rubbed the folded telegram message. He hated to read it, but he had to. No one else knew how to work the damn machine. Plus he was paid an extra two bits for knowing how to operate it.

Wish her Happy Birthday from me. At least allow me that much. Tell her I say it's from heaven if that's best for you.

Walter exhaled loudly, double-checking the back and front doors. The last thing he needed was someone stumbling upon Monroe inside the store, spreading the news to all the gossip queens in town. If people knew how many times Monroe frequented the store, he would be running them off with a broom. Monroe once told Walter he would sit behind a glass case at the back of the store for two pennies a gander. Walter never laughed at the idea. He spit on his floor. The carnival pier allowed Monroe the money to live well, but Walter wanted no part of it. The idea of his friend being laughed at and mocked made him sick. He spit again, thinking on the days Elizabeth still loved Monroe. His eyes teared up, but he dismissed the memories with the sudden urge to sell more American flags out front to the local rubes enjoying the day. He rolled the barrel out front, shaking away the image of Elizabeth smiling.

The first float was topped with Brother Phillip waving along with Reverend Thomas. The tall papier-mâché cross behind them lurched back and forth in the wind since no one saw the benefit of attaching a third safety line to it. The crowd began to laugh as the second string broke loose, allowing the thin tissue paper to fly off, exposing the chicken wire mesh. People laughed and pointed, yelling many different slogans:

"Jesus ain't in today!"

"That's never a good sign!"

"Ye who builds shoddy floats shouldn't face upwind!"

Reverend Thomas moved quickly. All those who saw it say it was the fastest he had ever moved in his life, trying to save the fleeing tissue. The effort was futile, as most of it hit the Rose Club float trailing behind them. Most of the girls on it were too busy staring at Brother Phillip to move an inch to save the cross's coverings.

With this sudden stop to the parade, my father took my hand and pulled me up from the spot I had spent days scouting out. I noticed Walter standing out in front of his store smoking along with everyone else. Some tissue blew into our faces as we jogged behind the church float and approached Walter.

"Steven, Steven," Walter said to us, putting out the cigarette on his boot heel. He pulled out two American flags from his barrel. "You guys want to buy a flag?"

"I'm not paying two cents for a stick and cloth. That's for the rubes."

Walter smiled, as they both got along well. They usually hung around Floyd's together—Floyd had a good line of whiskey coming in from Atlantic City straight from Canada. They said Floyd had gangster nephews living up there who loved their uncle more than their father. In a few years Floyd would be accidentally gunned down in a mob hit intended for his nephews.

"Walter, my wife and I were curious as to what you have to offer our son here for the summer. Any quick jobs?"

I gazed down at my shoes, hearing the possibility of work dangle over my head like the Sword of Damocles. Quick jobs were always a quick death sentence to horseplay because one job led to another, forcing one to mature fast. The last thing anyone wanted.

"You know, I do have one job that just came up. Simple paint job, it would take about two days," Walter gladly informed my father, and the sword just fell.

"Fantastic. Where and when?"

Walter lowered his head and voice. "Monroe House. I would say Thursday."

My eyes bulged with excitement. The prospect of work had enabled me a chance to gaze at the neighborhood's monster. A chance I would not waste. My father noticed the jubilance in me immediately.

"Do you have any other jobs?" he was quick to ask, but Walter could only shake his head.

"No, the other jobs require men of experience."

"I'll take it. You always said I have to earn some sort of responsibility," I declared to my father, who was kicking himself.

"Thursday, huh?" A brief pause followed, and the fear of spoiling this opportunity overtook me when my father said, "He'll do it." I couldn't believe he said that, and I tried to keep the grin on my face from showing.

"Great. I'll be there to get you started, and if I can trust you to do a good job, you can finish up on your own." Walter patted my head, enjoying the prospect of having a young kid to tutor.

"Thank you, Walter," Father said, bordering on sarcasm, as

my father hated the idea of me being within inches of the Monroe house's front door.

"This summer job idea was a good one, Dad," I said with a smile.

"Oh, shut up" was all he could manage to say as he led me away from my future boss.

Chapter 4

Growing up we had places we claimed as our own, where one could go to vent frustration or fish without adults telling us we were doing wrong. These places were holy grounds to adolescents the world over. Ours was called The Meadow. A patch of dead land in the middle of tall, overgrown grass rivaling corn stalks in height. A single tree grew over this patch, providing shade from the blazing sun above us. A small brook flowed over a slight hill to the east of it, and then emptied into a shallow pond. It was a great place to play pirate or navy battle, and sometimes it was just a good place to sit. We had gathered at this point to swim, when I divulged what had happened at the parade the day before. Billy was the first to speak out.

"Who would trust you with a summer job?"

"You can't even paint," Marvin added.

"It's not what you know, it's who you know," I responded with a cocky stride toward the pond, slipping my shoes off. "Walter knows good stock when he sees it."

"Celery stalk. You got as much fat on you as a bean pole. Skinny." Billy leaped into the water as he flung his shirt at me.

"When do you go?" Marvin kept his shirt on but his shoes off. He stuck a toe in the water and retreated.

"Thursday." I began to head to the water. I always checked for random bottles, and Billy always leaped head first. Once I heard Doug Malick lost a foot to a bad infection from a broken rum bottle. Ever since then, I made sure no random act of infection would hit my being.

"Would Walter be there?" Marvin put his shoes back on and perched on the log . Billy splashed him, getting him wet. Marvin showed no reaction; he took it in stride, as the heat was hellishly atrocious.

"Just to get me started."

"Then he would leave?" Marvin asked, wiping the condensation from his eyeglasses.

"I guess, sure."

"He trusts you? You know, not to do anything stupid?" Billy tossed Marvin a handkerchief out of the pockets of his pants lying on the sand.

"Yeah, he does, why not?" My mind put the pieces together as I stared them down with their conjoined brains already at work on a plan. "What do you want me to do?" I asked, flummoxed.

"Nothing," the two said in unison, like they were sharing a brain. I knew better. "That's rich."

"Okay… If you could go into the house, see what's in there, maybe grab something and bring it out," Marvin suggested, then moved to the side, allowing Billy time to add his idea.

"You could let us in on what you find." They both stood hip to hip, resembling Tweedledee and Tweedledum blathering on.

"If you're so curious, you guys do it." I turned my back on the two of them.

"No one would trust us with a summer job." Marvin seemed proud of this fact. "We don't have that mature sensibility you have. We're smarter than that." Billy was trying to get the water out of his ears, jerking his head side to side.

"Look, I'm not going to commit breaking and entering. And you guys can't tempt me with any amount of goading,"

"No breaking, just sliding on through." Marvin acted more and more like a suave businessman negotiating a deal he knows he'll get done his way. "Imagine, if you would, August 27th. First bell rings, you rush into Dillon's English class and sit next to Amber Hurley." Marvin handed the reins over to Billy.

"If this was last year, she wouldn't give you an ice cube in hell. But due to the story circulating around the school by said parties..." He pointed to himself and Marvin. Marvin took the reins back. "She would be obliged to not only stare at you but scoot her desk closer to yours."

"Because she'll conveniently forget her book, so she can brush against the Steven."

"The Steven?" I saw where this was going. I knew it was a trick deployed to seduce me into this wild scheme. Amber Hurley was a nice touch, enough to not only convince me to break into Monroe's house but walk through fire. The two cohorts responsible for my degradation of character moved closer, trying to see if any of this was sinking in.

"Your fame would be infinite." Marvin was quick to throw "fame" at me. It hit the right nerve, especially since most kids at our school didn't really know my name.

"In the school yard, but is there anything bigger? Nay, important?" Billy reiterated, forcing me to nod my head and imagine the possibility of going into recess with an unspoken respect emitting from all those little boogers playing hopscotch and kick ball, with Amber Hurley in the center, a radiant glow exuding off her freckled face.

"At this stage? No, there really isn't much else." I couldn't believe I went with their sale. Marvin and Billy had futures in the field of law. Or maybe they would be best suited to fraud or manipulation. In all honesty, the same field. "Okay, what do you want me to do?"

As I was agreeing with the Gilbert and Sullivan of adolescent manipulation, Monroe was walking up a trail to his cabin on Sunset Hill. A quarter mile spaced most of the cabins out, with a single trail snaking across and leading to all of them. Back in the teens, many a citizen bought a little piece of the forest. A way to get out in nature without having to travel sixty miles in any direction. Most people felt if you couldn't see your house from the hill, you were fine. They were cheap too and built quickly for the time. Monroe and Walter used to design and sell them before the War. Made a small fortune. But now, the past was forgotten. His present was what all remembered. Fellow owners sitting on their porches would see Monroe with his burlap bag over his head, treading up the slope. No one ever waved or said hello; they continued staring out at the trees, hoping he would just keep walking. He always did.

In his hand was a parcel small enough to be a doll. Everyone always smirked when someone mentioned it. A grown man carrying a baby doll up the Sunset Hill trail must be a little light in the loafers or worse. Truth be told, it was Monroe's pilgrimage. His daughter's birthday was the fifth of July. He needed to be at the cabin to place a gift on the bench standing in the foyer. It was a ritual that allowed him to maintain some part of fatherhood, even if it was a wasted gesture. The ritual was what mattered to Monroe. He didn't have many left.

In the doorway, Monroe gazed down on the bench littered with nine gifts still wrapped in their paper coverings. Spider webs had hitched themselves to the indents, and layers of dust resided on top. To Monroe, the dolls always seemed judgmental. A jury of porcelain peers all coming to the same verdict. Self-loathing brings a need for verification in wallowing in it. Monroe liked the idea of their black eyes staring, whispering foul things about him and his choices. Monroe shrugged them off, placing the tenth wrapped parcel next to the others. Laughing to himself, two more years and the jury would be full. He dusted the others off, blew the spider webs out of the indents, and smoothed out any flaws in the frail paper.

"Happy birthday, love" was all he could say, bent on his knees, facing the unopened gifts. He would spend the rest of the time drinking and crying.

Chapter 5

Walter knocked on my front door at six in the morning. I didn't realize the sun rose at this hour. It was a majestic panoramic view I could've lived without seeing in the summer of my youth. My father lifted the blinds fast, stabbing my eyes with bright daggers of ultraviolet waves that caused me to shoot out of bed.

"Walter's downstairs waiting for you. Get dressed in five minutes." He pulled the blankets off me and ripped the pillow from under my head. "I'm proud of you, son," he added after the psychological abuse he had just delivered.

"Thanks, Dad," I responded, with heavy lids focusing on my surroundings, getting a foothold in reality. My room was small but comfortable. Bed lined with the desk on the left, bookshelf to the right, toys in my ancient wood box handed down from Fisher to Fisher since old Lady Madison ran out the burning White House with the silver.

Downstairs, my mother handed me a bacon sandwich wrapped in a napkin; then she smiled at me and hugged me hard. "Your first real day of work. You're growing up too fast."

I remained in my early morning daze, chewing the bacon sandwich. Egg and cheese accompanied the pork fat on further inspection. The intermingling flavors exploded in my mouth, jostling the last remnants of crusties embedded in my eyes.

Walter slapped my back. "Good morning, Steven. I hope you wake up more on the way to the house." Mother handed him a bacon sandwich. Walter's eyes bulged, as he was not expecting such a hospitable gesture this early in the day. "Thank you, Wanda. That was nice of you. Usually I get an evil eye from the Misses waking them up so damned early."

"I'm always up this damned early. You think Dad can wake up himself? Just keep my baby busy with honest work," my mother added as we headed out the door.

The street was beyond quiet in the early summer sun. It was a still-life—a frozen image of the neighborhood. There were no kids playing in the yards, no laundry hanging from the lines, no Sheriff Tate driving his beat-up Motel-T down the pothole-ridden road, and not even a single person on their porch with a cup of coffee. Dead still. I realized, of course, this was due to summer. No one got up early because they didn't have to. Damn responsibility verging adulthood forces on us.

"Now this is when it's best to work," Walter assured me as we walked down the street.

"How's that?" I asked, hiding my indignation.

"No one is around to hear you curse." He laughed, chomping on his sandwich. "Oh yeah, me and the boys always have a real good time at the expense of the sleeping dumb shits."

I giggled a bit, immediately changing my discourse. This might not be a bad day after all.

Being this close to the house was odd. It was not fear but a certain anxiety, maybe due to the fact that I had to figure a way to break into the house. All I could hear was Marvin and Billy's speech in my ears. Hopefully, Walter would leave and allow me an opportunity. As I looked for a way into the house, my eyes fell on the painted words of teenage vandalism. Walter sighed loudly, popping open a paint can sitting on the steps.

"Stir this while I sand that off." Walter rose from his creaking knee, removing sandpaper from one of the toolboxes. "Thanks for doing this, Steven. Not many people jump at the chance to paint Monroe's house."

"What's he like?" I timidly asked while stirring the paint.

Walter was at a loss for words. He sanded, pretending not to hear me.

"When do I know this is ready?" I asked to see if he could hear that.

"When the color is even," he responded, letting me know he heard what he wanted.

"Okay, so what is Monroe like?" I reiterated.

"Nicest guy you could meet," Walter reported. "Does that paint look ready yet?"

"You tell me." I showed him the bucket.

"Keep going, maybe another couple of minutes of solid stirring." Walter had managed to erase most of the thick letters. "Look at that, barely ten minutes of hard scrubbing and presto, half of it's gone. Just goes to show you a little elbow grease goes a long way." He took one step to the left, breaking through the floorboard.

"Goddamn it!" he shouted at the top of his lungs. We both looked around, hoping no one overheard the utterance.

"See, I told you working in the morning was better. Shit! I'm going to have to get some boards from the shop." He pulled up his leg from the jagged hole he had created.

"Now?" I asked, hoping the window of opportunity was beginning to crack open.

"Nah, we got a few days to do this job. So what do you say? Another day of getting up early?" He checked his pant leg and noticed a slight tear from the fall. "Shit, now I need to buy another pair of pants."

"If it means more loud cursing, I'm there," I said with a smile. This old coot knew how to make me laugh.

"That's the spirit." He rubbed my head. "Now let's get started on this paint job. Hand me a brush." I gave Walter one of the brushes sticking up from the bucket next to the paint. "You saw how I sanded the door?" he asked me, handing over the sandpaper.

"Yeah."

"Start sanding the floorboards anywhere you see chipped paint. We're going to fix this whole damn thing before he gets back."

"What about the rest of the house?" I asked, pointing out the decay.

"One day at a time, Steven." He began to paint the first coat as I got on my hands and knees to sand. "And be careful not to fall through any floorboards. Some spots may be worse than others."

I rubbed my brow, dripping with sweat as the summer's humidity finally got to me. Walter handed me a handkerchief. "That'll work better than your hand." We were on hour three as the heat really kicked in, soaking the shirts on our backs.

"Thanks," I said, wiping off the sweat.

"Getting hot already. Damn summer. Just finish up there, Steven. I need to head over to the McHenry Mansion to check out the guys. They started about the same time as us, and most of them don't work as hard as you. Sweep off the shavings and be careful not to hit the door."

"Really?" I was amazed. All it took was five hours to gain this man's trust.

"Yeah. You seem decent enough." The word "decent" hurt momentarily.

"Thanks, Walter," I said, grabbing the broom.

"No problem, Steven. Remember, tomorrow at six in the morning."

"I'll be used to it," I reassured him, flashing a bright smile to add to the idea of my trustworthiness.

He walked down the street whistling. I waited until he was well out of earshot before I headed for the side of the house to look for a way in. Most of the windows were locked and the rest only rose two inches, with curtains hindering any glimpse inside. I got frustrated quickly, running around the sides of the house, when I spotted the back gate open slightly. This gate led to the demolished backyard, littered with patches of brown grass, dead flowers, and withering, overgrown azalea bushes. The back window was open and I checked to see if I could fit through. No dice. It opened into the kitchen sink, filled with wine bottles. I was hit with a pungent wave of vinegar. Falling from the open window, my feet hit hollow wood. Beneath my feet were two storm doors covered in vines and weeds. I tore them away, discovering a chain with a heavy lock.

"Shit," I cursed now louder than Walter. I checked my surroundings to make sure no one heard me, but it was still too early. I lifted the heavy doors to see how far they opened. They opened wide enough to squeeze through. I tossed the pulled-up weeds and vines away from the door, managing to fit through the gap quite comfortably and head into the belly of the beast.

Stone steps led down into the surprisingly cool basement. Lining the walls were shelves with hundreds of books, loose papers, framed pictures facing down, and old cigar boxes. Above the shelves, I noticed an odd painting. I checked the name underneath it: Picasso. No doubt another pretentious slob trying to sell doodles for pennies on some street corner. (My younger self had no appreciation for art.) A homemade wine rack displayed dozens of bottles covered in dust. Many of them were older than the town itself. Cognac crates were stacked up against the wine rack. In the center of the basement was a single desk. On top was an ashtray filled with cigar ash and crushed, soggy ends. A box of cigars sat opened, tempting me to grab one, but I knew better than to reveal my presence. A single blank page was held in the typewriter's grasp, next to a stack of over two hundred pages. I lifted up the top page and read it.

When I married your mother everything made sense. Mornings were brighter, night were bluer, food tasted better, and work was not a chore. I was living with someone whose life I impacted. It was amazing. Those first years were heaven. The farm sold right away after my parents passed on, allowing us enough money to buy a home and a cabin in the hills. We figured why not have another home amongst the trees within a mile's walk. It was far enough away to escape the town but close enough to allow us much needed time together. I was working nonstop back then with Walter Mitty, planning and overseeing the expansion of the town. We built the church offices, the McHenry Mansion, the post office, and the jail across the street from Walter's General Store. Within two years, we had changed the small village into a full-fledged town. We even began selling up land to big contractors wanting to build row houses on 1st Street.

However, all of it paled in comparison to the news of your imminent arrival. Your mother glowed when she felt you kick. My hand was pressed against her belly every morning until you came out. It was a wonder to feel something alive, moving around inside another person. You can't imagine it until it happens to you. The feeling inside burns through you, making the sensation of love between two people feel like a candle running out of wick. No love matches the love for a child, nothing matters more, and nothing stands in its way. But a young man doesn't realize this right away.

The house itself was just as cold as the basement. All the windows were closed with heavy curtains blocking the sunlight.

Wallpaper was peeling away, and only the imprints of old frames kept it from coming off completely. The frames themselves were on the floor facing in. Obviously, Monroe did not want to look at them. I flipped one over to see what was so horrible: a picture of a handsome man with a beautiful woman holding a baby. The house in the background looked pristine. A glimpse of what used to exist in this shell of a home. I put it down facing out, forgetting at once that the pictures were facing the wall for a reason. A mistake, I realize, but in the excitement and the passing of moments, I forgot my first rule: Don't let your presence be revealed.

In the dining room was a long table with candles, frozen wax dripping down the sides. The banquet table had an array of impressive crystal glasses and bowls. I opened the drawers to see a myriad of gold forks, knives, and spoons to rival an emperor's table settings. This was once a wealthy family's place to dine, now thrust into an unmitigated darkness. Plates were situated at the chairs, as if a holiday dinner was about to take place. A table set for no one. Unlike the rest of the house, the table suggested someone with care still lived here. But that was an illusion created by Monroe. A way to see the past physically. I never understood it, I was a child. But now, I knew. He wanted a mirage of someone taking care of him.

Adjoining the dining room was a well-furnished den. Like the basement, there were shelves lined with books. No Picasso paintings though, just more sad imprints of frames. Once, long ago, there must have been quite the collection of family photographs, but my curiosity vanished as I came upon a glass case in the center shelf. Three war medals rested inside: a Purple Heart, a Distinguished Cross, and the last one eluded me. It had to be an important medal, as it was bigger than the other two. The mystery, however, was short-lived, as I heard whistling down the street. It would be seconds before Walter reached the porch.

"Steven! Where are you, boy?"

I checked through the gap in the front window, catching him heading for the side of the house. I saw the opportunity to come out the front door. Luckily for me, it opened and closed with ease, not making even an iota of noise.

"Are you okay, son?" he asked from behind the house. I moved to the opposite end, running up to greet him.

"Walter?" I gave my best confused gaze.

"Where were you? Why didn't you answer me?"

"I was peeing. Couldn't concentrate with you yelling." I managed to lie rather well.

"Oh yeah, happens to me quite a bit. You can go on home now. I forgot to grab my extra keys." He pulled a key ring from deep inside the bucket of brushes. "I put them in there so no one gets wise to them, and here I am forgetting the damn things."

"That happens sometimes. Well, I'll be off. See you tomorrow morning." I waved and trotted down the street, hoping he didn't check the front door. I forgot to lock it on my way out. Walter paid no attention to it as he cleaned up a bit then began to head toward his store on the other side of the street. I breathed a sigh of relief.

Walking home, I was filled with some guilt. I had just broken into the private living space of another human being, witnessing the emptiness of it. I didn't take anything, but it felt like I did. The guilt stemmed from seeing the hollow nature of Monroe's life. Darkness had consumed a past life that was probably close to my current one: a loving home with two parents and crawling children playing with toys. And nights when everyone gathered around the leather chair in the den to be regaled by Father's stories. More than likely, he read those books aloud to his wife and child. Now just the decayed domesticity remained, slapping happy memories in his face every time he stood in the hallway. That was what hit me, the idea of a broken man standing in a hallway. It left my young mind as soon as I saw my mother putting up laundry on the front yard line.

"How was painting today?"

"Interesting."

Her perfected homing device for mischief attuned to the tone in my voice. "Wait. How is painting interesting?" she asked, coming down from her small stepladder and taking the clothespins out of her mouth.

"You know, it's amazing how many coats of paint a door needs before it's finished."

"Well, that's good to know because you'll find painting the backyard fence downright fascinating." She got me right between the eyes.

"Great," I said, walking through the front door.

Across the street, Cheryl, the same woman with the rambunctious child Dougie, came out of her home worried sick. Mother noticed and waved to prompt her over. "How are you, Cheryl?"

Cheryl had a sick look on her face, as if all of her instincts were indicating something was wrong.

"I'm okay. Do you know if Sammy came running through here? He's late for supper, and he always manages to come in from the park." She gazed into the distance, squinting to see if Sammy was running down the street. Mother noticed Cheryl continually digging into her thumb, the raw skin about ready to crack open with blood. There were only neighborhood children coming in from playing baseball in the street.

"I'm sure he'll be home soon. Everyone knows Sammy, and they'll send him on his way before supper gets cold." My mother tried to soothe Cheryl, but it didn't seem to help.

"Yeah, you're right. But if you see him please send him home."

"Of course I will. Now I have to go and make supper. Be careful not to lose your thumb with all that worrying. " Mother smiled at her, hoping to get one back. Cheryl just walked to the curb to sit and continue the nervous digging.

Mother came through the front door and noticed Katie standing on the stairs with a blanket over her head like an oracle at Delphi. I handed Katie a glass of milk per her request.

"What's wrong with Sammy's mom?" I asked.

"Nothing, she just worries too much, that's all." Mother pulled the blanket off my sister's head and wrapped it around her small body. "Now, let's have dinner."

Chapter 6

The second day of work was far from eventful. Walter stayed the entire time, loosening up old floorboards and replacing them with new ones from his lumber dealership. I spent the day learning as much as I could in one afternoon, but the house kept calling me. I wanted to walk in its halls again, to explore the upstairs, to thumb through his books and stare at the medals too. All those images kept entering my mind, keeping me from doing a decent job.

"Boy, are you paying attention? I need some longer nails," Walter ordered me, knocking me out of my daze.

"Sorry, I got 'em." I lifted the box out of the cart that Walter wheeled over.

"Are you okay, son?" Walter was genuinely worried.

"Yeah, it's just the Fourth of July and all. I was thinking about buying some firecrackers, but since I'm here I won't know if they're all sold out or not." I stumbled, but didn't stutter. Walter's expression didn't bode well.

"The hell you talking about?"

"Nothing. You need any help lifting those boards?"

"Yeah, toss these old ones in the shed next to the gate on the side of the house."

I lifted up the boards, lugging them over to the shed. I spotted the storm doors through the open gate. Temptation is a hell of a thing. I thought maybe I could run through the doors real quick, check the upstairs, and maybe see if he actually slept on a bed or the old, dry hides of dead animals. My imagination was going a mile a minute, but I was stuck with old pieces of wood digging into my shoulder blades, making the early morning sun feel even hotter.

"Steven, I got more boards for you, hurry up," Walter commanded me from the porch around the corner. I dropped the boards, exhaling loudly. I hoped this was a half day, but the crack of more wood planks, aligned with Walter's groaning, left me with a foreboding feeling there was more manual labor to come. After the sixth trip to the shed with boards under my arms, the need to know more about Monroe was overwhelming. I broached the subject to Walter.

"So, what's he like?"

Walter stopped his hammering, wiped his forehead, and gave me a strange look. After a brief silence, he cracked a smile, remembering Monroe fondly. "The nicest guy you could ever meet." He went back to hammering without giving me one iota of useable intelligence.

This not being satisfying at all forced me to prod further, "What happened to him?"

Walter went to the bucket of supplies, sifting through it, trying to get out of talking. That ended when I folded my arms and let loose both barrels. "Did he get that way from an accident?"

Walter dropped his hammer into the bucket loudly. He took the rag hanging from the back of his pants pocket to wipe the sweat and dust from his face, neck, and hands. It felt like an eternity of awkward silence.

"The war." Walter said it in monotone.

"How long was he over there?"

"He signed on for a three-month tour and stayed a year and a half. I was in intelligence, don't ask me why—they told me not to say it because it may open up an investigation." He went back to the floorboards with his hammer. "The war did that to him. Everything else came later."

"Did he have a family?" I continued to push.

"Why you asking that?" Walter scowled.

"Big house," I said meekly.

"A wife and daughter." He threw out two more old boards. They slammed against the sidewalk, echoing through the neighborhood. This sudden rush of noise silenced my interrogation. I went back to picking up boards, ending my pursuit of the issue. By noon, Walter sent me home. A blessed half day brought about from my questions.

The dining room stayed with me as I walked toward the meadow. No one had eaten at that table for years, yet all the plates were laid out with a wife's love.

"Did you get in the house?" Billy asked, breaking the ease the rest of the day would've brought.

"Yes I did, nothing to report," I said, throwing the line into the water.

"Is Monroe still gone?" Marvin asked.

"Yeah."

This led to the inevitable next question.

"Walter gone too?" Billy asked, never taking his eyes away from the stream.

"No," I said, sticking my pole in a hole properly dug out by us. I walked away from the two of them. Billy dropped his pole to the ground, cornering me against the sole oak tree.

"Come on, Steve, don't be a flat tire," Marvin said, catching up with Billy.

"Yeah, we got a chance to catch a darb, and I mean a real Grade A darb. This kind of chance does not come along very often," Billy declared.

"How about you guys not leave your poles behind," I pointed out, hoping they would rush off.

"We never catch anything out here anyway," Billy told me as his pole's line spun out of control, almost falling into the stream.

Marvin rushed back to the poles. "Why am I the one who always has to run back to hold everything?"

"Because you're the sensible one," Billy said.

"I know you're not," I told him.

"Yes, just why I keep pressing this matter. I want to go in and take a look for myself. You found a way in; let me know about it," Billy demanded.

"No, not at all. If you get caught, they'll know it was me who told you about the storm doors." I bit my tongue.

"Storm doors?" Marvin pushed his glasses up to his eyes. Coming back, whatever caught the line had let go.

"Storm doors, huh?" Billy has his hand on his chin, his mind churning to the breaking point. "They chained up?"

"Yes, but you could slip through them if you lift hard enough." I knew there was no way out of this, so I might as well tell him everything.

"I'll be the lookout," Marvin said, accepting his role.

"You're the thinker, not the doer, Marvin." Billy pointed out his tummy.

"Wish I wasn't so fat." He tugged on his own girth.

"If we do this, we need to do this now. Monroe is gone for another day, but I'm not sure on that." This bit of information did nothing to cease the excitement of the approaching crime.

"Whatever, we'll be in and out before the freak gets there." Billy never thought anything through.

At one in the morning, Monroe often came home from the carnival pier. Late trains allowed him to sneak past gawkers who waited around on the weekends trying to get a look. Some days he imagined they were waiting to greet him with open arms and ask for his autograph. Usually they would balk instead of gawk, running away with the fear that Monroe would actually strike them. A six-foot frame with a burlap bag over the head often produced an intimidating stance, especially if he stood still and face-to-face with another person. A person running away was always better than one asking for an autograph. Monroe accepted small perks to being mangled. One perk was pity for him in the black market. After every show, Monroe stopped off at the back alleys of the docks, digging up connections to bootlegged liquor. With cash in hand and face covered, people felt the need to get him plastered right away.

Monroe stepped onto the new boards placed on his porch. The fresh wood was clearly visible even in the moonlight. To test out the new boards, Monroe gave them a solid stomp with both feet. The door had a fresh coat of paint on it covering the word "FREAK." Monroe moved his fingers along the invisible word, and it was still there in his mind. His stomach rumbled, forcing him out of his daze. He removed his key to unlock the heavy door.

In the kitchen he picked up a red apple from the bowl. Rot had eaten one entire side of the once red fruit. Monroe threw it out the window into the backyard, hoping it would fertilize the lawn. He shuffled through the hallway, coming to the turned-out picture frame of his old self with wife and child. The anger swelled in him, not only because someone broke into the house but because they left the picture out, forcing Monroe to look. All the words his wife said to him on that last day hit him like a freight train. He kicked the picture hard, shattered the glass, broke the frame, and ripped the picture in half. Glass crunched under his feet as he marched up the stairs without looking back.

Once 6:30 PM hit, the sun was heading down over the horizon, forcing us to move much faster. We wanted to set off our own fireworks at home later. Marvin was the lookout, hiding behind the trashcans on the corner. Billy and I were going for the storm doors. The plan was to get in and out within ten minutes, enough time to quench Billy's thirsty curiosity.

"All right, Marvin, get those lips wet and ready for the blow in case anyone comes around," Billy said, tucking his shoelaces deep in his shoes just in case we had to run for it.

"Yeah, yeah, I got it. Just don't do anything stupid." Marvin knelt behind a trashcan.

"I'll be sure to watch him closely," I said, knowing how shifty Billy was.

We ran across the empty street, attempting to be stealthy. In the distance, the popping explosions of small firecrackers erupted. The bottle rockets exploded in the air, and the band played in the park. We came to the conclusion that our moms and dads wouldn't notice us gone until around seven, when the picnic blankets were laid down on the grass in time for the big show.

The two of us reached the storm doors. Before I lifted it, I forced Billy to look me in the eyes. "Ten minutes, that's it."

"I heard you the first ten times. You worry too much for a young man." Billy slipped through the crack in the doors.

"Son of a bitch."

Billy spotted the Picasso painting on the wall, sharing the same wonder I had. He shook it off quickly and headed up the creaky stairs. With each snap of settling wood I cringed, hoping no one could hear it.

"Where were the medals?" Billy asked.

"The den, it's next to the dining room," I whispered.

"Why you whispering?" Billy said in a normal voice.

"Just in case," I whispered.

Billy rolled his eyes and turned the corner, heading for the dining room, when I came across the destroyed picture frame and stepped on the broken shards. I figured we had a good three minutes to get out before we made enough noise to rouse the monster awake. That was, if it wasn't already too late.

"Billy, we got to go now," I whispered loudly.

"Stop whispering, will ya." Billy had the case in both hands.

"Who the hell is in there?" Monroe roared from the top of the stairs.

Billy dropped the case to the hardwood floor, breaking it. "Shit," he shouted, running for the door.

Monroe met us as we hit the door, swinging it open. Monroe grabbed my shoulder, squeezed down hard, and flipped me around to face him. Being eye to eye with him, all curiosity ended that night. The deformity was severe. His face was scarred and blistered as if a talon of fire had slashed it. His hair, matted at the top, flowed over the side in frazzled strands, and his upper lip was half missing to reveal yellowed and black stained teeth. With his nostrils flared he was akin to a demon from an old wood carving from somewhere deep in Eastern Europe. And his smell was drunken rot with a hint of tobacco.

"You little shit! Did you want to see the monster for free!" Monroe squeezed hard, making a bruise form immediately.

Billy attempted to pull me away. "Let him go, you freak!"

Monroe let go of my shoulder, allowing us a chance to run away.

"That was close, Steve." Billy said my name within earshot of Monroe. At the time I thought nothing of it, but Monroe closed the front door and remembered it.

Marvin came out from beyond the trashcans, shrugging his shoulders. "What's the deal?"

"No time, just run!" Billy said in passing.

Marvin sighed and ran as fast as he could with us. "Nobody said anything about running."

We ran all the way to the park and made it right on time, seven o'clock, on the dot. I waved to my parents as I caught my breath.

We were sweating as bad as Marvin. Anxious, but exalted by what we just witnessed. A local legend was delivered with a roar of a beast. No one would believe us. But we knew what we saw. And we laughed.

"You said his name?" Marvin asked Billy, heaving hard.

"Like it matters, it was dark. I mean seriously, how many Stevens are there?"

"Only one that worked with Walter Mitty, you idiot." I hit Billy over the head.

"Calm down, I'm sure that happens to Monroe all the time. He'll forget about it by tomorrow." Billy was never right about anything.

"You're probably right," I said, causing Marvin to frown.

"Are you crazy? No one forgets kids breaking things."

"Let's keep it down, parents are all over the place, and they tend to talk to one another." Billy trotted off to his family sitting on a large quilt.

"Are you worried?" Marvin asked me.

"Yeah. The last thing I need is Walter telling my dad about this. I'll talk to you later." I rushed off to my parents, who were sharing a pitcher of coffee with the neighboring couple.

"You guys catch anything at the pond?" Father asked, dumping about three ounces of sugar into his cup.

"Nothing bit. But we might go back later this week."

"Walter have any other work for you?" Mother added, not noticing my wince at the utterance of Walter's name.

"No, not this week. Maybe he'll let me help out at the McHenry Mansion," I lied. Hell, she needed to hear some good news just in case bad news came around tomorrow.

"Great. You keep this up you may make more than your dad." She smiled at me.

"Then I could retire early." My father lit a firecracker fuse and tossed it toward the Rose Club tent erected not ten feet away from us. The women dressed in fine white summer dresses leaped up in the air at the loud pop of paper and flame.

"I wish you wouldn't do that," my mother told him.

"They never once came to check out your roses for the town tour. Your roses are better than Miss Crowley's. Just because she runs the council, I say nuts to them." He lit another fuse connected to a string of firecrackers. "Here you go, ladies." He let the fuse go a bit before launching. In midair they exploded to the gathered crowd's amusement. A few actually clapped, and my mother broke her disapproval with a wry smile.

"Okay, that was actually pretty good." Mother and Father hugged each other and wrapped a blanket around Katie, pulling her closer to them. Katie yawned, resting her head on my father's chest.

The first set of big fireworks exploded over the park sky brilliantly. I stuck my hands into the picnic basket on the blanket. Mother packed a wallop of a meal tonight: fried chicken legs, potato salad, corn on the cob, biscuits, and apple pie still warm in the tin plate. I ate voraciously, never giving the fireworks two glances. It's not like I hadn't seen them before. What did catch my eye was Cheryl speaking with Brother Phillip. She had been crying for what looked like hours. He put his hand around her, comforting her the whole time and nodding to whatever she was rambling about. I wish I could hold her now, looking back, but as a boy, I just continued to eat. The rest of the town just stared up at the bright lights with mouths agape, enjoying the sight of exploding powder. The town would maintain this vacuous stare as the summer progressed.

A full twenty-four hours went by before Cheryl went to Reverend Thomas for aid in finding her son, Sammy. He didn't have time to help her look for him. It's not that the reverend didn't care; it was the fact that Sammy ran off for days at a time. He would often sleep in the tree house built by his father on Sunset Hill's front side, facing the town. It was a thirty-minute walk from the house and ten minutes away from the fishing pond, which always meant another couple of hours before Sammy would start back home. Sammy was taking the long way home when a man coaxed him into a long-forgotten shed on the dark side of Sunset Hill. This was about the time his mother Cheryl came out to the front yard and questioned my mother. Still to this day, no one really knows how he died and whether he was tortured or raped. In all brutal honesty, he probably was many times before the final blow. The local authorities would find his body with his eyes gouged out, floating in the river around three o'clock in the afternoon on the fifth. The discovery of the recovery wouldn't hit until later that night.

Brother Phillip was the only one in the church office the second day Cheryl came in asking for help. He listened to every quivering word that came out of her mouth; and he smiled most of the time to ease her worry. He decided to look for Sammy himself, and he promised to come to her first if he found him. In the park on July 4th, he told her he was still looking, but the search was in vain. He suggested the sheriff get involved, but of course she was against it.

"This isn't the first time he has taken off, but I feel something in the pit of my stomach. Something isn't right. Bringing the sheriff into this would be a waste of his time—what if Sammy is just sleeping in the tree house or fishing?"

This was her reasoning for not involving the law, so her small-town mentality got the better of her.

Brother Phillip held her hand tenderly and agreed with her. "The sheriff seems to me a little less than stellar anyway. You did the right thing to come to the church first. I can get a couple of people together to look for Sammy in the woods. More than likely he's fishing and getting to know nature firsthand. Which in my opinion often doesn't involve a mother but other boys in the neighborhood. And this always leads to nights away from home without a note." Brother Phillip poured sweet reassurances into her ear, calming her rattled nerves. But reassurances would only go so far by the afternoon of the fifth, when Sammy's body found its way to the river's edge.

On the fifth of July, the three of us were coming back from the Meadow on our bikes, enjoying the last day of small-town providence. We didn't really speak about Monroe until Billy opened his mouth.

"Well, I would say we made it out all right. Saw a freak, then some fireworks."

"You broke his medals, idiot." My anger rose out of the fact Billy used the word freak. It bothered me. I saw what he had looked like for a brief moment. A man with a family.

"And you said Steven's name," Marvin added.

"Idiot," I said, hitting him over the head.

"We'll be fine. Monroe doesn't talk to anyone, anyway. Plus, the glass case broke, not the medals. That's why they're called medals. I'm sure we made it out all right."

On cue, Sheriff Tate's Model-T popped with black smoke down the road alongside us. He gave us the eye, being the sheriff and all, as his Henry Ford monstrosity puffed more black smoke while kicking into third gear and passing us.

"He's heading for your house, Steven." Billy was worried now. "You think Monroe blabbed to the sheriff?"

"No, couldn't have." I pedaled faster. Marvin and Billy followed to beat the sheriff home, but the sheriff stopped in front of Cheryl's house, not mine. He got out holding abused, folded clothes.

"Looks like he got your jail stripes already picked out for you," Marvin said.

"Shut up."

Sheriff Tate headed for Cheryl's house with a nervous walk. He knocked on the door, the lights came on from the living room, and the door opened. Cheryl listened to what Sheriff Tate said, then collapsed, screaming, and suddenly our problems seemed irrelevant.

We rode over to try to help, but Sheriff Tate raised his hands to stop us.

"Boys, just go on home, you can't do no good here."

Cheryl shook uncontrollably, hitting her head with her fist and screaming at the top of her lungs. "Not my Sammy! No God! Not Sammy!" Her screaming woke the street. People came out of their homes to see what could be happening.

"Boys, please just get out of here," Sheriff Tate pleaded with us. His eyes focused on us for a long moment, as if we were on Death's door. "And stay away from the river for a while; the current might be stronger this year than normal."

"Is that what happened to Sammy?" Marvin asked, but Tate headed back to Cheryl, now in the arms of her husband.

"Just get out of here for now." He helped to carry Cheryl into the house. The door closed behind them, but the crying and pleading to God continued.

The three of us dispersed slowly, never saying a word. The muffled screams of despair didn't subside; an awful sound that lingered. God doesn't seem to exist when those shouts echo across an empty yard. When a tragedy hits, the entire world seems to shut down, and you feel angry seeing people smile and living life normally. It's not their fault to be human. Tragedy doesn't affect them when it's from a newspaper page, but being within earshot of Cheryl's screams made you realize all victims have mothers and they're broken forever.

Coming into the house, my mother and father rushed to grab me and hold me tight. They heard the screaming too.

"Where were you tonight?" my father asked, jerking me forward.

"We were at the Meadow."

"You got to start coming home earlier now. You can't just go off and do whatever you please. You are still under this roof, and we're in charge." My father paced back and forth.

"I'm sorry."

"Just be home sooner from now on," my mother commanded calmly. "Sammy ran off a lot too. We don't want you to do that anymore. If someone like him could get sucked up in the current, then anybody can."

This was the reasoning for Sammy's death: The current was to blame. The river was too much for a strong swimmer like Sammy to take, and that's what killed him. No one ever mentioned the part about his eyes being gouged out, or the very obvious bruises on his neck and face. The sheriff denied any of that when prodded. I think he knew something was wrong, but his years of minding the small-town atmosphere just took over his sense of justice. No one wanted to admit there could be a killer in their midst. That would deny us the simplicity a small town provides.

No one could sleep that night on 1st street. I lay on my bed with arms over my head and eyes wide open, still able to hear crying from across the street. I got up to my opened window; the breeze was coming in, and it felt good. I was angry now. Cheryl was still crying, forcing me to close the window and ending a once-in-a-lifetime cool wind on a July night. I stayed at the window for a moment noticing that the lights in every home were off, except for Cheryl's house. I closed my curtain too, blocking off any view. I still couldn't sleep, knowing yards away a mother screamed for her boy to come home. Luckily for me, my tired body yielded, allowing sleep to take over.

Chapter 7

The day of the funeral Marvin, Billy, and I watched the procession from up the hill leading to the church. Feelings of mixed remorse filled me. I hardly knew Sammy, but him dying so young hit me hard. Billy was blasé over the whole thing, and Marvin was smart enough to show respect but little else. We stood on our bikes watching the pallbearers carry the casket to the horse-drawn hearse. My eyes caught Walter staring up at me through the myriad of mourners pouring out of the service.

"This is bad. Let's take off," I suggested to the group.

"Show some respect," Billy, of all people, commanded me.

"My dad said they pulled him out of the river with his eyes poked out." Marvin was quick to dispense the gossip.

"Why would you think that would be worth telling?" I asked with a pint of disgust.

"It's odd, something you don't hear about often. I mean hell, that's pretty neat." Billy was quick to defend Marvin's revelation.

"Just keep that to yourself, would you?" I told them angrily. I pedaled away fast, leaving them behind.

"What do you think that was all about?" Marvin asked Billy.

"Walter Mitty was down there."

"Oh, makes sense he would be a bit sour," Marvin replied, giving Billy the stink eye.

"What?"

"You were dumb enough to say his name running out of there like a little girl."

"You didn't see his face. Hell, you would've pissed your pants. Oh, I'm sorry, your shorts." Billy pointed out the awful shorts Marvin was cursed by his mother to wear.

"They're the only size shorts that fit comfortably. My mom cares about my comfort. What about yours?" Marvin pedaled away quickly.

"Am I the only real man in this group?" Billy said to himself, shaking his head as he rode past the crying relatives of Sammy Miller.

I was heading fast down the slight slope toward Walter's General Store. It was fast enough to send someone to the hospital if I hit them, but I didn't care. All I could see in my head were Walter's eyes glaring up from the church steps. I knew he was judging me from down the street. He had to know what had happened. He would tell my father, forcing a beating on me for breaking the law. My mother would avert her eyes from me across the dinner table because I had failed her so miserably. I would be regarded as a common thug, a reprobate, scum never allowed honest work again. This plagued me coming down the hill, so much so that I didn't see Brother Phillip crossing the street directly in path with my reckless downhill plummet. I hit the brakes, skidding hard against the blacktop. He shot a surprised look, lifting his hands fast to grab the handlebars of my bike and settling me after the sudden stop. He was a surprisingly strong man, with a white-knuckled grip like iron around the metal of the handlebars. We both stared at each other, eye to eye, in the middle of the street. I tried to break the silence, but he was much faster.

"My Lord, child, you almost killed me," he told me in a soft voice. He smiled, calming me down in an instant. He allowed me to kick the stand down to regain balance before he let go of the handle-bars. "Why were you riding so fast?"

"I was just—I was trying to—" The addition of almost hitting a brother of the cloth caused me great anxiety, and I tried to slow down to catch my breath. Brother Phillip put his hand on my shoulder.

"Take it easy. A boy your age can't die of a heart attack, even if you look close to one. Relax. Calm down. Breathe." Brother Phillip breathed with me, in and out, in and out. My nerves began to subside, and my head cleared up fast. "Now, that's better. It looks like you were coming from the church."

"Yeah."

"Yes?" he corrected me.

"Yes."

"You saw the congregation gather?" he asked, cocking his head, awaiting my answer.

"Yes."

"And you feel sorry for that boy?" This time he spoke with a hint of a smile as if suppressing a laugh.

"Of course."

"Then you are forgiven. In some instances, when faced with hard times we either run away or face it with clenched fists. It seems you ran away, and there's nothing wrong with that." He smiled at me. His build would be imposing if not for the solid white collar around his neck.

"No, it wasn't that. I just…" I tried to find the words to explain the situation but instead throw up my shoulders to give the age-old excuse: "It's complicated."

"Complicated? Did it involve something mischievous? Did you do something wrong?" he asked, stroking his chin, with his eyes darting back and forth, thinking of the mischievous things children can do.

"Yeah, but—"

"No, don't tell me. I am a brother, not a priest. I have no jurisdiction over sins committed, but I can steer you toward the right path so that absolution can be delivered just in case your soul was in mortal danger. Is it in mortal danger?" he asked, exuding a charm I had never encountered. This was a man you would trust after one conversation.

"It might be. I don't know," I said, blinking in confusion.

Brother Phillip walked my bike to the side of the street. He sat at a bench, digging through his blazer, and removed a pack of smokes. "You see, a man is made by taking on what life throws at him. You are a boy and prone to doing dumb things now and again. But if you really want to grow up and show real moxie, you can't run away. You need to face it with clenched fists." He lit the smoke with an expensive lighter. "Things may go wrong for you of course, but don't let that derail you off your quest for redemption."

"Well, I don't want to disappoint my mom and dad. If they found out what I did, I don't think they would look at me in the same way again."

"Was this so-called sin an attack against your parents?"

"No."

"So, they were not the recipients of this so-called sin?"

"No, it didn't involve them at all."

"Ah ha!" He put his cigarette out on the sole of his fine leather shoe. "Then there you go. Maybe whomever you crossed will understand your plight and see to it that whatever the punishment for your transgressions, it is done with privacy. Just between the two of you." He smiled, nodding his head. "Yes, I like that. That would be the best advice I could give you. Go to the party directly affected and apologize. Beg them for punishment because forgiveness is never enough."

"You think that'll work?"

"Of course. This town seems to me to be very lovely and

forgiving. I think whatever small thing you did can be forgotten."
He looked at me with squint. "Then again, you may receive a penance for your transgressions."

I headed inside Walter's general store with my fist clenched like a real man against the world. I was ready for anything.

Walter was fast with the open palm slap. A strong sting shocked me. I stood there holding my throbbing face, and I could feel it turn blue and purple almost immediately. My eyes swelled with tears, but I did not cry or sniffle. I took it like a real man should. Walter, on the other hand, was not so proud of my newfound ability to take a slap to the face. His eyes narrowed like a Wild West lawman preparing to grab the guns at his side to finish off a lowlife. His lip curled, exposing his well-polished teeth, which let me know he was good and pissed off.

"I trusted you with work anyone could have done, and you squander it for a peek inside a man's home? Did you take money out of his pockets? His drawers?" Walter slapped me again. "You just got to give me a moment to clear my head." Walter ceased his attack, breathing hard, his face red with anger. "Hell with it, I'm going to leave it up to Monroe. His mind is more apt on how to punish people who sneak around his home, and if he wants to take this to your father, we will take it to your father. Now get on out before I hit you again." Walter went behind the counter, slamming down a bottle of scotch. Luckily, the Puritan forces weren't around to smash it. He took a quick shot, then another and put it away.

I walked out of the store seeing stars, with buckled knees and a raw nose from the hit, but I didn't feel it. I had accepted the punishment of a man I crossed and survived. Not many people would admit to what I did, so I already felt bigger than most people by the time I was thirteen.

Brother Phillip remained on the bench, with another smoke

dangling from his lips. "Looks like you received your punishment." He laughed a bit. "Looks like you can take a hit. You feel better?"

"Actually I do. I really feel better," I said, rubbing my face.

"Just put some red meat on that shiner. It'll go away before you get home." He put the cigarette out this time on the bench arm. "Your first steps to becoming a man… We're looking for some kids to help us out at the church this weekend. Would you be willing to come in for a few hours?"

"Depends on what's going on with my schedule. Likely the punishment will include working long hours under a hot sun with a loon as a boss."

"Fair enough, but please do tell your friends to come to me if they're interested in some honest work for the Lord." He began to head back up the road to the church. He turned around to give me another word of advice. "Remember, keep a clenched fist. Everything will be better for you if you do." He began to whistle a church hymn and put his hands in his pockets.

I watched him for a moment before I went to my bike. He had a pleasant quality to him that would force the most hardened cynic to smile, just as I did right there in the middle of the street. Then he made it over the slight hill and was gone from sight, allowing me to break off my amazement and ride home.

As I got closer to home, Marvin and Billy joined me. Billy rode slower than Marvin this time around and forced me to ask, "What?"

"You look a little beat up. Did you have a talk with Walter?"

"Yeah, I did."

"You didn't mention me, did you?"

"No, I didn't because it was my fault for listening to you in the first place. I realize this now that I'm a grown-up," I said with an air of maturity.

Billy threw me a raspberry. "Nuts to that! You broke in first, and I followed."

"You shouldn't have told him about the medals," Marvin interjected.

"Don't help me out here, Marvin."

"Look, Steve, you took the beating, and I thank you for it. But I still worry you might squeal." Billy stopped his bike directly in front of mine. He seemed to have a point to make. "I just want to be sure you'll maintain this newfound maturity, keeping me out of the shit storm that will come if my dad found out."

"Billy, you're an idiot." That's all I could muster as I rode away from him.

"Oh, looks like the maturity evaporated, you broken record," Marvin quipped, giving Billy a belly laugh.

"Hey, wait up," Billy shouted, riding to catch up.

I rolled my eyes at the two of them riding side by side. "I thought we were done
talking?"

"Come on, I just don't want to get in trouble, that's all."

"Don't worry about it. I'm sure you'll do something stupid later."

"Even if I did, I'm faster than any old man in this town. Just try to watch them hit me."

We rode a little while longer racing in the streets, doing tricks, and trying to see Amber Hurley through her window. On further thought, we realized this a waste of time, as the more developed ladies of the Rose Club had a propensity to air their bedrooms out when the summer wind blew into town on a night such as this. None were obliged to greet our hungry eyes with a flash of flesh. It seemed most were on dates with their boyfriends, leaving us wishing we were older. But the dreams of teenage carnality evaporated with the shattering of a bottle Billy smashed with a rock. Dozens of bottles lay about the train tracks where the hobos and railroad workers chucked their empty hooch bottles. We lined them up in phalanxes only Alexander could dream up. Launching wave after wave of brutality none had seen since the Great War. Defeating the evils of the world with grapeshot of stones ricocheting off the metal tracks, eliminating the quiet of summer nights. All one could hear was the laughter of children, the roar of imagination, and the wind through the trees. After this night, none of us would ever be able to hear that again.

Chapter 8

Two days had passed before any word came from Walter. I was hoping this trend would continue, but my punishment was only half paid. We were sitting at the dinner table, quietly moving the cabbage back and forth and trying desperately not to digest it. My mother was a great cook, but her cabbage would have made the Irish potato famine endurable. None of us had slept much either. We were all still shaken up over Sammy.

"You want to pass me the salt, please?" my father asked, checking the time on the clock hanging over the china cabinet. He had been doing that all night. He was waiting for something, which meant Walter would be coming over to deliver it. My nervousness began to rise.

"Here you go, Dad." I handed it over as he checked his pocket watch this time.

My mother dropped her fork against the plate. "All right, stop that."

"Stop what?"

"Looking at your watch. Are you catching a train?" she teased.

"I mailed away for something important. It should've been here by now."

"What is it?" My mother now showed a glimmer of excitement.

"Something to help us sleep."

"Not another tonic. You know those are outlawed," I told them.

"It's only illegal if it has cocaine in it. Damn government had to go and enforce the whole label law thing. But no, it's not a tonic." A knock rapped at the door. My father jumped up out of his chair. "I got it!" he shouted and ran to the door.

I sunk in my chair as the two men chatted it up at the door.

"Did it come in yet?" My father's voice almost cracked.

"Yeah, here it is. And if you could give this note to your boy." Walter didn't have much contempt in his voice when he uttered "boy." Maybe we were okay now.

"Can do, thank you for sending this over, really."

"Not a problem, have a good night all."

"Good night, Walter," my mother shouted from the table.

Dad threw me the note as he slammed a heavy parcel onto the table, shaking the glasses and plates. "Heavier than I thought."

"Okay, what the hell is it?" my mother demanded.

Father opens the parcel, revealing a purple brick. "A brick of wine. Finally, science has developed something for the masses worth getting excited about."

"I am not cleaning up after you," my mother informed him.

"This will be easy. All you got to do is add some water, sugar, and vinegar, I think. Maybe let it set for an hour or two. Then you got a grade A gallon of red wine. You drink about half that amount, and you're bound to be out like a light." He headed for the kitchen.

"Was that another job?" Mother asked me as I opened the note.

Monroe will see you tomorrow noon. Bring gloves.

The glove part worried me the most. "Yeah, another job. I'm a hardworking man now, huh?" I tried to hide my disappointment with congeniality. Luckily, my dad was making enough noise to mask the attempt.

"Kids, never invest in mail-away items. They're messy, never work, and cost too much to be worth all the trouble." A crash of pots and pans sent Mother running for the kitchen. "I'm coming in!"

"I got it!" my dad shouted back before a crash of broken glass hit the tile cabinet

counter. After about two hours of waiting, Father shouted through the closed door, "The wine is ready!" He had two glasses on a silver tray; very cosmopolitan it was. Too bad the wine itself left a milky residue on the rim of the glass with floating pieces of resin.

Mother could only stare at it. "I'm afraid to drink this." She brought it up to the lamplight, trying to uncover any obscure bacteria floating around. There were more than a few floaters in there.

"It's fine. Hell, I followed the instructions to the letter." He sat in his large chair, taking in the aroma and swirling the contents like a refined gentleman would. He took a drink and spit it out into the fireplace immediately. "This is poison." The bright red dye colored his white teeth.

"Look at your teeth!" Mother laughed.

He checked them out in the reflection of the silver tea set, and his face exploded in worry. "This isn't funny." My dad madly scrubbed his teeth with a handkerchief.

"This is why you don't buy mail-away items, kids." Mother dumped her wine into the potted plant in the corner. "Let's just stick to the whiskey." She pulled out the giant bottle from under the chair.

Walking toward Monroe's house, I kept looking over my shoulder. The new sense of paranoia did not stem from Sammy's death but was more about Billy and Marvin riding their bikes and discovering me without mine. They would eventually ask the question, *Where are you going without your bike?* Any lie I came up with wouldn't send them off. They would want to be a part of it because, like I have said repeatedly, this was a small town. There wasn't much to do when school was out. A kid could only go to the fishing spot and not catch anything so many times before it became maddening. I managed to get to Monroe's gate without anyone batting an eye, thankfully. I gazed up at the Victorian House of Usher. For a moment the sun seemed to dip behind it, engulfing me in shadows. My fear was getting the best of me until I remembered what Brother Phillip mentioned about standing with clenched fists. I clenched my fist, adjusted my belt, and opened the gate. It creaked loudly, forcing me to look over my shoulder again to see nothing. I carried on undaunted, taking the first step onto the sidewalk, then another, then another. I managed to make it to the door.

I knocked.

The door cracked open and Monroe's burlap bag came into view. The eye holes were engulfed in darkness, and the ripped edges had frazzled fibers like a scarecrow head. I couldn't say anything standing face-to-face with this beast.

"Well? Are you going to come in, boy?"

I walked into the dark recess of the foyer as Monroe closed the door behind me. He clicked the lock into the slot. "You can start by sweeping up the glass you broke in the den, and then clean up this mess." He kicked the broken frame.

"Where's a broo—"

He cut me off with a wave of his hand. "In the kitchen pantry. Dustpan is in there too. Sweep and dump it out by the shed." He walked to his den and slumped in his chair, sending dust up. His bag never came off. He folded his legs and waited for me to move. I didn't. I could only stare.

"Get moving," the bag emoted from the chair.

I rushed to the kitchen and noticed the big hole in the wall created by his fist, displaying his strength without his ever needing to move. But my fear turned to surprise as I discovered the kitchen was actually clean. Sunlight cascaded from the windows, making it feel cozy and warm, unlike the hungover monster slumped in the leather chair. There were no traces of dust or rotten food with buzzing flies, only the pristine display of a culinary world. There was a beautiful oak table in the corner, and a fruit bowl rested on top with fresh red apples and oranges. A huge block of cheese stood on the counter tile on a cutting board covered with red cloth, and a open bottle of wine sat next to it. A fresh baguette roll stuck out of a brown sack, along with a giant tube of salami. My mouth watered, but my hunger was interrupted by the shout emanating from the den.

"I don't hear glass being swept, boy!"

I swept up the glass and got a better look at the picture. The woman was more than just attractive; she was angelic, and her smile aroused as well as comforted. Her eyes, even in black and white, had bright color. The shape of her body was perfect through the tight dress. You could see the curves, the breasts, the thighs, and the legs. She was what any man with working balls would call a ten.

"What do you want me to do with the picture?" I timidly asked.

"Throw it away with the rest."

I lifted the picture and the dustpan to the kitchen door. Outside, the backyard remained a mess. I stepped over unkempt weeds and brown grass to the shed on the side. I dumped the contents of the pan, placing the picture down against the shed. I had a feeling no matter what happened between them, Monroe would be bringing this picture back inside. He was still sitting in the den when I got there to sweep up the glass from the medals. His head turned to watch me, which was easy to catch from the corner of my eye. The giant bag over his head was moving. Not even one piece of glass was pushed away from the honorary medals; he had just left them there for days. I swept the glass into the pan and got down on my knees to pick up the medals.

"Don't touch those," Monroe commanded me from his slump.

"I need to pick them up." I shook when I said this.

"Just leave them. Dump the glass and the case, but leave those. They're not for you to touch."

"Yes, sir." I did what he asked and left him. When I headed back toward the house I saw him standing in the kitchen door with arms folded. Even with the bag on I could tell he was smirking, setting me up for something much worse.

"Since you're out here, I would like you to clean up this mess. Pull the weeds, cut the grass, and plant those flowers over there." He pointed to dozens of potted plants against the fence. "Then water it all. All the tools you need are in the shed, so get cracking; it's only going to get hotter." He left me to the backyard hell.

"Shit."

"Don't curse!" Monroe shouted from within the house. I thought it was still too early for anyone to hear it.

Three hours later the yard looked phenomenal. The flowers were planted against the house, the grass trimmed low enough to see small green sprouts, the weeds gone, and water spraying out of the hose. My hands throbbed, my back was a wreck, my knees shook, and it made me proud of what I had accomplished. It was much better than anything the Rose Club could do in three hours. A clap began behind me. I turned to see Monroe sitting on the steps leading to the kitchen with a glass of lemonade in his hand, burlap bag still over his head. The drink glistened in the sunlight, and my mouth—dry as sandpaper—coveted the sweet citrus juice.

"A nice job, boy. Walter was right when he told me you would be the better worker." He stood up, surveying the landscape. "Not bad at all. You thirsty?" He offered me the glass.

I took it wholeheartedly and drank it down. "Thank you," I said in between gulps.

"Come inside. Let's have some cheese and salami. I feel you've earned it." Monroe stood on the steps holding the kitchen door open for me.

"Thanks, but shouldn't I work some more?" I couldn't believe that came out of my mouth, but I didn't think I could eat with Monroe next to me.

"Come and eat, then we'll see what else I can come up with."

I walked up the stairs and entered the kitchen, noticing the spread on the table: salami, cheese, fresh bread, a bottle of wine, and a pitcher of lemonade. My fear subsided and my appetite took control.

"All right, you win." I sat at the table.

Monroe cut some cheese and salami and put them on my plate. "Do you like salami?" he asked with no sign of disgust.

"Yes." My mouth watered uncontrollably. "Yes, thank you, sir." I sucked back the drool.

Monroe put the sliced salami and cheese on a silver-lined plate. Only rich tycoons ate off plates like these, usually garnished with steak and lobster. Here we were just eating a snack.

"What were you trying to do when you broke into my house?"

Luckily, I had a mouthful of salami, so I couldn't answer right away. I swallowed and shrugged my shoulders, "I don't know. My friend wanted to see what was inside more than me."

"Because *you* already walked through here."

"Yeah."

"Did my surroundings satisfy your curiosity?" Monroe had not eaten anything yet.

"I guess."

"Well, good, I guess now we can break bread together." He took off the bag to reveal his mangled face in the bright daylight. With the sun out the deformity made my stomach turn. Spittle dribbled out from his blasted, opened lips and his teeth were brown from tobacco and drink. His hair was matted by sweat and dirt. Hygiene was not as important when there was no one to notice and care. The muggy stench of sweat, urine, and vomit intermingled as the gust of air created with the swift removal of the bag suddenly hit me.

"Oh, it is so nice to get out from under that bag," he jested, trying to catch me staring. I could only look away. "Usually I smell much nicer, but last night I had a hell of a time with my friends, drink and misery."

"This is good salami," I managed, feeling queasy.

"I like the finer things in life. Salami of this magnitude is rare, shipped by boat direct from Italy. I buy it when I go to the city." He threw a piece of salami and a hunk of cheese into his mouth. Particles flew out of his disfigured lips.

"Sorry, this is why I can never invite people over for dinner. I would make them all sick." He drank some wine, cocking his head up so as not to allow any to spill out of his mouth. "The wine is much more expensive. And I don't share that."

I had not made eye contact once. He noticed and proceeded to rap his fingers against the table.

"Is there something wrong?" I asked, knowing exactly what was wrong.

"Not once have you looked me in the eye. I know why, but I would like to hear you say it."

"No reason." A stupid thing to say because there were about a million reasons.

"Is it because of my face?" he asked, leaning closer, the odor overpowering and his eyes ablaze. "Were you trying to be polite? Were you trying to have a bit of tact? Breaking into my home is neither tactful or polite, so why don't you look at me when you speak? Why are you such a respectful son of a bitch now? Look me in the eye, boy."

"No reason."

"Walter said you asked about me, so let me indulge you. I was in the trenches. One glorious but unfortunate day, I looked up to see if there were any approaching Germans. And bang! Dirt, fire, and shrapnel blast into my face. I don't remember the pain because I was knocked out on impact. I thought I was dead. I awoke days later, after the doctors had stopped the neck wound from gushing blood.

They did the best they could with what little they had, but my face was gone. My heart remained beating though, and now I am here enjoying a summer afternoon with you."

I remained silent for too long. He couldn't accept this, so he had to push the point further.

"Is this not what you wanted to see when you broke inside my house? Here I am giving you a free show; people would pay top dollar to see me up close without the bars."

"Why did you say glorious but unfortunate day?"

This caught him off-guard. Now it was his turn to be silent for too long.

"Glorious due to the fact that I was going home. I didn't need to fight anymore. Didn't need to be in a trench and didn't have to hear screams. Unfortunate because this is what I have left." He stood up, putting his plate in the sink but keeping the bottle of wine in his grasp. "How are you in English?"

"I get A's mostly." The tone in the room shifted. I think I kept surprising him.

"Mostly? What does that mean?"

"Two quarters out of four ain't bad... I read a lot though."

"If you did, you wouldn't use the word 'ain't.' What book did you last read?"

"I don't know, a school book. It's summer. No time to read."

"I agree summer is not the best time to curl up with a book. There's too much good weather and playing around to consider. Though for this punishment, reading shall be enforced. Come with me." He led me to the den.

"I need to read now?" I said glumly, shuffling my feet.

Monroe moved his finger along the spines of his leather-bound books. "Here it is." He pulled out a massive novel and tossed it to me. "Catch."

It almost knocked the wind out of me. I looked down on the

raised lettering etched into the cover: *The Count of Monte Cristo*.

"Every boy should read it before they turn fifteen. A rule my father forced on me."

"Why?"

"When you finish reading it, I'll explain."

My eyes met the grandfather clock ticking. Monroe was enjoying the awkwardness of our situation. The ticking clock was the only thing audible. It began to get to me, so I slammed the book shut just to hear something else.

"Am I done now?"

"Tomorrow, I have some errands for you to run."

"What time should I get here?" I put the book down on the table, hoping he wouldn't notice.

"Come on over at nine, gives us a little sleep-in time."

I headed for the door, but Monroe noticed the book before I could make a clean break. "Aren't you forgetting something?" He had the book in his hand.

"Thought I could make it." I grabbed the book, hating the heaviness of it.

"See you tomorrow, boy."

I never thought I would be walking home from Monroe's house with a book in my hand. Its weight was ridiculous. The leather cover had a minuscule layer of oil, causing it to slip through my hand a number of times. The heat also made the trip worse. What I wouldn't give to be unscrupulous. If I were, I would toss this damn book in the river and then follow suit to cool down. But this book was old and expensive. I couldn't do that to anyone, not even Monroe. Besides, he would probably make me work harder and longer to pay it off, and after today, I never wanted to work again. Every inch of me ached. I was thirteen yet felt like my father. Old and abused by manual labor. Yet with every pang of soreness there was a sense of accomplishment. A sense of joy. Pride for working hard.

Though my pride quickly turned as I passed Cheryl's house. Cheryl would just sit on the couch despondent. Her husband, Marshall, would watch her wither away by the year's end. Dougie was too young to know what had happened, so he would often ask for Sammy out of habit. This only pushed Cheryl over the edge. It got to the point when Dougie didn't exist to her anymore. She thought he was the ghost of Sammy, and she would scream and curse. Dougie cried more than Cheryl now. Drinking was not an escape, as booze was an expensive commodity. Mourning can take you so far and depression set in for Cheryl as the locals stopped checking up on her. By the end of the summer, Marshall left them, ashamed at what he blindly did at the White Lady Tree. Cheryl shot herself in the head on New Year's Eve. The grandparents in Rhode Island would take in Dougie, where he fared no better. Years later, I had heard he fell off the side of a bridge. Anyone who was there said he didn't fall with a shout; he jumped with a purpose.

Once I was through the front door I felt better. Now I could sit and relax after a hard day's work. My mother was dusting in the living room, and I marched upstairs quietly so as not to let her know I was available for chores. I made it to my room only to discover Katie playing with my toy soldiers.

"What are you doing in here?"

"Mommy didn't want me to mess up the living room. Bam." She killed my cavalry captain with a cannon.

"But this is my room."

"Read your book."

She aimed the toy cannon with its three-man crew at my fort near the bed. Pillows erected around the edges created a mountain terrain. My sister's imagination has always amazed me. She arranged the soldiers in a phalanx, in separate groups leading up the bed toward the stack of pillows. Roman centurions mixed with German infantry, all bad of course.

"Or you could be the bad guys." She pointed at the approaching phalanx on the bed.

"No, you have fun. I'll read." I left her to my toys. I was always a better brother than most.

Mother caught me coming down the stairs. "How was work today?"

"Good." I sat down in Father's chair and opened the book to page one.

"So, you're done for the day with Walter?" she asked, making me feel uneasy.

"Yeah, now I'm just going to read my book."

"A book? It's not school time."

"What if I just want to read to enlighten my mind? Feed my imagination with the words of illustrious poets of the ages?" I thought maybe the flowery language would pique my mother's feminine side, but to no avail.

"You've still got a backyard fence to paint."

"I didn't see any paint out there." I used a new tactic now. Also, to no avail.

"It's in the shed. Three buckets of white paint, you can't screw that up. Now go on, get a first coat on before dinner." She scooted the chair from under me, trying to get me up. "You can always read tonight. Besides, its cooler now and after working with Walter, this should be a breeze."

Her words failed to rouse any excitement from me as I went outside to paint. "All right, you win." The book fell with a thud to the wood floor. My feet dragged themselves outside to the yard. Buckets of paint greeted me on the lawn. The brushes stood by themselves, as they had not been cleaned since the last paint job eight years ago.

"This can't get any worse," I shouted to the heavens, turning my head to catch my mother laughing in the kitchen window, skinning potatoes.

Chapter 9

Monroe sat at his typewriter with his bottle of scotch. No wine tonight. Scotch was what he needed. On the shelf, he noticed the empty space where *The Count of Monte Cristo* stood, and he smiled. Someone was hopefully getting better use out of it than the dust. He shifted in his chair and drank a shot down.

We had just moved into the new house when your mother told me about you. I won't give you the details on how she discovered this, but this most joyous occasion began on a stormy night. The wind slammed into the shutters, rain battered the roof, and logs burned brightly in the fireplace. We shared a bottle of wine to celebrate the news. We were lost to the world in each other the whole night. Even the wind against the house didn't faze us.

"I love you," she whispered. It was the first time she ever said it to me. I held her close and kept her still between my legs, then looked in her eyes. We remained in this embrace for an eternity. Time is tricky when two people sit in each other's arms. Within a moment, the sun came up and the storm ended.

That day everything was amplified to the tenth degree. You can't imagine how wonderful it is to know a child is coming soon. So many thoughts run through your mind: what you will teach them, what they might look like, and what their first word will be. Any trouble you had the previous day disappears, and you're left with only the worry of the unborn future. It's a nice worry to have.

Walter already had cigars out when I came through the office door. The son-of-a-bitch bought the good ones with the company's money. Once the smell hit me, I was obliged to forgive him. They were pretty damn good.

"How the hell did you know?" I asked him.

"Your wife swung by here an hour ago and knew you would take your time getting to the office. She told me to buy the good cigars with the company money, of course." Walter lit up his second cigar, laughing.

"She's a quick one. What's the word on the McHenry Mansion?"

"We've sold it. They want us to move them in as well, so we need to hire a couple guys, and with the repairs I know they'll want before the year's end, we'll be looking good."

"Looks like you'll be able to buy a cabin on Sunset Hill."

"Summer is coming early."

"After the baby."

I saw Walter slump. He really wanted to sell that mansion by spring's end, allowing him to buy a new cabin. "That doesn't mean you can't buy one. You are entitled to fifty percent."

Walter rose from his slump and got out of his desk chair. "I'm buying it now. I'll be back before three."

"Take your time. I think we're all going to have a half-day anyway."

At the end of the half-day, I went to see my wife. I caught her checking out the stuffed toys on the shelves in the store. Her smile forced me to hesitate. I wanted to enjoy the image: a mother-to-be shopping for the child on the way. It's when you know you're a grown-up, when all those needs fueling selfish wants are gone. All I wanted was for you to be happy, and I would do everything to make it work.

She caught me watching. "How long have you been spying on me?"

"Long enough. Which one should we get?" I pointed at the stuffed animals.

"Which do you think is the softest? I like this one." She smashed a stuffed elephant in my face. Her laugh rippled through me like an ocean wind. Gooseflesh rose in me. Her eyes lit up, noticing my smile, noticing me. I loved her. She, in turn, loved me. I pine for it still. I hate thinking on it. But it feels good to. Damn it, it feels warm.

"Yeah, I would say that's soft." I picked up a lion with a feathery mane. "But I think this one is much better." I shoved it in her face.

We continued this display of affection for too long, forcing the shopkeeper to make his presence known.

"What the hell are you two doing? These are high-end items." He took them from our hands and put them back.

"Don't be such an ass," your mother told him.

"What did you call me?" The shopkeeper was shocked. His sensitive sensibility was rattled.

"She called you an ass, and rightly so." I put a five- dollar bill in his vest pocket.

"We're taking these two. Have a nice afternoon, ass." We both laughed as we headed out of the store, leaving the shopkeeper behind.

"I love you again," she whispered in my ear.

I kissed her forehead and grabbed her hand. The way she said it made me yearn to spend eternity with her, but time is a tricky thing. Within three years, we would hate each other.

Monroe stopped typing once the scotch bottle was empty. Reliving happy memories can really take a toll on a man out of booze. Monroe ripped the page from the typewriter, putting it on the stack. In the darkness he stood up slowly, his equilibrium off from drink. He put his hand on the back of the chair to gain balance. A round-trip train ticket for New York City rested on the foyer table. Monroe went for the last scotch bottle in the liquor cabinet as he picked up the ticket. He sighed loudly, hating the prospect of another trip to the freak show, even if it was good money. These trips allowed him to continue the drinking and keep the cabin. Some days he would rather burn it to the ground, letting the memories go up in smoke, but the face of his daughter interrupted his fantasies of pyromania. He drank up, dropping the ticket back on the table. He headed back to the typewriter and got ready to relive the moment of birth, the year things started to change. He reluctantly placed his hands on the keys but didn't type. Staring at the blank page comforted him. Perhaps she didn't have to read this part. If she did, the only real feeling produced would be hate for her mother. Monroe could not write this part with indifference or poetic license—it was too painful. Instead, he poured another glass and removed a cigar from his breast pocket. He bit the end off and lit up.

When the silence is all you have left in a house where long ago a child's giggle or a mother's song reverberated off the walls, the darkness is effective to hide in. Nothing can be seen or felt, and it forces a focus on the memory. Without any distraction, it can be a recreation. Monroe gazed off to the corner of the room where the rocking chair once stood. His wife sat in it, breastfeeding the child and singing a soft lullaby. The sun broke through the blinds, providing a soft backlight. He reached out to touch her, but the darkness emerged and sucked away this illusion. Nothing rested in the corner now. Just an old framed picture turned facing the wall. During the day, he could not bear to look at them, but when it was quiet and late, he often got sentimental. Drink always did that to him. It was the reason he wrote drunk. He couldn't remember for too long because his eyes clouded up with tears. The punishment for drinking too much as he sat alone, trying to summon up the image of his wife breastfeeding.

Nothing came, just an empty room filled with darkness.

Chapter 10

After Mother made me paint the fence, I collapsed on my bed without taking a bath. My clothes stuck to me. My hair was matted with sweat. My joints ached from the pain of manual labor. Now I smelled as bad as Monroe. I didn't care at all. I fell into my bed like a stone; the pillows provided enough comfort to pass out with little effort.

"You left this on the table." My mother's voice forced me out of the Sandman's clutches.

"And?" I said with eyes closed.

"It goes in your room. I don't want your things lying around my house. I just cleaned in there." She unexpectedly dropped the book on my stomach.

"Ah, thank you, Mother," I said breathlessly, my lower intestine smothered from the sudden hit of literature.

"It's a good book though. Now you have time to read it." She closed my door, showing some mercy.

I flipped through the pages, discovering small print. I rolled my eyes and threw the book down on the floor. Had Mr. Dumas believed in the practice of illustration perhaps I would've dived right in. My eyes were not too keen on gazing up and down an endless page filled with old English. Or, maybe it was French? Regardless, my peepers were not going to bow down to it, not tonight. And, if this work routine continued, I might never find the time to read anything again. My eyes were fine with that proclamation as the heavy lids closed and sent me to a blessed darkness.

My father woke me up with a shake on the shoulder, forcing me to erupt from sleep with the notion that work was upon me, sending a shock through my brain.

"It's time to get up," my father sang, making it much worse. "Another day in the land of adulthood. Learning a trade, being a man. Breaking your back, like your old man!"

"It's too early," I told him through closed eyes, pulling the pillow over my head.

"It's almost eight, I let you sleep 'cause you're young."

"Yeah, all my youth is being sucked out of me," I said through a sleepy haze. I rubbed my eyes and saw my father holding a cup of hot chocolate.

"I thought you might need this." He handed me the cup. "Mother made breakfast for us, so come on down." He kissed my head and my smell hit him. "Maybe take a bath first."

After a fast, hot bath and large breakfast, I trotted over to Monroe's house, hoping to make the nine o'clock start time I left the house at 8:45, figuring it would take ten minutes to get there, leaving me five minutes to spare. I made it in eight minutes. Not bad, considering I was jogging with a stomach full of bacon and eggs, as well as lugging good old *Monte Cristo*. I knocked on the front door with polite softness, but no answer. I looked over my shoulder and down the street, then knocked again a little louder. No answer. Flustered, I knocked louder and longer. I made it here in eight minutes. I would be damned if he didn't notice. I banged on the door loudly for another thirty seconds solid.

The door flew open. Monroe's hair was much more of a mess than before, his shirt stained with red wine, cigar burns, and ash.

"Why do you insist on knocking so damn loud?" He left the door open for me and slumped back down in his den chair. Three empty bottles of wine and two empty bottles of scotch stood on the dining room table, along with a typewriter and a stack of papers next to it.

"Drink and misery came by again?"

"You talk a lot for a boy your age. I hope this isn't a sign of things to come." He put his hand over his head, rubbing the bulge that was once a normal-shaped skull.

I handed him the book.

"I can't find the time to read this. Just take it back."

"Good literature is like religion; only a few get it right. Find the time to read it." He threw the book back to me.

"How can I find time to read it when I work here and at home?"

"Become a recluse and you'll discover all the time in the world."

"What do you need me to do?" I asked, cutting right to the point.

"I need you to go down to Walter's place and pick up some things. He has them ready. Normally, I pick it up at six, but as you can see I had a little party."

"Walter and I didn't part on the best of terms," I told him, rubbing my face with the memory of the beat-down still fresh in my mind.

"He won't wale on you again, boy. I had a talk with him and told him that you're a stupid kid who gets in trouble. Hell, he and I have done worse things together."

"Should I mention that to him?"

"Smart-ass. Go on and get my stuff. It'll give me more time to gain my composure and figure out how to torment you today."

"Yes sir." I headed out the door, leaving Monroe to deal with his hangover.

Monroe was right. The box of goods was already fully stocked. Walter stood over it with his arms folded, waiting for me with a scowl. Being greeted with such hostility made the time spent there awkward as all hell, even after eating with a disfigured veteran.

"Is this the stuff for Monroe?" I asked, not looking in his direction.

"That it would be." He slid it over.

"Thanks, Mr. Mitty," I politely added, hoping the scowl would dissipate.

"Monroe says you're a hardworking kid. You made his backyard look pretty damn good, considering no one has touched it in four years." He extended his hand. "Maybe we should shake on this and let bygones be bygones."

I took the hand, and we shook. "Thanks, I appreciate that."

"How's your face? It looks all right."

"Ah, it's fine. I just told my mom and dad I fell down a steep hill on my way home. I put some red meat on it, took care of it right away."

"You think you'll be able to carry that all by yourself?" He came around the counter, offering a hand.

"Yeah, it's not so bad." This was a lie. It weighed more than I did, but I wanted to gain Walter's respect again.

"I'm going to talk to your dad about maybe setting you up with some paint jobs over at the mansion. You may be of some use over there."

"Great," I said under great strain from lifting Monroe's crate of groceries. "That would be just great." The veins in my arms started to bulge, and specks of light erupted over my retina. *This must be what a heart attack feels like.* The strain was overpowering. Walter took it off my hands, placing it back on the counter. He laughed, removing the items from the crate until he got to the bottom. Out came three large blocks of concrete.

"I thought it would be funny. Monroe eats like a bird, but drinks like a fish." He handed the crate back to me.

"Funny. Almost threw out my back." I took the crate with ease now.

"Ah, it's what I do with most of the boys starting out. You should've seen this one guy, Stanley Kramer. This kid shit his pants lifting two heavy boxes of bricks. Oh Lordy, that was a sight to see." Walter rubbed my hair with a bear's strength. "You're a good kid. Oh, and before I forget." Walter went underneath the counter, pulling out two bottles of scotch wrapped in paper. "Hide these under the sack of beans, just in case any goody-goodies come around."

"Thanks again, Mr. Mitty."

"Boy, you need to start calling me Walter, especially after lifting that much weight without shitting yourself."

Billy was chewing taffy outside the general store. He ran toward me with nary a concern, bumping into two old ladies taking their morning stroll. "Sorry ma'am and ma'am." He dove into the box, ripping a piece of salami off the top of the tube.

"How can you mix taffy and salami?"

"It's a nice mix of sweet and sour." He reached for more, forcing me to pull further while swiftly kicking at him.

"Oh, come on, relax. I see you and Walt buried the hatchet?"

"He came close to burying it in my face last time. Now he's grown to like me. Even offered me more work at the mansion."

"What? This is getting silly now. You mix paint for one job and break into the house, then get promoted to paint the mansion. Where's my cut of jobs? This is a sad world we live in." Billy chewed on the salami, smacking loudly.

"Well, that's what happens when you grow up."

"Nuts to that. I got plenty of time to grow up. In the meantime, my mom and dad have forced some responsibility on me. I signed up with Brother Phillip. The church done and gave me a job," He beamed with pride.

"Idiots."

"You say that now, but come end of summer, I'll be knee-deep in choir girls."

"They don't start until the fall, moron."

"Even better. More time to wow the congregation with my skills."

"Skills of breaking people's stuff?"

"Keep it down. Walter has some good ears for an old man."

"He's forty."

"The last thing I want to do is work for that guy. I heard he puts bricks in boxes and bags to mess with the workers. One guy—"

"Shit himself. Yeah, I know the story," I interrupted.

He laughed a little. "He just did it to you, didn't he?"

I started walking away from him, and he just laughed.

"Did you get a stain, Steve? A big old turd stain on them drawers of yours?"

The two old women on their stroll gave me a look of utter disgust, as if I really did have a turd stain. "I don't." I tried to plead my case, but the old women kept on walking and gossiping. "Don't you need to wax the pews for Christ or something?"

"Yeah, yeah, I'm going. Thanks for the laugh and lunch." Billy took off toward the church.

The only real reason he took the job was the church's swimming hole in the back behind the supply shed. It was a little gully not more than four feet deep. In the summer, it was the coolest pound to swim in. I think the reverend blessed it so it would be chilly all summer. God's little gift to a small-town church filled to the brim with believers. Even though Reverend Thomas forbade any kids to swim in it. We did and discovered why he was so determined to keep children away. The gully was cool and shallow to hide crates of whiskey and beer from any prying eyes. It didn't much matter because even the sheriff bought his whiskey from the church.

After about three blocks, the crate began to weigh me down even without the bricks. I was taking a moment to relieve my muscles from the unwanted stress when Marvin rode up on his bike.

"Can you believe they gave Billy a job?" he asked me, adjusting his glasses after the sudden stop.

"No, I can't. I guess their standards are dangerously low."

"What's even worse, I don't have anybody to hang around with now. You work all day. Billy will be working all day. Hell, what am I supposed to do?"

"I guess you have to find new friends."

"I don't even want to think about that. I mean, have you seen what this town has to offer when it comes to kids our age? Jesus, why bother?"

"Well, there is always solitude."

"I may have to consider that if you guys keep this working thing up."

"Or, you could get a job too."

Marvin's face soured quick. The suggestion of working hit a nerve. "Are you crazy? You two got suckered into this deal. My mom tells me I don't have to work until after high school, that's if I don't get into college. But I will. So, enjoy your day of sweating. I'll be home reading."

"You're taking the recluse option?"

"Yeah, might as well. With this fat on me I doubt I'll be dating anytime soon. See you later, Steve." Marvin rode off, leaving me with the crate.

Reading in the summer was the greatest sin a child could make. Summer was designed to be played with, not looked at through the blinds. I figured this was why I had an aversion to the book Monroe gave me. Sure, my mother prevented me from reading for chores, but I would have thrown it to the ground anyway. I kept looking at the hunk of salami stolen by Billy. Monroe better not notice. His eyes weren't the best due to the whole deformity, but given a moment to complain, I figured Monroe's eyes would focus instantly.

Monroe lifted up the ripped salami tube with a quizzical look. "Hungry?"

"That was courtesy of my friend Billy."

"Oh, the same friend who has a knack for breaking my things." He removed the two bottles of scotch. "You can keep the beans."

"You did know about Billy."

"I'm not dumb. Walter knows everyone in town, and who hangs out with who. He used to be army intelligence, you know."

"He says not to ask about that."

"The army would be investigated."

"If you knew it was Billy, why isn't he working off the damages with me?"

"He's an idiot. You're the better worker. Walter says anyways."

"That was nice of him."

"I'm going to type a little down in the cellar for a while."

"What do you want me to do?" I asked, looking through the gap in the curtains, checking out the much bigger and messier front yard.

"I want you to read," he told me, unloading the typing paper from the crate.

"Read?"

"You told me you don't have time to read, so I am giving you the time."

I stared blankly at him, unable to add anything to that.

"What do you say, boy? Do you want to work all day in the hot sun or be whisked away to France for murder, mystery, jail breaks, romance, and sword fighting?"

"You make a good point. All except the romance part."

"That'll change." He smiled again but not to me; he turned his head whenever he showed a hint of emotion. "Head into the den and read in my chair. It's big, soft, and perfect for diving headfirst into a book. Off with you, and don't bother me until I call for you."

"You got it, sir." I saluted.

Monroe headed down the cellar stairs as I sat down in his chair. He was right—it was incredibly comfortable and smelled wonderful, like rain on cement in winter. You could fall fast asleep if you closed your eyes for too long, but I had a book filled with adventure to keep me awake. Within twenty minutes, I was engrossed in the story of Edmund Dantes. I'd never read so fast while still able to retain all the events and characters. I was there, in the middle of the story, enjoying the words more than I thought I would. Maybe it was the chair or the fact I wasn't doing yard work, but I enjoyed it wholeheartedly. The simple joy of reading conquered me with hardly a fight. The weight of the book became too much for me, and it slipped from under me. I fell asleep.

Chapter 11

Before you were born, I decided to take your mother to Europe. I had always wanted to go there and breathe in the air of the Old World. With the money we made from selling the mansion and the real estate on 1st Street, we took the train to New York Harbor. Life in New York was incredible to see. The towers of steel and glass were the stuff of dreams for a small-town man like me, and your mother loved it so much. She wanted to be part of the entire splendor. You could tell in her eyes as she looked up. Thankfully, we were only there for the night. On the balcony of our hotel room, I watched her hold her belly. She rubbed it, keeping her thoughts to herself. I didn't interrupt her, I just watched. A woman you love with a life growing inside her is much more beautiful compared to all the other days. I popped open a bottle of champagne, startling her out of her thoughts.

"How long have you been watching me?" she asked, still rubbing her stomach.

"Long enough." I poured the champagne into crystal flutes. She lifted it to her lips and drank. "You like it here, don't you?"

"The city?"

"Yeah, the city."

"I love it. Its busy, loud, there's culture."

"We're going to Europe, culture all over the place."

"But that's the way it was. Here is where it'll be going. Whatever they come up with will be here. Whatever changes made will start here. You can walk down any alley and find something different. Back home there are just the people you know."

"What's wrong with that?"

"Nothing, nothing at all. I just, I thought—everything is changing. I keep reading about what's going on in the newspaper. Seems so far away and yet, if we go in any direction for a few hours we could be in the thick of it. This is the thick of it."

"You want to march for women's suffrage?"

"No." She threw her arms up, tired of trying to explain herself to me. "Just forget it."

"No, tell me what you want?"

She paused for a moment, her eyes shifting over the lit-up skyline of the metropolis. "I want to leave the small-town life."

I couldn't tell her no right away. This was going to be a great trip, and already at the beginning of it, she wanted to leave our home and the foundation I built. "I think you got your first breath of city air and you like it. And great, I love it too, but living here for a long period of time would be a problem."

"Why?" she was quick to ask.

"It's the people, the noise, the space. I mean, hell, we couldn't have a house here like we have back home. It would be far more expensive than you can imagine. Why would you want to give that up for city life?"

She was quiet now, keeping the hurt inside. "You're right. I just got here and it got to my head."

"It would be nice to live in the city, but you're about to have a child, our child. That's not a good time to move to a new place, let alone a big city, hell, the biggest city. Would you want our child to grow up here? Yes, it has culture and different people on every corner, but it doesn't have what I built. It doesn't have my partnership with Walter, the real estate on 1st Street, or the McHenry Mansion. Here we would live in a tenement house, an apartment with three paper-thin walls and we wouldn't be drinking champagne now either."

"You're right" was all she could say as she drank her champagne. I hurt her feelings, but I was too stupid to notice. I was selfish, although it doesn't matter admitting it now.

We didn't make love that night. We just lay in our bed, looking up at the ceiling until sleep overtook me. Your mother was up all night think-ing about what I said, letting her anger stew all night. Though by morning she kissed me lovingly, forcing me to believe she had forgotten our dis-agreement about city life. Truth is, she was sav-ing it for later.

Monroe ceased typing to allow himself a moment to gaze at *Ambroise Vollard*. They stared at one another, separated by canvas and time. Monroe rose from his desk chair and headed up the stairs. *Hopefully the boy is reading*, he thought as he came up each wooden step. Maybe it was a mistake to allow this kid to rub his grubby hands all over a book much older than the town itself. After a moment of pondering, Monroe let go of his cynical nature. The boy being close to his daughter's age helped his case. Perhaps born in the same hospital room or better yet, on the same day across the hall. Thoughts flooded his mind and gave him a knot in his throat. He had tried so hard to forget love, but it was washing over him again. It didn't help matters to find Steven asleep with the book carefully clutched between his arms, a picture of innocence that would melt any deformed cynic.

"Well, shit."

He lifted up the book from under Steven, then tucked a soft blanket around the child, smiling all the while. Was this what could have greeted him if the war didn't happen? A child asleep in Father's chair, book in hand. He moved the hair away from Steven's face, seeing a child for the first time. Monroe, out of an urge to feel what his illusions produced most nights, grasped Steven's hand. He closed his eyes, pretending that the tender fingers belonged to his daughter. A daydream colliding with reality, but no electricity was created. Only the touch of a stranger: cold, limp, and foreign. His daughter didn't feel like that when he held her all those years ago. She was warm, alive, and his family. You couldn't create that with someone else of the same age. You could only garner respect but not love. Respect was nothing next to love. Monroe released Steven's hand, forcing him to mumble incoherently in his sleep. Monroe laughed and headed into the kitchen to crack open another round.

* * *

I woke from my sleep, amazed to find a blanket wrapped around me. I checked to see if the book fell through my hands, but saw it resting on the stand next to me. Sudden relief rushed over me and caused me to realize Monroe had wrapped me up in the soft blanket. I do believe I'd hit a nerve. Maybe this guy could be a giant softie after all. As soon as I put my foot onto the wooden floor, it creaked.

"You up, boy?" Monroe shouted from the cellar.

"Yeah," I replied, hoping the next words out of Monroe's mouth didn't include "front yard clean up."

"How far did you get?" he asked, still in the cellar.

"The Count is at the carnival."

"Keep reading. It only gets better."

I approached the stairs leading down into the cellar. I took a careful step down, afraid to invade his space when he was typing. "Do you need me for anything else today?"

Monroe was staring at his painting. He turned to face me; the light shining in from the window created an odd backlight, making him look much more like a monster than a man. Shadows engulfed his face, and the protruding skull and frazzled hair picked up a halo of light. It was a little frightening at first, but I contained my gasp.

"I want to give you something else, boy," Monroe told me, digging into the drawers beneath the painting. "I feel every boy needs one of these when they're young. Maybe it'll help you shut up more. Kids today tend to talk a bit too much; this will curb it, I think." Monroe threw me a Swiss Army knife.

"Wow," I said, pulling out the blade portion.

"Now don't hurt yourself playing with it or show your friends. The last thing I need is people talking around town. They say enough about me already."

"You'll be fine. Don't worry."

"Take up whittling. It'll allow you to think more clearly and shut out everyone else."

"Sounds fun. Thanks, sir." The image produced by the backlight had faded, and I saw him as a man now.

"I'm going to be leaving town for a few days. I won't need your services until next week. Keep the book and try to finish it before I get back. I wish to discuss it with you in detail." He headed back to the typewriter and sat behind it.

"Not a problem. Have a safe trip."

"I will." He typed. The clanging of the keys echoed in the dingy cellar. "Oh, and don't show the knife to that little shit, Billy. He would most likely break in again."

"Don't worry, I'm still pissed at him."

"Friends do that sometimes." The metal bang of the typewriter began again, allowing me the permission to leave.

Going the long way home was always a better way to travel. Forest trails, pine needles, soft dirt, and shade always greeted each step with the long way round. The trail would spit me out about three blocks from my house, providing sidewalk the rest of the way. Summer was the best time to take this route due to the shade the trees provided. In winter, you took the sidewalk. The last thing anyone needed walking home from school was a dump of hard snow breaking through the branches above. When that hit your head out of the blue, God could forgive the name in vain commandment being broken.

Though this time, taking the long way round brought me to Billy sitting on a rock alone, distant. His thumbs entwined in an eternal twiddling. His knee scraped, his shirt ripped, and his hair a mess. I rarely noticed my friend's looks or injuries, but this time it was obvious something out of his control had happened. My anger at him ceased as I felt a twitch in my psyche warn me something was wrong. But I didn't know what it could be. I had to smile to see if that would break his mood.

"Hey, Billy!"

"Hey, Steve, I didn't hear you coming." He never looked up at me.

"Yeah, I took the long way home." I decided to show him my knife. Maybe that would bring him out of whatever spell he was in. "Wanted to test out my knife." I pulled it out and flipped open some of the various blades. "You want to cut some stuff?"

"No, I was just heading home. I need some rest." He never bat an eye at it.

"The church got you working overtime?" I jested.

Billy feigned a smirk. "Yeah. They do that, don't they? Free labor, I guess." His attempt at levity was flat. Something was definitely wrong with him.

"Are you okay, Billy?" I asked, sitting next to him.

"Yeah, just tired, that's all. Had a long day." Billy threw a rock at a nearby tree. "How was your day?" The way he said it reminded me of Cheryl. Distant, cold, lost. Something was wrong, yet being young, I was not able to deduce what it was.

"I read."

"It's not school time." He finally looked at me, his eyes raw— he'd been crying.

"Well, sometimes you just need to read." This sparked some interest in Billy.

"Oh yeah? I should try it. Maybe it'll help me..." Billy trailed off, losing interest in what he wanted to confess to me. "I need to take off before my dad and mom get mad." He ran down the trail, never looking back to me.

"Have a good one, Billy, I'll see you tomorrow." If only I was older, I would've noticed he was hurt. But I was thirteen, too young to realize the obvious abuse. Trusting people was preferred to reality in a small town. If only I knew then. If only I could've been cynical. The real world was foreign to me. Its evil nature a distant thought, even if it was closer to me than I knew. Billy's behavior was too odd to let go. It stayed with me the rest of the way home and into dinner. Maybe Billy's parents fell on bad times. They always fought loud enough for people to hear it. Even then Billy would just shrug his shoulders and laugh it off. Yelling wasn't anything to be despondent over. I kept to myself, not wanting to induce any parental advice. They were not the best people for understanding emotional changes. It wasn't that they weren't emotional, it just wasn't their way. Keeping things inside was the best choice when it came to hard times or personal conflicts. People didn't care enough to help, let alone ask. I felt if something was wrong, I needed to seek help from someone able to provide it. And the only person in town capable and willing to provide sound advice was Brother Phillip.

Chapter 12

O n Fridays, the church office was dead as a doornail. Oftentimes, Reverend Thomas would close the church office so he could be at home with his rotund wife, doing what many holy men were forbidden to do. But today, the door to the office was open, and the man I was searching for sat smiling at me.

"Steven, did you come here to volunteer?"

"Maybe later, I still have another job. I needed your advice on something."

"Of course, of course, please come into my office." He opened the door wide and guided me in. "I guess my advice from before proved to be of some use."

"Sure did, thanks for helping me out on that one. I need to ask you about Billy. Did he do something wrong?"

"No, he's a great aid to the church. Why? Did he say something?" His inquiry seemed hostile but was covered up with a flash of white teeth.

"It was just strange. It looked like he was hurt, like maybe he fell down. Usually that wouldn't even matter, but he didn't want to hang out or anything. He just twiddled his thumbs."

"Billy is of the same cloth as many people living here. The best thing to do is ignore it. It will go away eventually. I would give Billy another day or so, and he'll be right as rain."

I come across a glass case on the bookshelf. War medals rested inside. The same three at Monroe's house, with a picture of Brother Phillip and his regiment standing behind it.

"You were in the war?"

"A lot of people were in the war, my young friend. That's why I became a brother. I hope you never experience a time like that. No one should. War changes men. It is the greatest evil humanity can muster."

"You have the same amount of medals as—" I stopped myself, not wanting to let slip that I worked for Monroe.

"Just as many as *who*?"

"Monroe—I work for him. He was the one I wronged. The one you helped me out with." I felt a pang of remorse for divulging his name.

"Oh, I see. Is he a member of the congregation? Would I know what he looks like?" Brother Phillip knew exactly who Monroe was.

"He wouldn't come. Too many people probably couldn't handle his looks."

"And why would that be?"

"His face was deformed by a shell in the war, but you get used to it after a while."

"I think it is very kind of you to help him. It shows great character, and it would make you a perfect candidate." Brother Phillip removed an altar boy robe from the closet. "I know the Catholics have what they call altar boys. Now I don't wish to continue practicing Catholic rituals, but this one seems to be a good way to rouse interest in God from the young boys in town. Try it on."

"Is there a changing room or something?"

"No, just change here, I was in the war, remember? I have seen everything. You should take off your pants and shirt because this garment is expensive, and I don't want it to be ruffled." Brother Phillip got closer, trying to force the robe on me.

"You know, maybe later, I need to go home. I'm already late. My mom will be worried." I used the old "mom will be worried" excuse, but he still pressured me to put the robe on.

"I'll write you a note; she'll forgive you." His lips pursed and his eyes widened as I attempted to back away.

"Brother Phillip, really—"

"Brother Phillip? Are you in there?" Reverend Thomas asked from behind the door.

"Yes, right here, Reverend." Brother Phillip put the robe back on the hanger, clearly upset. "Come right in. I was just showing Steven our new robes."

Reverend Thomas came through the door, beaming with hope. "Are you interested in helping out the church?"

"Yeah, eventually. Sure," I lied. Hell, he was a reverend, not a priest. "I need to go back home now. You know that commandment."

"Honor thy father and mother, yes. I do know it. The real question is: Do you know what number it is?" Reverend Thomas cocked his head, waiting to hear the right answer, knowing I never remembered the exact order of the Ten Commandments.

"One of the higher ones, right?" I ran off before any more questions could be asked.

* * *

"Maybe we should have a sermon on the commandments. It turns my stomach knowing the message of God is being lost on the youth," Reverend Thomas proclaimed to Brother Phillip, who was visibly perturbed by the interruption—until a new tactic came to mind.

"Then I suggest we have classes set up in the basement. It's big enough to hold a number of students." Brother Phillip's mood reverted to its congenial self.

"The only problem is who would we get to do it. Not a lot of people have the patience and the knowledge to teach children for free."

"I am always in the mood to teach," Brother Phillip said, putting a smile on Reverend Thomas's face.

"You're a good man, Phillip. Now I wanted to ask you, what sermon should I do on Sunday?"

* * *

Heading out on the train was always a hindrance for Monroe, especially when he wore the bag. The stares he received from people were bad enough, but the gazes of children were much worse. Little children excitedly walking along the train cars would clam up once Monroe passed them. His lumbering frame would freeze any child's wonderment of the steam shooting from the gears and whistle. Monroe felt his presence was a crime even if this was the only way to travel.

Calhoun, a greasy, crusty old man looking more dead than alive, lit a match against the train door. He took it to the tip of a cigar, sucking in the noxious fumes. He coughed loudly, and phlegm shot out of his mouth. He wiped his chin and waved to Monroe. Calhoun always met Monroe at the train car with a cigar in hand. His escort was vicious, quick, and cunning. If anyone attempted to fight or molest Monroe, he had to be there with fists raised and nails sharpened. Monroe was a priceless commodity to the freak show. He was the Marvelous Mangled Man—a weekend attraction that sold out the main tent on the carnival pier every time. He would, of course, receive 35 percent of the profits each night. A pay rate gladly given up to him by the proprietor of the show, Samson, an old war buddy. Though every time Samson gave him the cash, Monroe knew it killed him. Samson was a man filled with charisma, jokes, and drink, and one could easily tell when he was ashamed even if his shame paid.

"Shouldn't take the train anymore," Calhoun said, spitting again.

"How else am I to make the engagements?"

Calhoun pointed out a Ford parked. "By car. They make 'em faster every year. And you sure as hell can afford one, you cheap bastard."

"Never had the time to bother with one. Besides, I like trains."

"People give us looks, that's all. I figured another year of this, and I might not be able to get a jump on nobody. I ain't going to last much longer for this shit." Calhoun needed a hand up the step.

"Calhoun, you're too damned petrified to die." Monroe helped him up.

Calhoun laughed out loud, coughing up a mighty lunger. He spit up about three ounces of slime from his lungs. "Damn you, Monroe, I always do that when I'm with you."

"I've always been a laugh riot."

Their seats were in the back as usual. Monroe would always give up the window seat to Calhoun so he could spit chew or the mucus rising from his lungs out. The car itself was lightly packed with ten or fifteen people, most of whom were already settling down for a nap since the ride to New York always took three to four hours. Monroe allowed Calhoun to move in front of him. Stopping in the middle of the aisle was always dangerous because people got a better look at you when you stood up, especially with a bag over your head. They whispered to the person next to them and tensed up, thinking the bag might come off and reveal the monstrosity beneath. But Monroe never took the bag off his head, even when the heat became unbearable

"It's the middle of summer, Monroe. You should take that off." Calhoun spoke as if they were two casual businessmen.

"You know I don't let people gawk for free." Monroe sank in the seat next to Calhoun. The sweat droplets rolled down his face, and the stale, warm air was worse than a sauna.

Many of the travelers didn't turn around and just minded their own business. Monroe scratched his head. The temptation to take off the bag was great until a little girl two seats down turned to look at him. Her curly hair suggested youth, but her large green eyes suggested a mind beyond her years. She waved at Monroe and smiled. Monroe returned the favor. Her father scowled and looked back at him. Monroe turned away and gazed out the window as the train pulled out of the station. Every train ride seemed to place a little girl in Monroe's view, although this time she wasn't scared. This time, she smiled and waved, which was much worse. Monroe had grown accustomed to looks of terror. To finally receive a smile from a child made it all the more worse when the bag did come off.

"What's the matter?" Calhoun asked with a legitimate twinge of worry in his voice.

"Nothing," Monroe said, coughing to cover up the quiver in his voice.

"Samson wanted me to prepare you before we got there." Calhoun exhaled, hating to be the messenger. "He thinks the cage would be the better way to go this weekend. There's going to be a swell of dockworkers, all of which were paid in full, meaning the beer tents go up, quietly of course."

"Samson knows the deal: the more I sink into depravity, the more dockworkers drink, the more I get from admissions."

"Yeah, he was clear on that. He told me to let you know you'll get an even fifty percent."

Monroe was speechless. Fifty percent was overly generous, so he suspected something. "That's awfully sweet of him. Do you know what's up?"

"No, but I'm sure Samson's got something going. Hell whatever it is, it's good for you."

"Yeah, I know. Samson always knows how to make lemons into lemonade." Monroe got comfortable, adjusting himself in the seat. "Wake me when we get there."

"Don't worry about that." Calhoun folded his arms, tipping the brim of his bowler hat over his eyes. "You think you could spot me a couple bucks after the weekend?"

"I'm not paid yet."

The day you were born was as chaotic as you can imagine. Your mother was home alone because I was out helping Walter start up his store. Albert Huckley, one of the painters working for us, ran up to me and pulled me off a ten-foot ladder.

"What the hell are you doing?" I asked as I was being yanked out of the store.

"Your wife is going to have the baby. Sarah is riding with her to the doctor's." Albert was heaving horribly. He had just run about a mile, and being two hundred twenty pounds, it almost killed him.

"Don't just stand there, we got to run" was all I could say to poor old Albert, his head in between his knees.

"I just need a minute, I'll meet you there."

I took off like a bolt of lightning heading toward the hospital. "Okay, great—thanks, Albert!"

To call the medical facility in town a "hospital" was an insult to other major hospitals. It was a two-story stable, originally used as a veterinary hospital for the livestock and horses we relied on in the early days of the century. Progress forced the equines out and the sick in. Luckily, the town didn't have many sick people or else we would all be in trouble.

By the time I got to the delivery room, the doctor was already prepping her for birth. A bottle of rum was open and your mother drank freely.

"There's the man who did this to me." I remember her breathing heavily, as well as spitting as soon as I came through the door with sweat glistening off my brow. "Anyone not married yet?" she asked the nurses around her. They all nodded, except one.

"You, look at your future. Stay single, stay away from men." She then doubled over in pain.

"She's just drunk. Marriage is wonderful." One of the nurses patted my back, thinking it was a comfort.

"How many kids you got!" your mother screamed.

"One." The nurse kept her voice low to inform me, "Hurt like hell too. So be good to her."

"I don't think she'll let me be anything else." I smiled.

"What are you smiling at?" your mother asked through gritted teeth. "You're not the one being ripped open by a living thing."

"Doctor, should I stay here?" I sheepishly asked, hoping your mother wouldn't overhear.

She did.

"You're goddamned right you're going to stay here."

"That answers your question. Now hold her hand." The doctor pushed me over to your mother's side. Her grip was made of iron, and my knuckles went white.

"Push with all your might!" the doctor yelled over the screams.

Luckily your birth only lasted two hours, an

easy procedure compared to others the doctor later informed me. Your mother slept hard, mostly
due to the rum. When she awoke and held you for
the first time, she cried. I didn't cry, but I was
overjoyed. Everyone in the hospital got a cigar
that day. Being a father for the first time was
better than falling in love with your mother. I
held you against my chest, smelled your hair, and
kissed your soft head. When you coughed, I would
jump and rush to the doctor or nurse on duty.
They would smile, calm me down, and tell me it
was normal.

Your face made me laugh when I looked down at
you. It was so smashed and undeveloped. Your eyes
closed tight against the forehead. Your lips and
tongue smacked at the air, getting used to it. It
still makes me smile to think of you so young and
new.

Your mother would scold me for spending so much
time with you. It was just hard to let you go.

"What do you want to name her?"

She gazed down on your face and looked deep
within you. She was going through names in her
head, unlocking each possibility until she smiled
and settled on one.

"Mercedes. The love of Edmond Dantes' life would
make sense, especially for your daughter."

I never wanted that moment to end. It was the
first time I ever thanked God for anything.

Monroe kept waking up as the train car rocked back and forth.
The bag was still firmly secure over his head, making him itch with
madness. He wanted to take it off badly and feel the air hit his face
from the open window.

Calhoun noticed. "We'll be there in two hours. You can take it off then."

"I know. I know," Monroe said, scratching through the bag. "Cut a hole on the side, please."

Calhoun removed a knife from his pocket and cut a few holes on the side. Monroe inhaled loudly. Not one traveler turned around to say anything.

"You feel better?"

"Much, thanks. I guess I can spare a couple bucks now."

Calhoun laughed. "No need, I would just spend it on booze and women anyway."

"I would think a man of your looks wouldn't need money to woo women."

"I'm too old to woo; that's why I spend the money. It's to the point."

Monroe laughed, catching another glimpse of the little girl staring back at him. He didn't understand the gaze. Truth was that children knew more than adults. This little girl saw through the slits in Monroe's bag into the eyes of a good man. Her smile killed him. It was beautiful, innocent. It was like his daughter's from the crib. Monroe was lost in the memory, never noticing her father catching their exchange. He began walking down the aisle to Monroe and Calhoun.

"Is there a problem, friend?" Calhoun was always the first to speak.

"Yeah, there's a problem. Tell your bag-head friend to stop staring at my daughter. She don't want nightmares."

"She was looking at him. That usually costs a nickel. You got a nickel?" Calhoun had his hand around the knife in his pocket.

"Look here, buddy, I don't give a good god fuck what you charge per customer for this freak, but if he keeps looking it's going to be a problem."

Calhoun pulled out the knife, and the little girl's father stopped being tough. "Now listen here, sir. Sit down or else you're going to have to explain to your daughter why Daddy won't be able to give her a brother."

"Just don't look," he said, heading back to his seat.

"Had to bring out the knife?" Monroe asked.

"Always works, you know that."

"What if he was bigger?"

"Would've brought out the Derringer."

"Jesus."

"That's what they pay me for. Protect the talent."

Monroe laughed to himself hearing that. He had survived the costliest war in human history only to come face-to-face with an angry father. A funny way to meet an end. By the hands of what he always wanted to be.

Chapter 13

When I got home from church, my mom and dad were in the living room laughing and drinking coffee. It was a good sight to come home to. They both stood up to greet me.

"Steven, we've been talking and have decided to go on a little holiday," my mother said, giving my dad a heartfelt gaze.

"Yep, we've decided to go on a little trip to the city. We're heading to the carnival pier and then to the beach," Father said.

I nodded but was less than enthused. "Sounds good. We're not going to stay with Aunt Kathy, are we?"

"We'll never do that again," Father quickly pointed out.

"Steven," my mother scolded my father in low register. She always sent her decimal higher when she scolded me. "No, we have a hotel booked. It'll be a weekend getaway. I think we all deserve one." Mother sat back in her chair, letting the coffee do its job. I knew it had whiskey in it, even if they did hide it behind the chair.

My mother and father had memories of the pier that they never shared with us. I know it had to do with carnal activities, making me even more grateful they kept it a secret. This year, though, I think it had more to do with Sammy's death. Living across the street from a reminder of life's fragility is no way to spend a summer day. We all needed a weekend away from home. Away from the memory of Sammy.

"Bring your book. You'll have plenty of time to read on the way up." Father poured some whiskey into their cups of coffee as I headed upstairs; they always thought I never saw them breaking the law.

We got up at the crack of dawn to pack the family car with suitcases. Mother always over packed. A gift she possessed. Three to four sets of clothes were always required for a two-day trip, including six pairs of socks. A set of T-shirts for bedtime, two pairs of shoes, a winter coat, a sweater, and long johns were also needed. Even if it was summer, Mother always had a contingency plan set for a last-minute Ice Age. Father was easy to please and preferred one suitcase for the entire family so he didn't have to stress out tying the luggage to the roof of the car. With Mother, however, his dreams of one suitcase vanished as soon as she dumped four cases on the front porch.

"Is packing four suitcases a necessity for a three-day trip?"

"Always be prepared," Mother responded. "I still need to pack the overnight bag. Are you going to need a razor?"

"No, I won't need anything besides a shirt, another pair of socks, and a pair of pants. That's it. That's all."

"You'll be asking for more. Just wait and see." Mother rushed back into the house to pack more.

Father lifted one of the suitcases and rolled his eyes upon realizing its weight matched that of a small child.

"Where does she come from?" he questioned the sky as he headed to the car.

My bag was packed, my book was ready, and all I had left to do was hide my knife. The last thing I needed was Mother snatching it out of my hands the moment I took it out. I was leaving it in my room so I wouldn't be tempted to whittle some driftwood. The best place to stash it was in the cigar box under my bed. My prized items lived in there: my grandfather's Saint Francis medal, my baseball cards, loose change, and any picture of an attractive flapper that may have drifted to my possession. I was thirteen, mind you.

"Steven? Are you ready to bring your stuff down?" my mother asked from downstairs.

I was startled and quickly placed my knife over a picture of Clara Bow in a low-cut dress. "Yeah, I'm on my way." I closed the box and shoved it underneath the bed.

Katie clasped her stuffed animal under her arm and stumbled out of her room, her favorite bathing suit still on a hanger slung over her shoulder.

"Are you going to swim with me?" she asked, twisting. Four-year-olds tend to get excited over weekend trips, then quickly fall asleep when they get there.

"Of course, that's why you go to the beach in the first place."

"Good," Katie said as she grabbed a handful of toy soldiers and put them in the pouch of her stuffed animal. "For the beach raid." She ran out of the room, heading downstairs, still twisting side to side like a windup toy.

"Where does she come from?"

As I put my book on the seat, I noticed Billy down the road a bit. It looked like he was heading for my house but then decided to turn back. I rushed over to greet him.

"Hey Billy? What's going on?"

Billy's face looked more perplexed than anything else. He was squinting even in dim sunlight. His nose bruised, his hands shaky, and his knees terribly scabbed. "You're taking off?" he asked, crushed.

"Yeah, just for two days, maybe three. You wanted to hang out?"

"Yeah, but you're taking off, so I won't bother you." Billy kept his eyes on his feet. He had something to tell me, but I couldn't wait much longer to hear it—vacation was calling. His eyes kept shifting back and forth as he tried to find the words. His focus broke as soon as my father waved and shouted at him.

"Billy, how's the old man?"

"Great, Mr. Fisher. He's just great," Billy yelled with little emotion, a monotone response both my father and I ignored as we continued to put suitcases into the car.

"Steven…" Billy bit his tongue. "Have a good trip, okay?"

"I will. Look, just fish with Marvin. I think he's more bored than we are."

"I'll do that. Have fun, Steven." Billy turned and waved, allowing me one last glimpse of him. The next time I saw him would be in a coffin.

It always took about seven hours to reach the city. My father tried to impress us with a shortcut every time, but it only cut ten minutes. Mother had Katie on her lap, asleep after three hours of fussing. Katie would never sleep in a car by herself; she had to have Mother hold her to fall asleep. It was a sweet sight, but I am sure Mother felt pained by it, especially when Katie jostled and banged hard against her left breast. I was sitting in the back, legs strewn over the whole backseat, as comfortable as a king being escorted by his laymen. *The Count of Monte Cristo* kept me company, allowing me to be fully immersed in the action. By the time we were in view of the city skyline, I was almost finished.

"That good a book, huh?" my father asked in the rearview mirror.

I put my hand up to silence him. I was in the middle of a sentence.

"I guess it is," Father said, adjusting the mirror back to where it was focused. "Here comes the city."

Katie opened her eyes on cue, jumping with excitement and hitting my mother in the breast again. "The city!" she yelled as my mother rubbed her bruised boob.

"Thank God," she said, kissing Katie's forehead. "Katie, time to move you to the back. Mom needs a moment." Katie frowned but did what she was told and, in the process, hit me in the face with her shoe.

"Damn it, Katie," I yelped in pain.

"Don't curse," Mother said, hitting me.

"That's the same spot."

"Watch your mouth then."

"I may get some kind of brain damage, all this banging to the noodle."

"Doubtful, your head's pretty thick," my father said.

"Runs in the family, mostly on the male side," Mother quipped back, making Father smile. "What's the name of the hotel again?"

"Port Royal Motel, not hotel. Sounds prestigious, huh?" *Not hotel* was my father's way of informing us he booked a shit-hole.

Port Royal Motel was just what we thought: a shit-hole. It was on a slant held together by two red support columns with a matching red tile roof. It had seen better days. The front windows were encrusted with barnacles. New discolored rotting planks were nailed into the walkway, creaking with every step toward the door. Some had holes which gave one a great view of the murky water beneath. As for the rest of the exterior, wood was splitting from years of storms and bullet holes.

"You have got to be kidding me." Mother had her fingers tracing the bullet holes.

"Its rustic. Historic." Father pleaded his case. "Besides, those bullet holes are for show, just to scare off tourists not familiar with a local spot."

"The local reprobates," Mother quickly added. "This is the cheapest you've ever been."

You had to give the old man an "A" for being thrifty. Three slots were open for parking. Thankfully, it was on the street, not the dock. The motel itself stood two stories high on the rickety pier, which extended a mile up the coastline. The front office door had the Port Royal Motel slogan in blue paint: *You can't be a land lover at the Port Royal Motel.* You had to admire the slogan—very honest. Chances were you would sink into the ocean by the end of your stay.

"It could be worse." Father took a good long look at the motel and his face turned sour immediately upon seeing a dead seagull hanging from a light post with fishing line wrapped around its neck.

A fisherman with a long beard, sunken eyes with dark circles, smelling of the toilet and the sea, took the fishing line and flopped the seagull around a couple of times.

"Sons of bitching seagulls always attacking me when I make a big catch, so that teaches them a lesson. They don't bother me now."

Father was never one to be rattled easily, especially when the price was right, but a dead seagull hanging from a pole outside the motel was a big deterrent.

"I don't see why we don't just walk to the hotel over there." Mother pointed out the beacon of hope next door. A much nicer hotel, not motel: three stories tall with balconies wrapped around every room, each with a panoramic view of the ocean and city, with plants adorning most of the exterior. The paint job was brand-new; the chairs on the patio were wooden, polished, and pristine. Guests were playing shuffleboard on a long course, which extended along the side of the hotel. Even the water seemed bluer underneath. And to top it all off, smells of fresh baked bread mixed with the salt in the air.

"Looks expensive." Father reluctantly walked down the dock to the pristine hotel aptly named "Fresh Sundown." "What the hell kind of name is that?"

"I like it. It feels warm and homey." Mother defended the hotel before she even stepped into the lobby. "And no dead seagulls."

"We'll see," Father said, counting the money in his wallet. "If they can match the offer I have in my wallet, then vacation will be achieved."

"Cheapskate." Mother held Father tight and kissed him on the cheek.

* * *

Brother Phillip lit another round of candles at the altar. He did this often because the many people in his mind should be remembered for all the joy they brought him. He wouldn't pray. Instead, he would reminisce. Being a romantic, nostalgia appealed to him in ways most people understood. Only the reasons behind his recollections were very different. A man feeling the touch of a woman can be reminded of a first date or a first love. To Brother Phillip, feeling the touch of a woman reminded him of the first girl he ever killed. No one suspected a man of faith to be a wolf. Villagers were quick to hide their children with a man holding a rosary and humming "Hosanna in the Highest." When the parents died, no one was left to claim the hungry children. After his fun, all he had to do was throw them in a crater created by the Germans or the Allied Forces. No one could tell the difference between a victim and a casualty. All the nightmares he inflicted made him erect. Reverend Thomas placed a hand on his shoulder, killing his illicit fantasies.

"Glad to see you keeping a flame."

"Have to sometimes to remind those who forget. The coin box was empty though. Maybe I shouldn't be so cavalier with the matches."

"I wouldn't worry about that. Matches are cheap."

"What do you know about the local legend, Monroe?" Brother Phillip wasted no time. He needed to know where the reverend stood.

"Local legend? Is that what the gossipmongers say? I would suggest you ignore the women and children of this town, Phillip. They like to exaggerate a poor man's pain."

"I hope you don't think I am bearing false witness. Because the reason I ask, well, I saw him walking along the trails in the forest. Oddly enough, it was the same area where Sammy drowned." Brother Phillip was pushing his limits. He could see Reverend Thomas buckle with anger.

"I wouldn't suggest anything against Monroe. He is a quiet man, and keeps to himself." He began to walk away, not liking the conversation. "What happened to him is enough punishment for any man. Best to leave any whisper of accusation to yourself."

"No, no, I am not suggesting anything. I am merely curious as to what he does around town." Staying in step with Reverend Thomas, he cut him off at the end of the pew.

"You just said you saw him walking the trails where Sammy drowned. I'd say you were suggesting quite a bit. It's best just to leave him alone."

Brother Phillip knew this was going nowhere. "But is solitude not a path to darkness? He doesn't come to mass or give money. He just sits in a large house and does nothing?"

"I don't like where you're going with this, Brother Phillip."

"Forgive me, Reverend, I just came from a big city filled with shady characters. Perhaps I get too worried about small occurrences that in the end mean nothing. My suspicious nature is a sinful one, I know. But it sometimes does me well."

"If that is your way of asking for forgiveness, then you have it. Phillip, this is a small town with decent people, including those who stay away from church. I would just ignore what you thought you saw."

"Thank you, Reverend, I just worry too much."

"Worrying too much is not a sin; it's just not good for you. Come on, let my wife make you some dinner. Come to the house around eight?" Reverend Thomas calmed down, and his red face returned to normal. "Please say you will come."

"Of course," Brother Phillip said, smiling.

He would be lighting two more candles soon.

Chapter 14

War erupted overnight in Europe, but here everyone turned a blind eye to it. They all ignored the bigger world around them and felt it was none of their business. America was a place of virtue and new beginnings and not a place to be bothered with the rest of mankind's mistakes. Your mother thought that way too. It was an uphill battle trying to convince her America would have to intervene to stop the bloodshed. Too many boys were dying on the fronts from the modernization of the war machine, but they weren't our boys. They were the sons of the old world, still clinging to the ideas we Americans abandoned in search of new ones. Xenophobia played a part, though mostly it was the arrogance of a new super power learning the tricks of empire. As the debate raged in the States, there were machine gun embankments slaughtering entire regiments in minutes, mustard gas bombs choking the life out of soldiers, and barbed wire strewn around the forests and plains like fishing nets, catching huddled men trying to cross lines on a map. It was a new type of hell America didn't believe in, didn't accept, and hoped to ignore until it ended with little fuss. But it didn't go away. It went on and on, swallowing Europe back into a dark age.

Your mother shouted at me many times in 1915. She was tired of me. The young love had worn off, and the adult mindset had taken over. No more nights of passion, just a cold separation. We would share a bed faced in opposite directions for a month. We would not eat meals together for three months. You were barely two when all this took place. Most of the time I spent at home was with you. Your mother stood outside on the porch chain-smoking cigarette after cigarette, and biding her time before the inevitable fight over the newspaper began. It got so bad Mother eventually cancelled the subscription.

Walter would come over quite a bit to calm the waves we created. Your mother was afraid to shout at me when company was there, so she would just keep herself quiet, calmly building up her rage to dispense when Walter left. She did with a vengeance. Looking back, I don't know why I kept aggravating her. I just kept pushing and pushing until she cried. Our arguments escalated to hitting. She would strike out at me. I would hold her back, and then slap her across the face. She would bang her head into my chest, wetting my shirt with her tears.

"Why don't you join up with those bastards?" She came out of the rage with a smile. "Bleed for them, Monroe. You don't want to be here? You don't want this small town under your feet anymore? Fucking leave, hypocrite. Go explore the world while I stay here with your daughter."

"Maybe that's the only way for you to understand

what's really at stake here," I shouted back, drinking straight from the bottle. The heated rage of argument filled me with delusions of grandeur. Medals adorning my chest as I would parade down the streets with an American flag wrapped around me, basking me in nationalistic pride. The dreams of a hero lost in the fantasy of romance for war.

Your mother spat in my face. "Everything is at stake here. Remember all those good times? Those nights with just us? I seem to be losing most of it." She walked away, wiping her face.

I didn't say anything more about it. I didn't even shout back. I was too angry to breathe. In retrospect, I see now we were both young. Too set in the ways of the past to accept change. It was my weakness, and I dragged your mother into it. Why I write now. Living in those moments again and again to see if there were other alternatives. But there was nothing to be done. I had failed already.

The next day I went to Walter and asked him what he thought of all this. He was of a similar mind. He knew it would take American intervention. It would come to that two years down the road anyway.

"Would you serve if they called on you?" I asked him point-blank.

He hesitated a moment with his eyes closed, his breath leaving him momentarily.

"I would go if they told me to. I would fight if it were all that could be done in the end. Everybody dies, but not many die in a blaze of glory, if you could call it that." Walter was coaxing himself. He didn't want to go. In the back of my mind I didn't either, but I was pig-headed to the bitter end.

"I'm joining up." He never attempted to stop me, nor did he say anything. He just stood there without blinking. A few moments went by before he opened his mouth again.

"That's a good service, but you have a goddamned daughter to think about. I've heard how many men have already died in this war. You plan to not be included in those numbers?"

"By the time I get there it will be mostly finished. I just need to get away, Walter. Maybe if I leave and come back, things will be different." Sound logic to me at the time. A man faced with change believes that it is in the running where the change will happen. Never understanding that change is not from running, but in standing still.

"Sometimes things don't change with time, Monroe. It's either working or not. That's just life. You shouldn't do something stupid on account of the hope that things will turn out better."

"I joined up already and training starts in a few months."

Walter threw his hands in the air and spit. "Christ, you're going to force me into this with you. I don't have the luxury of waiting to be called now."

"Walter, don't be stupid."

"You mean, don't be like you? Shit, you leave me with little choice, Monroe. I'm going to join up with you, and if we get separated or routed off to different parts of the big show, I'll still do everything in my power to keep you from trying to be a war hero."

"What a friend I have in you."

"Don't get excited. The first chance I get to shoot my own foot, I'll take it."

Your mother didn't speak out when I told her. She just laughed and then lit up another cigarette on the porch, an empty bottle of whiskey at her feet. She could keep her liquor, mind you. It made her quiet and resentful. I went to your room to get away from her dead gaze.

The music box was chiming on the nightstand as you were dozing off. I put my hand on your stomach and chest to feel your breath and warmth. Right then and there I regretted signing up. I was a fool. At that moment you smiled at me. It caught me off guard, and I started to cry. I heard a creak behind me but never turned around. Your mother stood in the hallway and watched me weep. She never said a word and never offered a hand. We were through that night.

Pier 34 was an ancient dock that had stood since the revolution and it had seen many phases throughout its long history. Sticking with the façade of a carnival lately. A myriad of tents hugged the borders of the dock. The Ferris wheel stood high above the water, casting a shadow over the tents at high noon. Game shacks stood erect down a single row in the center, painted in a typical circus palette: lots of greens, reds, and yellows danced on every piece of naked wood. It was a sight to behold for a tourist but an eyesore for any local. A petition to shut the carnival pier down had been thrown in front of the mayor's desk many times. Each time it was rejected because the carnival and freak show still had an economic value to the community. Located in the back, thirty yards from the end of the pier, was the main attraction tent. It was the place circus-goers paid a nickel to view the oddities gathered for their amusement, standing almost as high as the Ferris wheel. It could fit a hundred people on a slow day and three hundred people during holiday months. Summer was the busiest time of year, and the money kept rolling in. This was always a plus for Monroe, who saw a decent cut of the profits.

The cabbie stopped the car. A large clown face entrance greeted them with an open mouth, bulging eyes, and a glowing nose. It was a bitch to power, but a spectacle nonetheless, especially at night or when the sea fog rolled in. Bird shit decorated it now and Calhoun would have to wash that off later.

Calhoun opened the door for Monroe and threw the cabbie a couple of ones.

"Hey, I thought I got a fin if I got you here in a hurry?" the cabbie asked, collecting the singles.

"You could've done better." He flipped him a nickel. "Buy your wife something nice."

"Circus folk." The cabbie pulled off and sped down the dock.

"Cabbie's got a real personality problem. I hope it don't spread to the rest of the city," Calhoun said, unlocking the gate.

"Bigger cities, bigger chips on the shoulders," Monroe added, taking the bag off his head. He breathed in the sea air, cracking his neck. "About time I get out of the fucking bag."

"If Samson sees you out of it, he might yell at ya. You know how he don't like you spoiling the surprise to bystanders."

"Samson is my friend and partner. He can yell at my dick, and I say that with all due respect."

"Is that a fact?" Samson said from behind Monroe.

"Yeah, I would say so." Monroe smiled, turning to greet him.

Samson was a large man, tall and round, his hair nicely slicked back; his suit and tie screamed legitimacy, but his chubby fingers wrapped around a bottle of bourbon contradicted that thought. His dwarf assistant, Murray, was a Middle Eastern gentleman with a handlebar moustache. He held a tray and two glasses up to Monroe.

"Please have a drink with me, old man." Samson took a swig right out of the bottle, and Calhoun and Monroe drank from the glasses.

"Good bourbon? What's the occasion?" Monroe asked, tipping his glass to Murray. Murray grabbed the bottle from Samson's hand and filled it.

"We'll talk about it upstairs. You enjoying the sea breeze?" Samson pointed at Monroe's face in plain daylight, while grabbing the bottle back from Murray.

"I've been in a bag for about ten hours. I needed a fucking breather."

"I would too. Hell, I need one now. Let's head upstairs and talk about the future."

Monroe's good eyebrow shot up, perplexed. "The future?"

"Come on, we'll talk alone." Samson waved Calhoun and Murray away, and the two of them headed down the fairway between the tents.

Samson's office was a wooden tower that was added to the pier back in 1778 as a lookout post to watch for British ships. Most of the floors were storage for powder kegs and rations. Now Samson found them to be a suitable place to store his extra crates of posters, tarps, costumes, toy animals, sea salt, and corn kernels, all stacked neatly against the stuffed and manufactured animal oddities. He liked variety in his oddities, and never showed the same one twice. Money was also important too, leading to the nefarious economic process of bootlegging. Twelve dozen Canadian Whiskey barrels loaded into the tower through the false floor beneath the dock added a nice cushion for the carnival pier's finances.

"The good bourbon?" Monroe pointed out the barrels.

"Street value, ten bucks a bottle. Got to drink right when you listen to jazz." Samson removed a massive ring of keys from the hook next to the office door. "What if I told you your tenure with us could end?" he told Monroe with a smile and found the right key to unlock the door.

"I would ask to see the freak better than I."

"I hate that word, but it sells. If they only knew Murray down there was an accomplished pianist. You know Grace, the pinhead?"

"Yeah, I know Grace."

"She paints better than most artists with recognition. Hell, even better than that Picasso you got. You still got that, don't you?"

"Yes, and for the last time, I'll never sell it."

"Fine."

Samson unlocked the rickety door, which could easily be broken down if one was so inclined. Inside the office, air whistled through the cracked windows, and the ocean wind rocked it back and forth. Shelves were tied up to hooks in the ceiling, papers and books were stacked along the walls for insulation, and Samson's desk was large enough to take up most of the back. It was a wonder it didn't break through the floor. A fresh bottle of bourbon stood in the corner, book-ending several ledgers and a glass case with two war medals.

"You heard about a surgery that could reconstruct your face?" Samson threw a pamphlet at Monroe.

"Plastic surgery?" Monroe flipped open the pamphlet to reveal illustrated examples of deformities created by explosions, gunshot, or shrapnel. "This can't work."

"Office is right here in New York. They've already fixed a few guys with facial damage. It's like you told me on the front: the two greatest words in the English language were wait and hope or am I paraphrasing?"

"I was paraphrasing. It does look promising, but I already have an idea of what they'll say. Damage is too severe to fix." Monroe couldn't take his eyes away from the brochure. He read it, allowing himself to hope for the first time in a long time.

*The subject's damaged face can be reshaped with a new process re-
ferred to as a skin graft. Living tissue from one part of the body can
be placed on heavily scarred tissue, including sensitive facial tissue,
to produce a new face. It will be as if the person never had the accident that befell them. Several tests have been conducted to ensure
the success of the procedure and the results speak for themselves.
Pages three through five of this pamphlet contain photos of before
and after the procedure, all of which had eighty percent recovery
ratings. Though these results do vary for each individual, the difference is negligible. You too can rediscover your former self through
the power and wonder of medical science.*

Monroe flipped to page three and found men just as bad if
not worse than him. Their faces mangled by war, mechanical accidents, or lifelong deformities. Next to their mangled forms were
their new faces, human and intact. All of them smiling in the after
pictures.

"Tomorrow, Murray and I are taking you over there. Don't be
pessimistic either, two greatest words, remember?"

"Wait and hope," Monroe repeated, folding the pamphlet and
putting it in his coat pocket.

"Well, I was always impatient." Samson sat in his swivel chair,
rolling up his pant leg to reveal straps and buckles connected to a
wooden leg. "Remember?" Samson unlatched the straps and pulled
off the prosthetic limb. He pointed the nub at Monroe, laughing.
"You saved my life out there. I want to extend the courtesy."

"You've already done that with this job."

"This was nothing. You're not an idiot. You're not even a freak.
You're more of a man than me, and I've always thought that."

Samson and Monroe were quiet, hearing the wind filter through
the holes in the wood.

"This was a way to survive, Samson. Without you I would've

died, maybe worse." Monroe read the label of the whiskey bottle. "Ten bucks, huh?"

"Only the best for you, my friend."

"Only the best," Monroe repeated, pouring another round.

Samson pursed his lips, thinking about the cage Monroe had to perform in. The act consisted of screaming like a mad chimp and throwing mud at the audience. All in the elaborate body suit created by Samson. The work was ahead of its time. Samson fancied himself a modern-day Lon Chaney, especially since it had a twisted, deformed hand that Monroe had to bend lightly to use as a gimp arm. The rest of the body suit was a series of scars and twisty stitches designed to look like a series of mismatched body parts, hence the Marvelous Mangled Man moniker. Samson was inspired by Mary Shelley's Frankenstein. He figured since Monroe read only the classics, he would see the charm.

"Jesus, enough of this nancy talk, let's drink some more." Samson drank.

On the pier at six o'clock, the lighthouse would come to life and cast its beacon out to the ships at sea. Monroe loved to sit and watch it from a bench below Samson's office, situated a good distance away from the tents and any onlookers wanting a free glimpse. Smoke rolled out of his mouth from the giant cigar as he contemplated the future. He removed the pamphlet and flipped through the pages, getting excited like he used to at Christmas as a boy. Horns from an approaching ship tore his attention away from the pamphlet for a moment. Its bow ripped through the low fog and glided across the water. Its lights glowed a weak orange and yellow before the lighthouse beam guided it home. Wait and hope. Such a simple phrase to shape a lifetime even if it is nowhere near that. Time is funny when you're in hell. Being alone takes a toll on a man. Not being able to feel a woman's touch or hearing a woman's voice say

"I love you" makes a year feel like an eternity. Monroe had nine of them.

But, now in the cold night, he was a happy drunk with hope in his heart.

Your mother saw me off at the train station, while you were sleeping quietly against her shoulder. We didn't share a lengthy goodbye or a passionate kiss. We just stood in the center of grieving mothers and wives watching their husbands and sons run off to war. We stood there eye-to-eye, knowing there was a chance I could be dead soon. Your mother and I both silently ignored the possibility. We just looked at each other, hoping the other would break the stoicism first. The train whistled for the last time, forcing me to jump on. She only stood there, cradling you. I should've kissed you that day. I didn't know what the future would hold for us. I should've told your mother I loved her. I wish I had broken free from my youthful indignation to kiss her on the mouth once more. We were both stubborn people; it was the reason we got on so well in the first place. My anger was still fresh, as was hers. It was all a battle of wits in the presence of farewells. All of them lost to the idea of war. Your mother and I were lost to the past, and how it fell apart for us.

Training was fast. There was a sense of arrogance throughout the American ranks because we were the ones being shipped out to save Europe. After clinging so long to our isolationist stance, we felt more entitled to the spoils because we held out for so long. It was a foolish way to feel, but it was there nonetheless. Britain had done the worst of the fighting, and we were sent to pick up the pieces. We were saving Europe from an impending apocalypse after all.

Walter joined me in boot camp after a week. Poor old bastard could barely run the ten miles each morning. Eventually, he bribed the corporal in charge of keeping count in order to sleep in. He figured running ten miles was not going to make him faster than a bullet fired from a rifle, so to hell with the 4 AM run. Word got around to those in charge, and he was promoted to intelligence.

By May, we launched from New York Harbor ready to kill any Hun we saw. The bloodlust imprinted on many men was lost on me. I was too busy daydreaming about our trip to Europe from the very same dock. I was alone out here this time. I forced her not to care, and I was a lonely son of a bitch, feeling the sting of consequence. It was my fault but on that quarterdeck, I still hated your mother and what we lost.

When I put my feet down on solid ground, I was foot deep in mud. A premonition not lost on me. To get a foothold in Europe was not going to be easy, even if our bloated sense of self kept creeping forward. The British regiments we joined with had the look of lost children. Many of us Americans dismissed it as fatigue. But when one looked closer in their eye, into what was left of their souls, one could see remorse. It was the loss of whatever made them human. It was not romance and glory beaming from them, it was shame. All of them were sinners of the worst kind. All of them had to live with it. And they were too tired to stop us from doing the same.

The first weeks of battle left us all shaken. None of us were prepared, none of us. The cold dimmed us all. We would make decisions none of us in life would dare conceive, let alone set out to accomplish. We would steal from one another if it meant warmth. Once, a man crawled out into the battlefield just to get a coat off the bloated corpse of a young man barely sixteen. You couldn't smell the rot or the dried blood or the fecal material—too cold to even try. One couldn't say anything in offense.

As the weeks progressed, the British began to open up to us. Divulging stories they would never tell their children or wives back home. Stories of ordered executions of their own men, their friends, who awoke from the dreams of death and country to find themselves adrift in Hell looking for a way to run back home where life made sense. No one believed them. War was a costly endeavor, and to kill your own men made no sense to us.

But it was true. These men killed deserters. Not by choice but by the obligation to the hierarchy and their laws of war. Any tone of defiance meant a discharge by firing squad. So they were forced to live with it. To accept their orders, never telling themselves: *I murdered a fellow soldier. I shot a friend.* But in war, a life written on paper as a statistic is less damning. A statistic has no history, no family, no idea of future. Just a slot that needs to be replaced due to a flawed character defect: fear.

Eventually, the British changed their tune, seeing us Americans catch up with the hell they knew. They cheered us up with stories of brothels along the edges of bombed-out towns. Most of them were erected out of former churches now lost to sin because the world was ending. I was skeptical that a church would stem any eroticism but was surprised when three months into the campaign, I walked through a modified church of the flesh. The doors were encased with patches of steel and other random metals to protect it from occasional shelling. I discovered sectioned-off quarters all the way to the former altar. Every "room," if it could be called that, was a section separated by canvas or other stitched material. Most of the artifacts were removed, stolen, or blown up. Most of the men lost any semblance of respect after seeing the multitude of flesh hanging out from ripped clothes. Most of the men were married, but in war when you murder every day, adultery is just a drop in the bucket. We spent a good many days in the arms of women hiding out from the harsh reality outside. It was better to sell yourself than be raped by roaming soldiers or bandits scattered across the landscape.

I was in the middle of pouring bourbon for my new purchase when a man bumped into me, knocking the bottle from the table. It spilled all over the patch of tattered carpet covering the cold tile floor of her small section of former church altar. I was incensed because I spent a good deal of money on that bottle.

"Jesus Christ, I do apologize. I was looking for Sophia." He eyed my companion for too long. "You think you would be apt to share a glass of my booze, as a formal apology." He raised the bottle of French wine, and not a bad one, but wine is not the drink for drowning out the feelings brought about from sleeping with a village whore. "Now, don't think me a thief in the night trying to swindle your girl. You, sir, are much more attractive than I. I, being Samson, how you be?" He extended his hand to me.

"I be Monroe; you be leaving." I shook his hand as a formality.

"American boy? Great, please say you're from New York State." Samson sat against the altar protruding through the sheet and acting as the back wall.

"You would be correct. New York State, but from a small town, not the big city."

"Yeah, yeah. Small-town boy hates the big-city life but ended up all the way out here because he wanted to see the world. Romantic as always."

"Not really. I had seen the world before. This was just a way for me to get out of the house."

Samson laughed. "I like that. You know, you've got quite a speaking voice. You should be on the stage or something. Small-town life can be boring, so if you're ever in New York City, give me a call." He handed me a business card.

I laughed out loud. The silliness of the situation hit me. Outside, not four miles in any direction, death and chaos erupted into every walk of life, while here, out of hell came a man with a business card into the church brothel.

"Entertainment? I mostly work in real estate, and it proves to be far more rewarding." I smiled, reading the card again.

"They say that, but entertainment garners girls and booze, occasional opium hits. Hey, it's not everybody's thing, I know. But, if you want to clear the shit out of your head in a quick fashion, call a Chinaman. Real estate though, not a bad form of income from what I've heard."

"You have no idea." I drank some of his wine straight from the bottle.

"You have a sweetheart back home?" he asked me as he lifted the sheet separating the neighboring room. A redhead with large breasts was washing herself. She said something in French and threw a piece of tile from the floor at him. "I don't speak the language, babe." He threw the tile back, splashing water from her bucket onto her sheet wall.

"Why ask a question like that in here of all places?" I asked, feeling guilty at once.

"Why not? Love is not a replaceable commodity, but pussy is. It's why we're all here while the bullets whiz by not two hundred kilometers away. I say most people cling to love but don't work for it. There is no honest love when a man can get his hard-on worked on for a small fee."

"You have a way with words."

"The entertainment business does that to you. People can be fooled more easily if you've got a way with words, something us entertainers do well. How long did you get with this one for two cents?"

"An hour for a nickel, which was starting to go somewhere before you came in."

"No man can go for an hour, and I have been to the Orient. Whatever they tell you is a lie, they can't fuck for hours." He stood up, stretched out his calves, and cracked his neck. "So, if I don't see you later, Monroe, have a good night. And if you see me on the battlefield with a blown-up leg or arm, just shoot me in the head because I don't want no peg appendages. How about you?"

"Sure, shoot me if you see me with no arms or legs."

"Got you." He walked out of the small sectioned-off room.

"That was odd," I tried to say to the French woman, who had no idea what occurred. She was too busy stealing half the cigarettes from my pack.

"Just take off your top, would you?" I said, pantomiming the act.

Days later, we left the whores at the church of fornication to march into the gunfire twenty kilometers away. Samson and I marched side by side as luck would have it, and he gave me a once-over before realizing it was me.

"So how did she do after I left?" he asked.

"Limp like a dead fish."

"They all are, but hey, don't hold it against them. Most likely, their sweethearts are all dead. No one replaces love, remember?"

"Unfortunately, I do. What about you?"

"I don't have a sweetheart back home. Just have lady friends. They seem to like me well enough. Any good wife material steer clear of me, but I don't seem to care either."

"Is that the entertainer in you?"

"No, it's mostly the drinking. It's one in the same if you think about it, but it always makes me funnier, hence the lady friends over the wife material."

"Wish I had your skills."

"You don't need them, like I told you, you're better-looking than me." At this time, one of the soldiers gave us both an odd look.

"Don't say he isn't—just look at him. Handsome!" Samson shouted, making me laugh. I guess I did find something good out of the front after all.

Chapter 15

T he hotel room was far better than any of us had hoped for. It was luxurious: a small suite with a kitchen unit, a couch, a new radio, new wallpaper, and two bedrooms situated behind the living room. A large window gave us a sweeping view of the Atlantic and the carnival pier to the east. The lights were beginning to flicker to life in the distance, and the revelers of summer were lining up along the cobblestone roads. The music from the bands echoed off the hulls of docked frigates, and the smell of cotton candy and pop-corn lifted onto the sea breeze. I was dying to be a part of it, my leg twitching anxiously as I sat on the couch watching my father play with the dials for the radio.

"I'm trying to find something. Stop your damn leg jumping," my father commanded me, jumping off the jittering couch springs.

"Sorry, it's just the carnival pier isn't that far off, and I made enough money with Walter to go buy some cotton candy." Whimpering was a last-ditch effort at getting what I wanted, but it never really worked.

"No, no, not at all," my mother said from the bedroom. Katie had finally succumbed to the Sandman's call. "You are not heading out there by yourself."

"Why not? I walk to Walter's store all the time by myself, and that's three times the distance."

"Yeah, but this place has ten times the scum," my father interjected, finally finding a station worth listening to.

"Oh come on, I know not to go down any dark alleys or into any warehouses. I just want to head for the pier, that's it. Please? I work now, doesn't that mean anything?"

"It's up to your mother." All fathers have a wonderful escape clause with those five words.

"Don't leave this to me. He's your child too," Mother said from behind the wall, her legs sticking out from the bed.

"Then I say he'll be fine." Father winked at me, cracking the window open.

"Oh, make me the bad guy because I care for the safety of my child," Mother retorted, slipping off her shoes with her feet and getting ready for bed. This moment of fatigue granted me the permission I normally wouldn't receive. "Have fun, Steven. Don't follow anyone down an alley or back room. Stay in the lamplight and be back in an hour."

"An hour?" I whined, again to no effect.

"Be happy I'm allowing you to take a single foot onto the dock." Mother and her feet got comfortable in bed.

"All right, one hour. Thanks, Mom, Dad." I leaped out of the room like an escaped convict eager to kiss the ground outside.

The docks at night were scary, but the lurking strangers I had been raised to fear were mostly drunks and old men with no cares. They paraded around in the darkness like moths to a light, enjoying the solitude it provided. It was the cover needed to escape all of life's little problems. I heard vomiting, cursing, and the grunting of men and women in the back alleys but never wavered in my step. I felt like an adult. Finally, the small-town kid was forcing the city boy out and becoming less and less afraid of things that go bump in the night. Each step brought me closer to the carnival pier, and my excited nature penetrated through me, giving me gooseflesh. I was about to pay for myself and for the first time ever. A small feat, I know, but for a thirteen-year-old boy it felt like a real workingman enjoying the fruits of his labors. The line to the carnival pier overtook my attention, killing my excitement. It ran fifty yards down the pier and almost hit the street. There were dockworkers, whores, whores with dockworkers, squatters from the tenements around the corner and their dirty children, and a smattering of decent folk who I assumed paid for their homes and were taking a weekend stroll along the pier. They all stood shoulder to shoulder, dovetailing one another. I stood behind a behemoth with arms as big as tree trunks, so tall he would no doubt hit the hanging sign above the entrance. This was the guy Paul Bunyan was created for. He immediately looked down at me as I stepped behind him.

"Hey, kid, this your first time to the pier?" he asked in a baritone voice.

"No, I've been here before," I lied. The last thing I wanted to do was play tourist.

"So you know about the Mangled Man?"

"No, I always seem to miss that one," I lied again, although the title Mangled Man intrigued me.

"Well, this time you should see him. Word on the dock is he's an experiment by some German surgeon. The Kaiser tried to make an undying monster, but it didn't take till after the war."

This intrigued me.

"Maybe I'll see you in there?" He burped the last word.

"Sure. Get some cotton candy. It's the best in the state."

"I knew you hadn't been here before." He laughed, checking out a nearby woman walking down the cobblestone way. "What's your name, darling?"

"Ain't free-Mona. Or cheap-Mona, neither," the woman said.

"How about comforting a dockworker who just got paid-Mona?"

"Then we can have some fun." She smiled with teeth rotted to the gums. Her eyes were sunk into her skull, but her breasts were full and perky, which was hard to do because the bra was not around yet.

The world around me was a bright neon glow. Tents blocked the bright lights beamed from the ships in port, and the lights from the city cast a warm backlight, destroying the harsh shadows emanating from this shady underbelly of amusement. Children ran around me in circles, chasing rats and dropping popcorn kernels along the way. Men drank, cursed, and spat in the beer tents, lighting cigarettes and watching the women pass by with their husbands or boyfriends. All of them dressed scantily because the humidity was thick in the air. The dregs had their mouths open and drooling over the sweat-soaked white tops and bottoms clinging to the feminine shapes. Even I was getting aroused, although the roaming Sisters of temperance quickly repressed my discovery of titillation. Dressed in black, with rosary beads wrapped around their wrinkled, vein-encrusted hands, racked with rheumatism, looking down on me with the eyes of judgment fit for a murdering bandit. If only my father were there, he would've given them an earful. In the center of this parade of sultry sensuality and witch-hunting was the raised podium where the carnival master bellowed his sales pitch to the gathered fools eager to waste their hard-earned money.

"Come one, come all to the fabulous, frantic, freakishly, fanciful foray into the sideshow spectacle. You shall feast your eyes on the perverse and the weird, the amazing to the frightful! God's creations made pacts with the Devil, and they smile with glee for your nickels! But don't be quick to judge on price—I only ask for two pennies! Two pennies for the passport into the odd, where the id is the norm and the norm is the id!" He hooked the fools with ease, me included. I dug into my pockets and pulled out two brand-new pennies.

"I got two pennies, mister."

He ceased with the charming showman act. "Two pennies per tent, kid."

I went back into my pockets and pulled out a more diminished dime. He grabbed the dime quick, replacing it with five tickets.

"You have successfully secured five tents for your viewing pleasure. Go, my son, walk down the valley of the shadow of death and witness what the good Lord wished he didn't create, and be sure to purchase some candy."

I was inundated with brass band music as well as the shouts of the various ringmasters trying to coax more money out of me. There were animal oddities, bearded ladies, topless girls tents, and the deformed. In the center of the pier was the main event tent standing high, almost eclipsing the lighthouse in the distance. Its twin flags flopped in the wind. The ropes securing the tent were taut, being tied around the raised posts from the dock itself. Too many people were huddled around the topless tent for me to see the marquee for the main attraction. No one wanted to see the bearded ladies. I didn't care to see deformity, I had been there and done that. The only thing I hadn't really seen before was animal oddities. An old man stood at the entrance smoking a pipe and sucking on a stick of chew. The stench he created overtook the animal droppings emanating from within the tent. He spat out the chew and blew smoke into my face.

"You pay the two cents for this tent, boy?" Calhoun asked, dipping into a canvas bag at his feet and pulling out a bottle of bourbon.

"Of course. You the tour guide?" I tried to bring a touch of levity to my voice, but the old man spat again, wiping the bourbon dripping from his chin.

"That's what they pay me for. I tend to wait for more people to come on over before I indulge." Calhoun stared me down, and his drinking continued unabated even when the temperance group dressed in their Sunday best stared him down with Bibles in hand.

"Evening, Sisters, would you like to view a goat with bigger balls than a man?" The Sisters removed their gaze from Calhoun. "That works every time. All right, come on. Nobody ever comes in droves to this shit. Too many of them looking at a set of girl's tits—no need to see twelve tits on a goat."

Two dimwitted men arrived behind me; both of them stared across the way to the topless girl tent. Calhoun spotted two pigeons with his experienced eyes.

"You two should calm those feelings down before you head over there. My boy Carl broke three noses on men twice as big as you with twice the hard-on. So, cool it and have a gander at some animal mistakes the good Lord failed to rectify, like those three broken noses from Providence." He opened the tent, allowing admittance.

Immediate disappointment greeted us all as we feasted our eyes on the spoils of the taxidermy world. Every animal of interest was a stuffed recreation of mythical creatures fables informed us about. There was a griffin, a two-headed cow, a centaur that wasn't badly constructed, a merman in a bottle in the center with a single bulb shining above to show it off, the twelve-titted lamb, and a goat with abnormally large testicles.

"Merman?" I asked with disbelief because in the light you could see the stitching and bolts. I'd give them an "A" for craftsmanship.

"Caught it off the coast of Portugal. Shot that centaur in Morocco and raised that goat when I was a wee boy." He spat on the wood chips littering the ground.

"I've seen that two-headed cow before," one of the idiots said.

"We get some of these on loan sometimes. Everybody should have the right to view oddities at least once in their life. Reminds you to appreciate the abnormal."

I approached the glass enclosing the merman and tried to get a better look, but Calhoun grabbed my shoulder and pulled me away. "Don't touch the glass, kid."

"You make that yourself?"

Calhoun smiled and leaned lower, forcing me to be eye to eye, smelling his stale breath, a mixture of tobacco, bourbon, and puke.

He lowered his voice to a whisper, not alerting the idiots ogling the two-headed cow.

"If you want to see reality, head on over to the main show. The Marvelous Mangled Man is something no one could create in a shed. He's the genuine article of human atrocity. He's the one, the only one of his kind in this state. Hell, he might be the only one of his kind in this country. Men like him used to be shackled in the dungeons, but now he is in a cage for your viewing pleasure. Go see the Mangled Man; he'll be worth the remaining dime you spend."

My sense of wonder was at its zenith. I wanted to know more about this Mangled Man, but Calhoun opened the tent and scooted me out.

"Go on, kid, this tent is too lowbrow for someone of your intelligence, and be obliged to drop a nickel into the coin slot for the Mangled Man. He don't ask for it, but he does need it." As soon as I was out of the tent, Calhoun turned his attention to the two idiots gawking at the centaur.

"Shot him dead in the Congo. The son of a bitch killed three of my guides before he fell."

The line leading out the main tent edged along the dock, forcing many staggering drunks to cling to their dates, not wanting to wind up another drunk drowning statistic. Two-hundred-pound men made monstrous, like ancient Roman gladiators, from lifting cargo losing their equilibrium from drink was not where I wanted to be, especially with the Atlantic Ocean twenty feet below. I was saved by the large dockworker I had met earlier at the front of the pier.

"Hey, boy! What the hell you doing back there? Come on up here with Mona and me!" he shouted with a bottle of beer in one hand and Mona in the other. Her gaunt cheekbones were brought out with cheap rouge; her breasts were pushed up and her nipples hard from the cold sea breeze. It almost warranted a second look, but the smell coming off her was far from good. "You briefly met my date Mona earlier, so now I shall allow a formal introduction: Mona, boy, boy, Mona. There, it's like we've known each other for years."

Mona kept rocking back and forth, bumping into me as cheap booze dribbled from her chin. Her arms were bruised all the way to her chest from constant fights with Johns, her shoes were ripped and held together with wire, her knees scraped over from falling on hard, cracked cement, and her lips chapped and cracked from the sea wind blowing on hot nights. Her name wasn't Mona, but it didn't matter. She probably forgot her real name long ago.

* * *

Monroe stood beside the back flap of the tent. There was a large slit in the center where any curious stagehand could view the crowds. He glared at the line waiting to view his act. A good gathering this time around, but summer always provided that. Many of them drinking and rocking back and forth. Monroe always prayed they would just fall over the side but then remembered the money. Drunks were okay in the end, he figured. He was one of them too but without a date.

Murray came up behind Monroe, clearing his throat. "Are you ready yet?"

"Yeah, yeah. Are we doing the mud on my chest thing again?"

"I think so. It worked last time. Stay away from the corners of the cage. We put the horseshit there for effect, and try to stay away from the hay bale in the corner. We don't know what could be living in there."

"Never sit on that damned thing; it's older than I am." Monroe gazed at the wheeled cage that existed as his stage. A silence befell him as it always did the moment before a performance. The only thing keeping him from running away was the deal he made with Samson and the lines reaching the end of the dock, but he still needed a reminder.

"Why I should throw dignity out the window again?"

"Half the money at the door for three more shows. That'll be more than any of us make in three months, and none of us show no ill will toward you for receiving that amount." Murray slammed a fistful of mud on his exposed chest.

"That is fucking cold; prepare me next time." Monroe got a chill but recovered. "What's the opening act tonight?"

"We got the dog show, then we got Juggling Jimmy, and then we got those twins from Russia. You know, the guys that lift each other with the moustaches, and then you."

"Fantastic. Make sure no one has bottles again. The last thing I want to do is relive the front." Monroe tapped mud on his face, and the cold actually helped him relax.

"We always check, Monroe." Murray opened the cage door. The metal clanged against the wooden planks of the dock, reverberating in Monroe's mind. "You greased it up good, Phil, fell right on smooth. After Monroe's done, we got to switch the signs for the tigers."

"You guys got tigers?" Monroe asked, genuinely impressed.

"Well, the zoo ordered them, but the train dumped them here first. A full weekend with Mindy and the tigers means breaking even after your deal."

"Samson was always the businessman. All right, let's get this shit on the way."

Months went by so fast, I didn't even notice. I was too busy dodging bullets to think about the passing time. I didn't write one word to your mother, and she never bothered asking why. I found out a year later of course, but by then, there was not much I could do about it. All the while, I was surviving every tour of duty I was given. Not one scratch on me. It's an odd feeling, surviving so long when every corner could mean death. I don't know if it was divine intervention or dumb luck. Whatever it was, I didn't care to thank any of the Fates or God in heaven. I just marched over bodies in the snow. When 1918 appeared on the calendar, I had seen five tours of duty, losing roughly seventy percent of those who served with me. I received a few medals for that, but it was hardly exciting. The men in charge stood up a busted ammo crate to announce my bravery to the dozen or so tired soldiers nodding off during the ceremony. Samson and Walter were both present.

"You son of a bitch, you'll have more medals than me by the end of this," Walter told me, pouring us all whiskey straight from Scotland.

"No small feat, five tours. Lucky fuck," Samson said as he smelled the whiskey from his mug.

"Hardly luck. I always stood at the back of the lines so the machine guns would run out of bullets, thus sparing me from an early grave. I sure as hell ain't going to die in the cold."

"Well, I'm glad you kept yourself alive. Hell, I can't run the business all by myself." Walter had something on his mind, I could tell.

"Something the matter, Walter?" I asked with a smile. It had been awhile since I forced one across my face.

"Nothing, just gossip. Letters from home are always full of it. Best not to even talk about it, all bullshit anyway. Samson, could you give us a minute?"

"Can I take the bottle?"

"Sure."

"Take ten."

Walter handed him the bottle of whiskey, then sat me down. "Emily has been telling me about your girl. She's fine, healthy and jumping around in everyone's yards."

"Good."

"She doesn't seem to know about you. The months keep going by, and she doesn't understand where you are, so she thinks you're gone. She tells people she's never had a daddy."

"Her mother doesn't say anything?"

"No." Walter knew more but he kept it from me. "You should write a letter to her."

"What's the use?"

Walter squeezed my shoulder and looked me square in the eyes. "A daughter should know who her father is regardless of disagreements or fights. Elizabeth should know that, but you pissed her off so bad. I can't scold her too hard. Write Mercedes and tell her you're her father still."

You're her father still stayed with me as three weeks rushed by. Nothing had happened to hinder a letter. The Front was quiet. No screams. No explosions. No death. Maybe that's why I didn't write. The sound of silence was a new concept. Without the command of firing, I was forced to attempt a letter. At first, it was foreign and uncomfortable. But when I scribbled your name on the cheap paper, words came. My clenched and ruined hands began to write a letter you never received.

Dearest Daughter,

Nothing comes to mind as I think of how I should begin to tell you about war. It's a war I thought needed to be fought, but now I feel your mother was right. So many men could have done things beyond this, but they're all buried in mud. I'm alive. Not much else to say, really. I think about you during these dark days, knowing there is a light at the end of all this. I hope I can hear you laugh again, and I hope to hear your heartbeat. Remember me, daughter, because there is always the chance of me not coming home. At least give me the understanding that you know me now in whatever way you can.

Love you always
Your Father

After I finished the letter, all the happiness created with your mother flooded into my head. I was crying beside a tree. There I was in central Europe, dreaming of you and missing your mother. I loved her despite the fights we had. I thought of the past so vividly it drove out the present. It gave me hope, a yearning to return home so that all the pain I created would heal over and be forgiven. Time was the factor needed in repairing the love we had. The youthful dreams we clung to but lost to the realities of the world began to take shape again. But the war was not over. The monster was not created. I was still a whole man in the cold.

RICHARD PIRES

As the last lines on the map drew closer for an Allied victory, we found a ruined estate in the thicket of forest God forgot about. I pined for basic comforts. Hopefully the bed would be intact and not soaked from the elements. War makes nature an evil bitch. She spews out all her aggression on mankind's folly when he is trapped in her darkest of hearts. Cold in war is made colder, and the constant rubbing of limbs to create friction only yields cracking bones and ligament failure.

Rain turned to snow, then to ice. Each sheet bigger and harder than the last, smashing into your face so much you grow too numb to feel blood drip down your skin from a bullet hole. The need for a reprieve from nature was damning. A man could be understood if he killed his best friend for a fireplace and a chair. A point I was at.

When the estate came into view, I dismissed it as a mirage. A lie created by my crippling sanity, but then Samson saw it too.

"Jesus Christ on biscuits," he cried with the same gusto reserved for a sermon filled with snake handlers.

"You think there might be hostiles in there?" I asked out of routine.

"We're better shots. So to hell with it. You got the papers?" Samson was always on the lookout for spoils. He was a businessman. I was too, but was not interested in stolen loot. The argument was lost on Samson; he figured he wasn't stealing anything from the living if they were already dead.

"I got the papers, but the boys with the crates are two days away." Of course if you took spoils you had to ship them. The military had a great mailing service designed for such needs. This was a bonus for us young romantic war hawks.

"Which means, anything in there is up for grabs, and I was always quicker at spotting valuables than you. You ain't got the eye of a sultan."

"Ain't?" I asked, heading toward the house.

"It's cold. When it's cold, I get de-educated."

"I doubt there's anything of value left in there. Anyone with half a brain would have taken anything shiny by now. I just want a bed and a fire."

"Booze?" Samson asked with a smile.

"Always the next thing missing after shiny things."

"All right, enough dreaming. Let's squash our hopes with reality." Samson raised his rifle, checking for any sharpshooters.

"I'm optimistic for the booze." I followed suit, keeping Samson covered as we headed toward the demolished stone walls of former nobility. The exterior of this mini Versailles was appalling. Scars from small arms fire, shattered windows, and crumbling marble pillars greeted our eyes as we stealthily approached. We pushed rotted wooden doors down and were immediately hit by the smell of decay.

"Well, that bed idea might have been premature." Samson spat as the aroma of mildew and rot hit his nostrils.

"Keep an eye out and trigger finger ready." I headed first down the once-illustrious hallway, seeing the imprints on the walls where paintings had hung. The smell was getting worse as we got deeper in the house.

"This place has been wiped clean." Samson had

his hands over his nose, keeping his gun lowered. "Too many refugees have made this their toilet. Need we continue any further?"

"Never know what could be hidden." I smiled, giving Samson a thought.

"The spoils go to the victor, and we have been victing lately." Samson made a left down the hall as I headed right.

The smell of rot was getting stronger. Once I stepped over the dug-up tile and ripped carpet into the dining room, I saw where the smell was coming from. Three decomposed bodies of a family tied down greeted me. What was left of the husband sat in the head chair at the upturned table. The back of his head had been caved in with blunt force. The brain was visible and frozen. Yellowed ice stuck to his face and bare chest. Whoever killed him urinated on him. A final act of depravity for a man who spent the last hours of his life in hell.

His wife, or what I assumed to be his wife, was tied to another chair, her legs spread opened and tied down to two blocks of marble. She had been raped repeatedly. Her long hair ripped off in clumps at her side. A bullet hole remained in her temple. Her face was contorted in eternal sobbing. Her wrists were torn open from the rope burns as she squirmed. Legs bruised from repeated gropes.

The third victim was a child. His face buried in the molded pillow in the corner. Blood had stained it as his throat had been cut. Judging from experience garnered from seeing death up close for almost a year, I was able to realize the child was the last to die. He had to see his parents murdered. He had to experience their pain, even if he didn't know what it was. My feet came to the edge of the boy. His pants were pulled down around his ankles. The blood and bruising pointed to the act of forced sodomy.

I sat in the middle of this crime and took it in. I didn't cry, or shout to Samson. This was the aftermath of pure evil forcing me to face reality. The reality of man. There may not be a hell, but we create it just the same. Heaven was nowhere in this old world. And I forgot God in it. Or maybe he had forgotten us. I stepped back from the boy, coming down on the floor with a loud thud. In doing so, I realized the floor beneath me was hollow. I stomped my feet to the floor a few times to make sure I wasn't hearing things. I wasn't.

My hammer came down on the wood, smashing through the boards, discovering the edge of a frame beneath a heavy cloth. I pulled two paintings from the floor. As I did so, jewels and coins tumbled down from within the cloth. Samson came running.

"What did you find?" he asked with excitement as he rushed past the hell around him.

"Paintings, jewels, gold, and death."

I didn't look at the corpses or Samson. I kept my eyes on *Ambroise Vollard*, the cubed portrait created by Picasso; then I shifted to *The Red Room* by Henri Matisse.

"Jackpot." Samson was on his knees digging through the gaping hole I had created.

"Should we bury them?" I asked.

"I don't even want to look at them." Samson opened his bag and shoved the jewels and coins inside. Then he removed the forms. "Fill these out to make it legit." He handed me the form.

After we had diverted the mailing service from a critical post in Daumont, we were shipped to a border patrol post. We had looted and did it right, but the powers that be saw it as a tasteless act of piracy. Fortunately, my paintings had already shipped, and Samson cashed in the jewels and coins.

After about three days of huddling in the station with a potbelly stove, I looked at Samson. "Did we do wrong in that house?"

Samson laughed, pulling a blanket higher to his chest. "Nah. It's just a way to compensate us brave men in the heat of battle. The generals know about it. They just probably saw a public relations nightmare coming and needed to pin a penance on our sin to show those who care. That yes, the men in the trenches can be reprimanded by a chain of command."

"But did we do wrong?"

"Yes, we did." Samson hated the heat stemming from his self-conscience. He got up and threw the blanket on me. "I need to take a piss. Keep that blanket warm for me, would you?" He walked out of the station to a corner bush.

The first bullet hit his shoulder, then most went below his knees. Samson went down screaming as bullets rattled the station, blasting the potbelly stove. Embers and burning wood flew onto me. The fire caught quickly, forcing me to run out the back door, firing blindly at the darkness around me.

Samson was firing his weapon as I crawled to him. I saw that his leg was badly wounded. Blood sprayed out against the wall of the station. The bullet had hit the artery.

"Samson, can you move?" I screamed, unloading my rounds into dark shadows running from a nearby clearing.

"No." He fired two more rounds, sending one of the shadows down to the ground.

"Come on, this place is compromised." I grabbed him by the collar and pulled him up.

"You think a bullet can stop me? I've died on stage too many times to let something that pedestrian kill me." He let loose a final shot and then dropped his rifle. He went limp in my arms, passing out from the pain.

Hours later, Samson awoke. He cried while looking at his leg but stopped as soon as he saw I was awake. His leg had gotten worse overnight, and the smell of rotting cheese floated in the air. The infection was permeating through his leg fast.

"You need to get to the medic fast," I told Samson, packing whatever supplies I could find.

"To hell with that—the nearest medic is ten American miles away. I can't do that."

"You're not. I am." I tried to lift him, but he hit me in the face. His right hook was not infected. I shook off the stars and grabbed him harder.

"Just leave me."

"You stubborn fuck." I tasted blood in my mouth but couldn't care less.

"No. I am not going to be responsible for you dying on my account."

"Have a little hope, would ya? How many times did you die on stage again?"

"I had two legs to carry myself off stage."

"Just shut up. You'll weigh less if you don't

flap your gums." I lifted him up over my shoulder. It was no easy feat.

"This is more painful. Shit, just let me hook around your neck. If I strangle you, just say hey." We readjusted. "Better."

Both of us headed out onto the dirt road, praying no ambush lay in store for us. As the hours dragged by, I was getting more and more tired of carrying Samson on my back. His body heat mingled with mine, providing thirty added pounds of sweat. Samson went in and out of consciousness, which weakened his hold and forced me to wake him with a violent jerk.

"Just leave me, you dumb son of a bitch. I don't want to live with one leg anyway."

"You're supposed to be the entertainer here, Samson. Make me laugh while I save your life."

"Too tired to be funny."

"Nonsense. Funny people are born funny, no skill required. Just make something up."

"You're out of your goddamned mind. Are you doing this for another medal, you glory fuck?"

"See, that was funny, keep going."

"Just let me sit on the ground for a bit; just let me take a nap."

"The moment you fall asleep, you may not wake up. That infection is spreading fast, and resting will probably kill you."

"Let me fucking sleep!" He shouted in my ear this time. I didn't stop or slow down. I took the sonic hit.

"Go ahead and shout if you want. It just keeps you awake longer. We got about six miles left before the next checkpoint. We'll make it."

"Hope so. We'll just have to wait and see."

"The two greatest words in the English language: wait and hope."

"Don't be an asshole. Just because you read some books doesn't make you any smarter. For Christ sakes, look where you are right now. You should be home with that love of your life, you dim bastard."

"You make more sense when you bleed a lot."

"Close to death. Maybe that's the secret to life." He laughed, then shook uncontrollably. "I'm getting cold here, Monroe. Just let me die on the side of the road."

"Shut up, Samson. Last thing I need is you dying on my conscience. I always need friends."

"You get me out of this, I buy the booze from now on."

"Don't drink that much."

Four hours later, we made it to the checkpoint, where the soldiers on duty informed the medics of Samson's condition. The infection was contained thanks to my quick thinking, garnering me another medal. Samson was quick to take credit for it.

"They should have given you the Congressional Medal of Honor for saving a priceless treasure like me," Samson said. He never mentioned how he felt about losing his leg. When they fastened the peg onto his stump, his pleasant face turned bitter. As the years went by, he would start arguments with strangers just to prove he could still fight. His disability shamed him and made me realize why he was such a good friend to me after the bomb deformed me. Inside it was the same man, but no one would ever know what he was before because they spent too much time focusing on what he had become.

Chapter 16

"Please, ladies and gentlemen, do not aggravate the performers. They are professionals of the highest order and demand respect for their craft." The ringmaster tried to soothe the mob but only received a chorus of "boos," sending him to the back of the tent.

"Goddamned drunks. Every time they get paid, we have to deal with this shit," he said to Murray at the back entrance.

"They spend more money when they're drunk. Mind them for now, and we'll get steak tomorrow." Murray spat on the ground and headed back to Monroe, who was still standing and looking out at the sea behind them.

"They sound ready," Monroe said with his back to Murray.

"They want a show, but they can wait. We still need to be courteous to the Lynch Brothers. They're doing their thing right now."

The women were excited to see two muscle-bound acrobats throw each other in the air, causing many men in the audience to feel inadequate. The Lynch Brothers were in the middle of balancing each other by their feet, displaying their talent for strength and dexterity when the first bottle flew by them. They maintained their balance while the main tent security, three men with bigger arms than the behemoth, thumped the guilty man's skull. They carried him out over the roars of laughter and claps.

The main tent was at full capacity. They had to move the

bleachers into the main square two feet from the performers. The dog lady was making her poodle do an array of tricks but to the chagrin of the crowd waiting for the Mangled Man. I was still sitting with Mona and the behemoth.

"We've seen these tricks!" a man shouted in the back.

"Put that bitch away and the poodle!" the behemoth shouted, getting a big round of laughter, prompting him to throw a beer bottle.

"If the gentlemen drinking would be so obliged not to throw bottles at our performers, as it destroys the illusion," the ringmaster reported from the curtain, using it as a shield, as he bellowed into a cone. "Knuckles and Charlie will escort anyone they see being unruly outside, where the carnival has no legal authority as to what they do to you." The ringmaster pointed to Knuckles, a large man with handlebar moustache and massive arms folded in Zen calmness and Charlie a shorter man holding a large lead pipe, a twitch in his eye signaling little Zen calmness.

I laughed enjoying the foolishness of the elderly. They were not too far away from what Billy or Marvin would be doing. It made me feel mature. It made me feel adult.

"Give us a few more minutes to bring out the Marvelous Mangled Man!" The ringmaster shouted, heading back behind the curtain.

"This is taking forever." I said dismayed.

Monroe lowered his head and stepped into his cage. The mud was beginning to dry to his chest hair. Inside the cage, he scanned the surroundings. The slop bucket in the corner smelled like old shit, and the hay was borrowed from the llama cage. A family of rats took refuge in it.

"Why does it always have to stink?" Monroe asked, pointing to the slop bucket.

"Authenticity," Murray said, looking down at Monroe's shoes. "Need to take those off, they're too nice."

"Christ, don't get these near that fucking elephant or llama. The damn things piss more than an old man." Monroe pulled off the shoes and socks, his feet touching the cold, steel floor and sawdust between his toes. "Remind me again, Murray."

"Half of the door." Murray held the shoes and socks against his chest, protecting them like the crown jewels.

"All right, I'm ready. Wheel me out to those sons of bitches."

Three men pushed the cage to the edge of the tent opening. Monroe could see through the gap slightly. The array of people in the seats made him sick: another round of dockworkers with their week's pay, holding their hired dates for the evening.

"Christ" was all he could say as the spotlight crashed through the gap, blinding him momentarily. He didn't care. It was better to see spots than people.

Murray stood next to the cage, cueing the ringmaster to begin Monroe's introduction. He caught the cue in between drinking a few shots of rum to calm his nerves. He gave a thumbs-up, then walked to the center of the tent. The Lynch Brothers tumbled off stage, cursing the crowd in Russian.

"Sorry, guys, you know how the Friday crowd works," Murray told them.

"You think the bottle throwing will subside now?" Monroe asked.

"It just means they're drinking more tonight."

"I should've asked for half the beer money."

"Samson would never give that up. He ain't crazy."

The spotlight moved to encompass the ringmaster fully. "Now, now, ladies and fine, fine gentlemen. You want the state's greatest attraction? If P.T. Barnum were alive today, this man would be the centerpiece of his illustrious Museum of Oddity! This man, if you can call him that!"

"Was that necessary?" Monroe asked.

"Samson wrote it."

"It's just a bit melodramatic."

"No room for subtext here. Melodrama is all simple people can take."

"Now for your viewing pleasure, the Marvelous Mangled Man," the ringmaster shouted proudly. The cage pushed through the gap, and floodlights and gels came to life, capturing the Mangled Man in colored light. Monroe started his act yelling inaudible gibberish while running up and down the cage and keeping in mind not to put his naked feet into the hay or knock over the slop bucket.

* * *

When the lights hit the cage, I felt the air leave me. Seeing Monroe screaming like a deranged fool was sickening. I never stopped to think it could've been him. Any excitement I had for the night evaporated the moment he shouted grunts while hugging the cage like an ape. He drooled too. The wet stream of saliva glistened from the lights as did the tears forming in his mad eyes.

"Come on, kid, stand up. You can't get a good look sitting on your ass," Mona told me, laughing at the Mangled Man.

"Goddamn, that is one ugly son of a bitch. Bet he eats his own shit!"

I was frozen with hate, watching the gathered dregs of the docks howling with laughter and hurling insults. But how could a thir-teen-year-old tell anyone bigger than him to stop? Monroe kept his act going until the lights dimmed momentarily. One of the bulbs popped, giving Monroe a clear view of me. The act stopped dead in its tracks as his eyes adjusted to the view and saw me right smack in the center of all the laughing drunks. He stood there staring at me, but I couldn't return the favor. The drunks around me were angry at the lack of Monroe's indignity. They started yelling obscenities, then throwing popcorn, peanuts, and beer bottles. Many bottles shattered against the steel bars, leaving Monroe soaked with warm summer beer and wine. None of it mattered to him. He could only stand in the cage, lost to everything, seeing my shame.

* * *

The bulb was replaced, allowing the bright lights to block out the crowd, but it was too late. Monroe had never felt good about this work, but now he felt ashamed. Before, this was all about surviving and making enough money to live as comfortably as possible with his deformity. Now the illusion was gone. The gravity of the situation was apparent when glass shrapnel hit Monroe's face. Murray ran out with Knuckles and Charlie and broke up the gathered mob.

"Goddamn it!" the ringmaster yelled through his cone, running with the crewmen from behind the tent to get Monroe out of there.

"You all know the rules, no throwing. You've been warned once, but not no more. Show's over, get out of my tent." The ringmaster threw his hands up, heading through the gap in the curtain.

The crowds tried to instigate a fight, but any uprising was quickly squashed as Knuckles and Charlie smacked heads into wood seats and broke fingers with brute force. Most of the people headed out in an orderly fashion, laughing at the screaming of injured men holding their bleeding heads and twisted fingers.

"Well kid, too bad you didn't get to see the entire show. Take it easy." Behemoth rubbed my head. "Come on Mona, let's ride the Ferris wheel."

Murray inspected Monroe's face as blood streamed down his check. "It's not too deep, thankfully. I thought you were supposed to be checking for bottles," Murray asked the ringmaster, wiping the sweat off his face.

"What do you want me to do? Frisk every person in line? That would take money and time, neither of which Samson wants to cough up. No one got hurt, so consider it a good night."

"Monroe's bleeding."

"It's not deep, Murray. Just grazed the skin. I've had worse," Monroe said.

"Was something wrong, Monroe? You froze up. You've never done that before," the ringmaster asked with genuine care in his voice.

"The lights, that's all it was. It was the lights."

"I'm going to talk to Samson tonight. We need better security," Murray said.

"What was the take?" Monroe asked, taking Murray by surprise.

"What?"

"How much did we rake in?"

Murray whistled to the box office girl—a short, stubby woman most would mistake for a man—from the booth adjacent to the entrance. She rolled her eyes, walking to Murray with a ledger under her arm. Her eyes never met Monroe's. The box office girl kept the money box near her nether regions at all times, a rule Samson required her to follow. His reason being that her looks were so distracting one would never think to look for the money near her honey pot. If they did, they deserved the money.

"Looks like more than last weekend." He closed the ledger and handed it back to the masculine woman. "Do you have the box secure?" Murray kicked her in between the legs, smacking against the steel. "Good."

He slapped her ass when she walked away. It was the only action she would get in the next month.

"You know when they get paid, they all come to spend it on you. You've always been the star in this tent," the ringmaster said, drinking from his flask.

"Got any more of that bourbon lying around?" Monroe asked. "The twenty-dollar stuff."

* * *

I was alone on the pier after the show. I managed to move past the ropes to sit on a lone bench and watched the water crash against the rocks under the lighthouse in the distance. The cold air hit me hard. It was still July, but the wind suggested otherwise. I folded my arms as chills went through me. A shadow fell over me. I knew who it was even before he spoke.

"At night the ocean is the best thing one can look at because it lets you forget everything else. You thirsty?" Monroe jiggled a bottle of bourbon at me.

"I don't think I want that."

"It'll keep you warm. The ocean breeze can chill you to the bones. Besides, one swig won't kill you or make you drunk off your ass." He handed it to me. I drank, then coughed. My nose and throat burned as the alcohol went down my gullet, and the aftertaste hit me like a hard punch to the esophagus. My face most likely turned green.

Monroe took it away from me, fast. "Or maybe it will."

For a moment, we stood staring at each other under the dock light. The yellow glow was not helping Monroe's disfigurement. He looked angry and sick as the shadows played against his folded skin and protruding bumps of scarred tissue.

"I didn't know you were here. I didn't know this is what you did." I was being honest with him. I truly wished he were a morphine addict. If it were that simple, my shock would've been less severe.

"Doesn't matter. It's all a show. Half of the grunting monsters in cages are more intelligent than the ogling crowds, but if you ask a person to talk to something born with a pinhead or a man with no arms and legs, they more likely stare than talk. Ears go numb when you use your eyes to judge. It's the way of the world though." He sat next to me, lighting a cigar, then handed it to me as soon as it was lit.

"Doesn't have to be." I took a puff from the stogie. The smoke was smoother than the bourbon and warmed me. Monroe tried to take it back, forcing me to swing at him. He smiled at my newly discovered love of smoking.

"Why not? It pays better than any other job I ever had, including the army. I owe Samson. Old army buddies can come in handy. Without him, I would have lost more than just my wife and daughter." It pained him to say those words. I don't think he'd said that out loud in years.

This was the moment for me to finally break through his barriers. "What happened to them?" I asked point-blank.

He was slow to respond. He smoked a few puffs, took a swig, then exhaled loudly. "Read my memoirs."

"My mom always said night is the best time to tell the truth because you're too tired to lie. But I understand—"

He interrupted me with a raised hand. "Shit, might as well tell you with a piece of sage advice like that." Monroe spat, wiped the slime off his battered chin, then looked out onto the ocean trying to conjure up his last moments with Elizabeth.

"My wife worked in a factory when the men went away. The old man running the place had a son who seemed promising to her. At first it was friendship, but it eventually grew to more. By the time I returned from the war, she was ready to marry him. She left me for the West Coast, with her David. My face made her guilt subside." Monroe threw the bottle against the dock, and the booze created a large puddle at his feet. "Damn, shouldn't have done that."

"It wasn't that good."

"You're too young to love bourbon. Give it a couple years, and you'll find it does the trick."

"Why don't you just write them?"

"Write them all the time, but it never works. I just get replies telling me the same thing: we've moved on."

"Sometimes we just have to wait and hope. The two greatest words in the English language, right?" I thought I was being smart, but Monroe just stared at me with dark eyes.

"You're not the first person to feed me that bullshit today. Hope never works when you're facing something that can't be changed. The ones who live deal with it the only way they can, through reading and paraphrasing the words of wiser men. That is all I have left. So, spare me the regurgitated words of a Frenchman who never knew what losing love really felt like. Who wrote about revenge as opposed to truth. You lose what you love because nothing lasts. Anyone who believes in something more is a sucker. Never sacrifice a goddamn thing for any idea or person. You'll always be wrong and live with the aftermath of your choices... You'll be alone."

"Just wait then." I walked away, leaving him to the lighthouse and waves.

There was nothing a thirteen-year-old boy could say or do that would matter right now. I had forced the bad memories to return to him. Memories that were pushed down deep into his mind. It was hard for me to realize he had so many good memories, causing the present to be torture. Monroe lived a life foreign to me: a removed one. The chill grew colder, but to a man like Monroe, it wouldn't stir him one bit. He just puffed away on his cigar, kicking the shards of the bourbon bottle over the side.

* * *

Samson was heading up the stairs. "Broke your bottle?"

Monroe smiled drunkenly, turning his head. "You got another one?"

"Why is it that you take up drinking when it costs so damn much?"

"I'm an expert at pissing people off."

"Like that kid?"

"You saw that?"

"You shouldn't have been so down on him. He was right, you know." Samson pulled out a flask, sharing with Monroe. "It's too damn cold out here to be morose. You should get some sleep. We got a busy day in the morning, or are you reluctant to start new memories?"

"What does that mean?" Monroe was honest in his questioning.

"I know you well enough. I think the only real reason you keep coming back here is to find something new to hate." Samson picked up the broken shards. "I don't want the kids to play with this broken glass." He dumped them into the trash can.

Monroe kept his eyes on the sea, finally feeling the cold chill creep into his bones. "I got tired of seeing her face." He pointed out his mangled face. "So, I used this one against her. It was good at first, enough to keep me from blaming myself. Having these sons of bitches gawk at me put things in focus. It makes me realize most of what happened was my fault." Monroe pulled his coat up against his face in an attempt to block the tears forming in his eyes. "Always a pain in the ass, admitting to yourself anything truthful." Monroe wiped his eyes, shaking off the hurt. "If this procedure works, I don't know what I'll do with myself."

"Live again." Samson smashed the cigar into the bench, splashing embers against his shoes. "What most men never get."

Samson walked up to his office to let his stump breathe. It was a pain in the ass to stand on that platform shouting all damn night. And he was tired.

Chapter 17

B illy woke up in a pool of sweat. For the last week he had slept a total of four hours, give or take. The bags under his eyes were darker than the average child his age, but all those who noticed just ignored it. It wasn't their concern what a boy was doing up at all hours of the night. People talked about it behind his back of course. Being a small town, gossip flows quicker than a deluge. Though any time one of his parents was within earshot, the talking quieted quickly so as to not be rude. His parents were even worse. They figured the best thing for Billy and his unmentioned problem was to spend more time at church with Brother Phillip. They figured a man with his background would be more apt at discovering the problem with Billy. They never once thought Brother Phillip was responsible for the sleepless nights and the bruises that showed up on his arms and legs. Billy couldn't defecate normally either. Blood would flow down the bowl of the toilet, forcing him to spend frantic minutes cleaning up before anyone would notice. By day three of his abuse, he was used to the pain. Even the shame was becoming commonplace.

Before Billy died he had a special day. This day was like the ones before Brother Phillip because it had a sense of hope. Billy stole a knife out of Walter Mitty's General Store. He stuck it in his belt underneath his shirt. He patted it gently against his skin, making sure it was still there. He felt bad for stealing, so he purchased some random items to make up for the stolen one. It was his way of saying sorry to Walter.

He rode his bike to the church, beating Maybelle, the church secretary walking with a veil over her head. She had been mourning the death of her husband for the last three years like he was the saint of all saints. Everyone else remembered him as a drunk who died in the arms of another woman, but Maybelle ignored the truth, recreating her husband in her own image. She was a sad sack of an old maid.

Billy parked his bike and ran into the office, heading downstairs to the basement and passing Brother Phillip, who stood in his office doorway. Brother Phillip licked his lips at the thought of Billy being so quick to run to the basement. It cemented his theory of the town: with a little nudge, they would do anything for him. With a little more nudging, they would be inclined to blame someone else for the evil plaguing their town. He could stay longer here than he anticipated. With the reverend gone, he could snake his way into the hearts of the congregation. The town would follow him to any conclusion and ignore any evidence that suggested anything foul about him.

The basement was being converted to a classroom for the Sunday school Brother Phillip envisioned. A dozen desks gave off the smell of freshly cut timber, rolls of carpet leaned against the brick walls, wheeled chalkboards stood in the corner, and various religious paintings hung on the wall. Billy went to the window and unlocked the latch. He opened it and made sure it didn't stick. It moved up and down with ease for a quick escape. He took the knife out and palmed it. The blade hid behind his arm.

Brother Phillip came down the stairs slowly; his shadow engulfed Billy as he stood in the slim doorway.

"What brings you here so fast, Billy?" Brother Phillip asked, removing his belt.

Billy just turned around and faced the wall, keeping the knife hidden as best he could. Brother Phillip noticed the window slightly open.

"Put your palms against the wall."

Billy didn't know what to do now. He never asked that before. He had no choice but to act ahead of schedule. He swiped up the knife, missing Brother Phillip's chest by three inches. Brother Phillip could only laugh.

"Got a pig sticker, boy?" He let Billy stab a couple more times, knowing full well he had the upper hand. "Billy, what will your parents say to you now?"

Billy lunged forward, and Phillip hit him over the head with his fist. He took the belt and wrapped it around Billy's throat and squeezed. Billy's neck broke quickly. Brother Phillip didn't even break a sweat. He went to the window and locked it. Then went upstairs, leaving Billy's body below.

Maybelle was typing the church newsletter when Brother Phillip put his hand on her shoulder. "You scared me, Brother Phillip."

"Forgive me, Maybelle, I was just wondering if you got a letter from the reverend regarding his mission retreat?"

"Yes I did, it was in the mailbox today. Says he's having a great time."

"Fantastic. Did he have any passages for me to read this week?"

"A couple. I left them on your desk."

"Wonderful. Maybelle, go home early today. I sent Billy home early too, so don't think just because you're older means you have to work harder."

"I don't mind. I love working for the church."

"It's a bright day, which leads to bright evenings, and I got something for you in the meantime." Brother Phillip went into his office, returning with a dozen tulips wrapped in plastic. "These are for your husband's grave. I think you both need some time to enjoy the blessed day."

She smiled at the tulips and then at Brother Phillip. Her hand touched his, and she started to cry. "I appreciate that. Who told you it was the anniversary of his death?"

"People talk all the time here, Maybelle. You just have to keep your ear open."

"Bless you, Phillip." Maybelle took the flowers and left the desk.

Brother Phillip waited until she was out the door to wipe the hand she had touched. Old people always bothered him. They were easier to kill, but they smelled worse than children. Old age was not a stage he looked forward to at all. With Maybelle gone, he had ample time with Billy. The rush of murder had subsided, leaving Phillip feeling empty. Murder was always too quick. Savoring it was dangerous, Phillip knew. But to have an entire afternoon removed from the ears of people with a body in the basement was heaven on Earth. He had to be content with the limited fantasy fulfilled and deal with the aftermath: a dead body.

Billy's eyes bulged too much. No one would believe a simple drowning was responsible. Brother Phillip had to be creative now. If he plucked out Billy's eyes, a pattern would be suspected and he didn't want that. He looked around the room, finding the perfect way out. Brother Phillip wrapped Billy in an old rug. Billy's body was heavier than the last one, but Brother Phillip didn't mind too much. He needed a workout. Sitting at a church desk all day got on his nerves, not to mention adding weight to his midsection. He managed to walk up the top peak of Sunset Hill with no one watching. Most of the cabins were rented out during the winter. The summer months produced too much heat to spend in a stuffy cabin, and the brook was a mile down the trail.

Sunset Hill had a few steep points, leading down rocky crevasses. One particular crevasse led into the river. Billy would be the victim of a cliff jumping accident. His eyes would be crushed into his skull, and hopefully, the blunt force of the rocks would break his neck to ensure the bruise around his throat was written off. He unrolled the carpet and lifted the body over the side, dumping him. The body fell straight down, never hitting the side of the cliff. There was a light thud and then a splash as the body flopped into the brook where the current would do the rest.

Brother Phillip would head into the sheriff's office in two days to inform Sheriff Tate that Billy didn't come to work the last two days, and he was worried. He'd tell them that Billy complained about being hot and wanting a dip in the water. He suggested the pool in the back of the church, but Billy wanted to dive from high up. Brother Phillip would say he had talked him out of cliff jumping, but boys will be boys. This often proved fatal, especially in a small town with nothing else to do. Then he would drop a note into a slot when the time was necessary, divulging an eyewitness account of a man seen dumping a heavy load over the cliff and into the river. All he needed was time and Monroe.

Chapter 18

Monroe sat in the doctor's office staring at the tile wall: green with a white border and not even one was dirty or sticky with condensation. This was the cleanest, most sterile doctor's office he had ever seen, especially with this much tile. This was the mindset Monroe was forced to have, sitting in a gown with his ass hanging out. His flesh was prickly from the cold, but it was his worry that kept him shaking. What if this was his last shot at anything? he thought to himself over and over again. A glimmer of hope being dashed can kill a man. Here, the last glimmer was shining

The nurse was a petite woman around thirty, very cute and robust for her size. Monroe always blushed when an attractive woman was within eyesight of his mangled face. Her smile soothed him, even though he knew it was just professional. Inside, she must've been disgusted.

"Monroe, how long have you had this deformity?" Her eyes went back to her clipboard, writing furiously.

"I would say nine years."

"Any physical pain attributed to the deformity?"

"At first headaches all the time, soreness, and hazy vision, which just added to the headaches."

"Okay." She flipped through the pages of the file, quickly

scanning them. "They grafted most of the skin from your face over the exposed bone. Is that why there is so much scar tissue?"

"The field surgeon did the best he could with the tools he had."

"Yes, I can see that. But don't fret, in all honesty we can fix you up easily," she said nonchalantly.

Monroe sat up in his slump, not believing a word she just said. "What do you mean, fix up easily?"

"Exactly that. You were lucky your skin wasn't burned off completely. You would've died. The bone damage in your face can be repaired somewhat. It will still be sunken in around the cheek and right eye, but the lumps around your skull can be reduced easily. We can make it as normal as it ever was. Your lips and teeth can be repaired as well, although once the procedure is done, you won't be able to eat solid food for a couple weeks until the tissue heals and covers over nicely."

"I can live with that. I mostly drink, anyways." Monroe realized the joke one could take from it.

"Well, good." She didn't know if he was being funny or not. "Doctor Steinberg will check you over in a moment. He will be operating on you, so just answer all his questions. Any fears you may have with the procedure, bring them to his attention."

She began to walk out of the room, forcing Monroe to speak up before she could leave. "Thank you, nurse. You don't know what this means to me."

She turned around and smiled once more. "We bring hope back to people now, Monroe; it's the plus side to modern medicine."

Monroe smiled, no longer interested in the tile.

* * *

I sat on the beach watching my sister build a sandcastle with my father. My mother read through *The Count of Monte Cristo*. She'd scanned through most of it in two days.

"I forgot how good this was."

"I didn't know you were a reader," I told her.

"There's a lot you don't know about your mom. I've read probably more books than your dad."

"Well, it was either eat and live under a roof or just read all day. Call me crazy," my father retorted, making me laugh. "Besides I read that—it was all right."

"Are we heading for the pier today?" Mother asked.

I didn't answer the question because I didn't want to go back there. Monroe had destroyed any future ambition to explore carnival tents.

"Are we heading for the pier today?" Mother repeated.

Katie frowned at the prospect, along with my dad. He rolled on his stomach, looking up at Mother with a squint. "I like lounging here for now. What about you? Do you really want to spend more money?"

"Well, when you put it like that." She went back to the book.

"Steven, you went last night. Is there anything worth seeing?"

"No, not really, most of it is fake. The rest is just sad."

"Yeah. How much did you spend?" my father asked, bringing everything back to spending money on a holiday.

"Like ten cents, I guess."

"Too much."

"Stop being so damned cheap," Mother said, never lifting an eye away from the words. "Who spent three dollars on shipping for a brick of wine a few weeks ago?"

Father lifted Katie up from the sand and rushed for the water. "We're going swimming."

"Works every time," Mother said, going back to the page she was reading.

* * *

Murray and Samson stood against the flatbed truck in the loading dock of the hospital. Both of them paced up and down the concrete, chain-smoking cigarettes. Samson sat on the garbage can, rubbing his stump through the gap in the fake leg. With the passing of time, Samson had become accustomed to the idea of having one leg. It was no longer a sore spot for him but a reminder of the Great War. In the early days, when fights erupted over nothing, Samson usually won. His fists were far from crippled, and his other leg had no problem keeping balance.

Now though, he was tired of fighting. It gets old after a while, he concluded. Sometimes, the best thing to do is let time pass and not give credence to the old saying "Time heals all wounds." Usually wounds scar over or get infected, killing the poor son of a bitch. No, the reasoning for letting time pass is for the individual, not the situation. Samson had a theory on mankind: give them a day to think about killing, and they won't do it. The problem is that every man rushes into it because of the situation. He was a wise man, once you got past the smell of alcohol and tobacco.

"This will work, right?" Murray asked, flicking his cigarette away.

"It better. God knows he's been through enough."

"You did a good thing for him."

"Stop saying that, would you."

Monroe came out the back door without a bag over his face. Samson and Murray were both startled to see his display.

"Good news, I take it?" Samson said, coming to attention.

"How can you tell?" Monroe asked with a grin.

"That's the first time I've seen you smile in daylight in about eight years. I like the old you better." Samson laughed, pulling out a bottle of bourbon from his leather satchel. "We'll drink in the truck."

Monroe, Murray, and Samson all sat in the cab of the flatbed, passing the bottle.

"So what should you do for me now?" Samson asked.

"Well, I have become quite the capable typist. Maybe I could come up with some banter for the shows." Monroe knew how to get under Samson's skin. The writing was his job, and he took pride in it. He usually spent a good four- or five-day session racking his head against the typewriter, smoking three packs just to finish a paragraph.

"He could write the shows better," Murray said.

"There's nothing wrong with the shows. People like melodrama, especially inside a tent. Anything close to realism makes them nervous and ashamed. No one ever wants that. And I can't have drunks think and ponder over the subtext of a freak show."

"Monroe could write the shows better," Murray said, downing another shot.

"He does make a good argument," Monroe said.

Samson did a double take at the two of them and exhaled. "I hate the typewriter anyway."

* * *

Spending time in a hotel room with family can be nice, but once day two hits, the familiarity of family becomes oppressive. You don't have your own space. You don't have a backyard. You don't even have a kitchen to go and sneak a snack. All you have are four walls, two beds, a sofa and a desk with a radio and a lamp. The balcony was not an option because Father claimed that zone. Sitting in his chair with cigar in hand, reading the paper or drinking a cocktail next to Mother in her chair. I just watched from the sofa as Katie continued to play with my toys. My thoughts kept going back to Monroe too. We didn't part under good circumstances, which caused my guilt to rise. With the boredom brought on by the hotel room, I decided to head back to the pier to see him.

"I'm heading out," I said casually.

Mother and Father had a good laugh at my nonchalant attitude.

"Where you going, man about town?" my father asked with a raised eyebrow.

"Back to the pier. I didn't get to see it all." I maintained my nonchalance.

"Did you get to the main tent?" Father asked.

"Yeah."

"You saw it."

"I thought you said there wasn't much to do?" Mother asked.

"That was before I got bored."

"Read your book."

"I did. Mom's got it now."

"Oh right, my educated better half."

Mother hit him with the book. "I don't know, Steven, once was enough. I wouldn't want to chance anything."

"What is there to chance, Mom? I already went when it was dark. It's only three in the afternoon now."

"Don't remind me. I still can't believe we let you go." Mother said.

Father's face grew long and pondering. His eyes washed over with an idea as he noticed Katie nodding off, and then whispered in Mother's ear about a certain marital obligation only achieved when the kids were either asleep or out.

"Katie, it's time for your nap," Mother said, rising from her chair.

Katie fell to the floor and hugged the pillow that was a fort for my soldiers. They tumbled off in groups, as if the earth opened up and swallowed them in their realm of existence. "Okay, Mommy," she said, closing her eyelids tight and figuring sleep just came once you focused with your eyes closed.

Mother whisked her off the floor, kissing her check repeatedly. "You can go, Steven, but be back before dark."

"I will. Do you want me to pick up some whiskey for you two? They got a tub full of it in one of the warehouses."

"Two jugs," Father said, still seated on his wicker throne, never turning around from the view. "You know what? I really like this hotel."

It was daylight this time on my way to the pier. All the dark corners were bright, the dockworkers were still working, and the roaming strumpets were nowhere to be found. What I did find was the chained-up entrance to the pier. It seemed the carnival opened at dusk, still three hours away. I walked to the side near the edge of the pier, discovering a gap big enough for a boy my size to climb over. Once achieved, I used all of my stealthy infiltrating skills to make it thirty feet up the pier before the old curmudgeon from the animal oddity tent tripped me with his boot. He was smoking a pipe, sitting on a box behind one of the tent folds blocking his presence from my view.

"Wanted to see the merman for free?" he asked, not helping me up.

"I came to see Monroe."

The old man's face was confounded. "How the hell you know Monroe?"

"I help him out back home. I need to ask him something."

"What? You could tell me, I'm his confidant." The old man spit near my feet.

"I need to ask him. I'm sure you'd forget halfway down the pier." I was tired of being polite with carnies.

"All right, he just got back from the doctor's office up in the city, so hold on." He turned around immediately. "If he don't know you, I'll kick your ass over the side so you can swim back to the beach. It ain't that deep."

"He knows me."

"Should he know your name?"

"Steven. What about you?"

"Calhoun," he yelled, heading up the pier.

* * *

Monroe sat in his wagon, gazing at the empty bottles of booze lying on the floor and shelves. This place was always a mess once the late show was over. His self-loathing would crescendo into an all-night bender when he worked the carnival. It was customary to see Monroe vomit over the side of the dock in the early morning. Everyone ignored it and left him alone. Now he stood looking down on a wasted lifestyle. There was no more pain inside, just hope. For the first time in nine years the word "hope" made him smile.

Calhoun knocked on the door, hoping Monroe got good news from the doctor. When he saw Monroe open the door without a frown or vomit-stained shirt, he smirked. "There's a boy out here says he knows you."

"I know him. Send him on up to the bench, but before that, I want you to have something." Monroe went into his drawers and pulled out three boxes of cigars along with three bottles of sealed bourbon.

He threw them to Calhoun, who caught each one with an ever-widening grin. "Cutting back would be a good idea, I think." The last cigar box stayed in his grip. "I'll keep this one though." Monroe put them back and locked the drawer.

"Enough for me, I ain't no glutton." Calhoun ripped off the seal, pulling the cork with his teeth. "But I am thirsty."

* * *

Calhoun came back with arms full of cigars and booze. He had already downed half a bottle from one side of the pier to the other.

"He'll see you at the bench." Calhoun marched to the corner of his tent, opened the cigar box, and sniffed the tobacco. "Three-cent cigars. Monroe knows how to live." He bit the tip off and lit up.

Monroe was sitting at the bench with his face in full daylight. He had a cigar box tucked under his arm, puffing away and seeming to be far away from where he was sitting.

"That can't be good for you," I said, pointing to the cigar.

"Lungs feel fine. You want one?" He presented the box to me.

"Sure." I grabbed it without a thought, biting into the tip just like Calhoun. Monroe threw me some matches, and I lit up with joy. "Not bad, three cents?"

"These are the ten-cent ones. Calhoun wouldn't know the difference."

I didn't know what to say to him. My excuse for being here had to be a logical one because the last thing I wanted Monroe to do was get mushy with me. "I had to ask you about Cristo."

"What about?"

"I finished the damn thing, and now I want to know why I had to read it in the first place?"

"My father told me to read it before I was fifteen. This was his rule, and I agree with it. The story is important to any boy starting out on the path to manhood, and it usually hits around fifteen. All the dreams and love you had can be taken from you by the powers that be—be it God in the sky or men with their pens. There are always risks. It might sound paranoid, but it's true. Though Dantes prevails, allowing himself to discover there can be something better than what was before, it just takes two words: wait and hope. In the end that's all we really have."

"In the end, what did Mercedes have?" I said, feeling lightheaded from the cigar. Monroe noticed and took it out of my hand. "If he loved her, why didn't he try to talk her out of leaving everything behind?"

"Love is sometimes a piece of the past. When you stand next to it and feel what used to be, you realize it is an aftershock and not what is there now. Even if all the memories you shared were good. If enough time passes, anything you had with the woman you loved is lost. It's just something that happens. In situations like that, wait and hope isn't enough. Finality is what you can muster. The end of what used to be. Some people can't deal with that. I used to be someone like that." Monroe lifted his crooked lips into a smile, and genuine relief washed over him in the moonlight. "I don't have to look at the past anymore. I can finally wait for the future with hope. A nice feeling."

"Wait and hope." I looked up at Monroe for a long time and saw him change into the young man he was before the war. "You seem happy. I don't know how to take that."

"They can fix me. Make me what I was," Monroe said, tapping the enflamed end of my cigar lightly. He was going to save it. They were ten-cent cigars after all.

"When?"

"Soon. Probably within the next few weeks." He put the cigar back in the box.

"Are you done with this place?"

"Yes, let someone else be the star."

"Most of the people living on the port are uglier than you. You should have an open call."

Monroe laughed out loud, a good sound to hear. "I think I have a new book for you."

I rolled my eyes. "Is it as long as *The Count of Monte Cristo*?"

"All the best books are long."

"Which one?"

"*Ivanhoe*."

"Sounds boring."

"You complain way too much for a kid your age."

"We're supposed to."

"That's the problem with your generation, too much time on your hands. Use the time to get smarter, would you?"

"I'm smart."

"Keep lying to yourself." Monroe patted my shoulder and laughed.

Chapter 19

Brother Phillip always had an ear out to the women of the town. They were a talkative bunch, filled with gossip and spite for many people in town and a perfect way for Brother Phillip to look for a scapegoat. He had done this multiple times, making him an expert in who to listen to more intently. Edith Mayer was the one woman in town with an eye out for anything suspicious. She would judge anyone with quickness and was always the first to spread bad news. Good news was boring and unsensational. Edith knew the women coming to her beauty shop were in need of other people's problems. Life was boring if not for the bad news. Brother Phillip made her a special project.

Edith was in her late forties but told everyone she was thirty-two. Most knew better. Her body still had the curves and the boys in the neighborhood noticed, which only added fuel to the fire. Brother Phillip first came into her boutique for a haircut the third day he was in town. He knew the type of person she was from the get-go. She was the one to find his scapegoat, and by the third week, she delivered.

"He's always been distant, that one," she said with a mouthful of muffin.

Brother Phillip told her he had seen Monroe walking the trails by himself, as if he was retracing his steps. Edith ate this up with a fork and knife. Her eyes went wide at the prospect of a child murderer in their midst.

"Distant," she repeated. "I would bet he had something to do with it, but we're just talking here, no bearing false witness… That kid had his eyes poked out, right?"

"That's what I heard, but who knows if it is true." Brother Phillip cut his muffin with a knife and spread butter on top. "What do you mean by distant?"

"Oh, just that. He doesn't come out of his house at all. He has Walter deliver his groceries to him. Oh, he's deformed too—did you know that? Face crushed or blown up, something like that." Edith checked herself in the mirror, making sure no crumbs were resting on her face.

"I had heard a shell blew up in his face." Brother Phillip couldn't hide his irritation at this woman's ignorance, but he was quick to put on a friendly face.

"Yeah, probably. You know what's stranger though is that he left right before Sammy disappeared and went up to his cabin. Convenient, huh?"

"Very. Maybe someone should tell Sheriff Tate about that."

"No, no need. Tate loves Monroe. He sold him his house and helped out with Tate's election for sheriff before he took off to the war. But we're just talking here; no one is accusing Monroe of anything."

"Not at all. False witness, mind you, is a sin."

"My favorite one." Edith laughed. "But still, people have dark sides, even people who have friends in law enforcement."

"Especially those with friends in law enforcement."

Edith bit into another muffin, shrugging her shoulders. Within twenty-four hours, she had spread her suspicions to three local women, who, in turn, told their husbands and planted the seeds of unrest.

Sunday morning service could not ask for a better day outside. The sun was golden, the sky was blue, and the people were seated together with fans in their hands, listening to wonderful Brother Phillip. He had made a name for himself these last few weeks since taking over for Reverend Thomas, who was still not back from his sudden holiday. Most people didn't even notice the weeks going by; they all just loved being in the presence of such a charismatic leader of Christianity. He would sing loudly and drown out the choir. Everyone especially loved that. He told stories from the Bible many knew by heart already, only he told them with such panache, many forgot they had heard them before. He always provided refreshments to the people outside the church after services. Brother Phillip was a miracle for this town and a blessing from God. Since Billy's body was found that morning, the people needed a man like him to help them overcome these dark days.

"Brothers and sisters, I have heard ramblings around town of heinous acts not brought to light. With the absence of Reverend Thomas, I have been given a cross to bear. I have been given a congregation with much trouble on their minds. This is a town that has embraced me like a true brother, but I want all of you to cease this bearing false witness. As Christians, you must embrace all of those around you, even those who choose to stay away from the light of the church. Those who stay away from the parades, the picnics, and the holiday festivals. Those who remain hidden should be brought to the light. They should be questioned with a Christian heart. You need to ask why. You need to seek out those who shy away from the eyes of our loving gaze. We need to bring them to the forefront. We need to make sure their hearts are pure, because to welcome an unknown into your heart can be dangerous."

Walter sat in his usual place: the back. He was always late to church—things had to be done before ten in the morning, so he would often sneak into the back and hunker down as quietly as he could. This morning though, he wished he'd never shown up. Hearing Brother Phillip's sermon stirred his paranoia. It left him with a nagging sensation Brother Phillip was buttering up the people to make them side with him if it came down to it. Walter had always been one to question the cloth. It wasn't because of his agnostic tendencies but due to his distrust of most people. It was why Monroe and he got along so well. When the sermon was over, the choir rose to sing, forcing him to ignore the feeling and read the newsletter.

Many of the gathered flock were morose with the news of Billy's death. Many whispered outside the church walls, not wanting to be disrespectful. Brother Phillip maneuvered around the people, keeping his ear out to listen to the growing speculation of a murder most foul.

"Sheriff Tate is leaving town," one woman said, keeping her eyes out for Billy's parents. They were not in church that day, nor would they ever return. All faith was lost with Billy's death. Two weeks later, they sold their home and moved back to Maryland where Billy's mother had been born. Years later, I heard they had another son, but I never spoke to them after that summer.

"Another kid drowned in that damn river. They need to block off the trails," another man said, keeping his voice low to his wife.

"Children shouldn't be out there by themselves anyways," his wife replied.

Brother Phillip couldn't enjoy this more, as he continued to shake hands and overhear the crowd's paranoia rise. As soon as he saw Walter, he rushed over. "Walter, I don't think we've had a chance to speak before."

Walter gave a courteous hand, keeping his smile to himself. "No, we haven't really had the opportunity to speak. My fault, I don't really participate much."

"Reasons for this?" Brother Phillip maintained his congeniality.

"Not at all, I am just busy working on too many things. The day passes by too quickly to make church a priority."

"Well, church is never a priority, it is an obligation. I hope you don't feel obligated to always sit in the back."

"I'm always late, so it's easier to sit in the last pew."

"I can save you a spot in the front or middle, if you like." Brother Phillip wanted to get a rise out of Walter. He looked him straight in the eyes, seeing if they gave off a hint of dislike or trust.

"Not at all. Call me an old man stuck in my ways." Walter showed teeth, now knowing it would piss Brother Phillip off more.

"Of course. There are always habits we develop that never go away. I understand completely." Brother Phillip shook his hand again and bowed to him. "It was a pleasure speaking to you, Walter. I wish to do it again very soon."

"As do I, Brother Phillip, as do I." Walter smiled and watched Brother Phillip head back to the church through the sea of people. Every old woman received a hug and every old man a handshake and a few words. The town loved this man. Walter did not.

* * *

No use in cracking a lock at Monroe's house. Brother Phillip found a way through the storm doors. With his first step, he looked up at the portrait of Ambroise Vollard and squinted. An ugly painting if there ever was, no matter who the hell painted it. After the viewing he went to the typewriter and moved his finger along the edge, feeling the cold metal.

Next to it stood the stack of pages. The smudged words didn't speak to Brother Phillip at all. He rolled his eyes and wiped his fingers on his pants, heading toward the bookshelf against the wall. Dozens of volumes lined the shelf, an occasional cigar box full of nails, other random items, stacks of deeds from the many homes on 1st Street, and a file wrapped with twine. He pulled out the file carefully, unraveling the twine wrapped around it. Inside was the deed to the cabin on Sunset Mountain, number 5. Brother Phillip memorized most of the information written.

The kitchen was nothing special, but the den proved otherwise. The medals in the new glass case shined on the center shelf. Brother Phillip noticed most of his were the same. He scanned the books, seeing a number of first editions Monroe had picked up in his years of solitude. Brother Phillip, being an educated man, was going to return to steal most of them once Monroe was dead.

In the hallway, his feet touched the edge of a framed picture. He lifted it up, catching the light cutting though a crack in the curtain, to see Monroe standing outside his cabin with his wife and daughter, barely two years old. Brother Phillip put it exactly where he found it and proceeded upstairs. Each step creaked as Phillip's heavy shoes hit the ancient wood. Upstairs was bare: three empty bedrooms overpowered with the stench of mold, rotted wallpaper peeling on all sides, and curtains thick against the windows, blocking sunlight or air from coming through. The master bedroom had a deck overlooking the backyard, the door leading out to it crusted over with age.

Brother Phillip sat on the unmade bed, putting his hands on the sheets. They were cold. No one had slept in this bed for a few days now. Brother Phillip lay down, looking up to the ceiling. It was yellowed and cracked. Rainwater had created a scar that cascaded down the wall to a bucket in the corner. There were scratches in the floor indicating the bed had been moved and Brother Phillip saw why. A large sinkhole was forming where the water had dripped originally. This place should be condemned. He grew bored and went back out the way he came. There was enough in sight to round up any suspicion against him. He almost felt sorry for the man, pained by fate to suffer even more and be remembered as something worse than a monster. Then again, Brother Phillip liked living, so his remorse quickly disappeared.

* * *

The train rocked back and forth as it sped past the scenery. Monroe kept his eye on it firmly now. It was the first time it had appealed to him, all the greens and all the blues; even the heat emanating from the sun on this humid day pleased him to the degree of giddiness. Calhoun kept drinking, and his eyes remained on those staring at Monroe. Nobody approached though, no need to whip out the blade.

"Have you ever looked out the window, Calhoun?" Monroe asked.

"Yeah, all the time. Not much else to do."

"It feels like I'm running really fast."

"Are you sure you don't need a drink right now?" Calhoun unscrewed the top of his flask, shaking it in Monroe's face. "You sound a bit off."

"No. I just want to stare at the day for once. Got any sights worth mentioning?"

Calhoun put the cap back on the flask, stowing it in his bag under the seat. "You'll be coming up on this great farmhouse. Two stories and a stone barn. I haven't seen too many of those still standing, but it's there all the same."

"You ever step out and see it up close?"

"How the hell would I be able to do that? Pull the cord?"

"Humor me, you crusty bastard."

Calhoun smiled for a moment but returned to his standard toughness. "No. Just from a distance. Better for me. Never been too good at being up close to anything. It'll be coming up in a few minutes, so keep your eye out."

Monroe was smiling under his burlap bag as they passed the two-story farmhouse with the stone barn. It stood out, removed from the house with ivy growing over it. Moss had already claimed most of the stones on the outside, but through the crumbling east wall, one could see the inside still maintained a gray color.

Calhoun exhaled, "Damn, looks like it's starting to fall down. Can't keep anything decent up anymore."

* * *

Marvin stood in my driveway with his mother when we pulled up. He had red eyes, puffy from crying, along with his mother. I got out of the car first, rushing up to Marvin, and asked what was wrong. He told me Billy died. I didn't cry at first, the shock was too fresh. I did fall on my knees, feeling the air leave me for a moment. By the end of the day, after Marvin told me when the funeral would be, I was left alone in my room and cried into the night.

* * *

Walter packed old lady Vickie's kitchen cupboards with fresh supplies. He did this often for the elderly in town, always delivering their groceries in person and putting them away where they directed. It was never a burden, until old lady Vickie asked Walter what he thought of Monroe.

"Why, dear?" He kept his politeness in check, feeling the presence of Brother Phillip.

"I just keep hearing stories about him," old lady Vickie said, going over what Walter did in her cupboards.

"Stories?"

"Someone said they saw him walking up the trails where those two boys were found dead." She removed two items from the cupboard and relocated them on top of the icebox.

"He has a cabin up there, and he always walks those trails."

"Not on that side of the hill."

"Come on now, Vickie, aren't you too bright to be listening to people talk gossip? You know Monroe."

"Years ago I did, but I hadn't seen him lately."

"You old women got to stop gabbing in those sewing circles and just sew."

"No fun in that. Half of the things we knit get thrown away, damn kids."

"Monroe does nothing wrong, Vickie. Tell them that next time you all get together," Walter said, grabbing his crate and heading out the door. "I'll be back next week with a fresh load for you."

Walter walked back home, looking over his shoulder and eyeing anyone who might be speaking in hushed tones. He knew the people of this town were quick to forget anything worth remembering. Most of these people got good deals on their homes when Monroe sold them; others were given employment, and others were aided in charitable causes spearheaded by Monroe before the war. None of that mattered to them. For the people in this town, if the shoe didn't fit, they would manage to smash the baby toes trying it on. It made sense to blame someone different. Walter knew if he wasn't careful, and if he didn't at least warn Monroe, there could be consequences. How severe the consequences were was still the question. Walter didn't want to wait and find out. When Monroe got back, he figured he would have at least a week to get out of town before the gossip became gospel. Though the problem with best-laid plans is they go south quick.

Chapter 20

T he trail to the cabin was easy. There was not much uphill climbing, just a steady incline. Brother Phillip jaunted up, inhaling the fresh air. Being summertime, all of the cabins along the trail were empty. There weren't a lot of people interested in renting out the small hot boxes on the hill, allowing Brother Phillip time to whistle his way up to Monroe's cabin without a witness. It was nothing to envy from the outside; the brown paint job was peeling worse than Monroe's house. The front window had a ratty hanging curtain, a rocking chair on the porch, and a pile of wood against the steps leading up. How could anyone consider this a slice of heaven? Brother Phillip pondered this with a scowl. People made him sick when he thought about them. Their hobbies, their dreams, and their cabins on the hill. All of it worthless in the long run. People didn't realize that their prayers and hopes were all for nothing when men like him existed. It made him laugh. He was a joke to himself but, to others, the worst creature ever created.

The dolls greeted him on the table in the foyer. Dust-caked, stitched cotton dollies with button-eyes lying limp against the wall. To anyone it would look pathetic. He walked the area along the dining room table, near the corner sofa. Three books stood on the shelf. He didn't dare touch them but read the bindings: *Boys Scout of America Field Guide, Crime and Punishment,* and *Alice in Wonderland.* The second was too good to be true, and Brother Phillip had to stifle a giggle. There was only one bedroom in the cabin located down the narrow hall. One bed stood in the room and in the corner was an antique crib, pristine compared to everything else in the cabin. It had fresh polish, fluffed pillow, and pressed blanket, as if some kid was coming there tonight. He had seen enough to know what to do. This town already had ideas about Monroe, and all he had to do was point them in the right direction.

* * *

Matisse replaced Picasso on the wall when Monroe came home this time. He didn't feel a connection to it anymore. It was becoming an afterthought. He had Walter provide him with a shipping crate stamped with Samson's address. The son of a bitch gave him this newfound hope, so might as well give him something in return. He drank his last whiskey shot in honor of Vollard, then dumped the rest in the sink. He could've sold it on the black market, but hell, who had the time or patience to meet a shady character in a dingy alley.

Walter had his arms folded in the doorway and watched this unfold. "I know people who would've bought that."

"Made enough this weekend for a while. Did you get my telegram?"

"Yeah. You think they can really do it?" Walter's question was not negative, just curious. He didn't want this to end up another dead end.

"One way to find out." Monroe threw the bottle into the garbage bin outside the kitchen window. "It's strange to think after all this time, I could be myself again."

"You were always yourself, Monroe."

This caught him off guard for a moment. "Maybe that was the problem."

"Things change sometimes. I never interfered with your affairs, regardless of what you did to her or what she did to you. I stayed out of it. I still do."

"Just delivered those telegrams."

"I always did."

Monroe shook his head, feeling the rush of foolishness in sending a barrage of telegrams. He was given the address from a private detective three years ago. All he wanted to know was if his daughter was comfortable. She was. With the passage of time, Monroe found simple questions answered but needed more. A message from Mercedes, the girl he last saw from a street corner, pulling away from the window in fear. He wanted a link, a possible reconciliation to allow for a new future. Hope sprang forth in him, creating tears in his misshapen eyes.

"I had a dream last night. I was in a restaurant or bar. There was a party with lots of people dressed nicely and attractive. They were drinking and eating around this one woman who stood in the center. She looked familiar to me in the dream, but I couldn't make her out. So I walked toward her, passing every guest. When I got to the woman, I saw Mercedes. She was older, but it was her standing and staring past me. I turned around and saw no one in particular behind me. Then I looked around and saw everyone else look away from me."

"What else happens?"

"I woke up."

"What do you think it means?"

"That it wouldn't matter either way. Even with a human face she wouldn't know me."

"Are you getting cold feet?"

"What would you suggest?" Monroe asked, uncorking the last bottle of bourbon and pouring it into a glass. "You seem to be the more stable of the two of us." He laughed, pouring the expensive liquor down the drain.

"I think it makes sense to let her go. You'll confuse her. She probably has a good relationship with a man she thinks is her father. You coming back into her life now would be inappropriate."

"She's my daughter."

"You've said that many times."

"And I won't stop saying it."

"Then why do you even ask me? To be honest, you've always had a mind to do whatever the hell you wanted anyways, so don't start asking me what you should do now." There was a long silence between the two. Monroe poured another glass and drank it down. Walter followed suit, frowning immediately after.

"You frowned at perfectly good booze. You don't do that unless you're thinking hard."

Walter noticed the crate against the wall. "I see you're finally getting rid of that damned painting. I always thought it was ugly."

"Worth something, I hear." Monroe, out of habit, began to fill another glass of bourbon. He stopped the pour and then poured it out in the sink.

"People are talking about you." Walter blurted it out. No need to tiptoe around it.

"What else is new?"

"This time it's not just talk."

"I never listened to it, Walter. You told me not to. Follow your own advice." Monroe had a tinge of doubt in his voice.

He had heard about the recent deaths, and like everyone else in town was convinced they were accidents. Nothing nefarious, nothing evil. Just the tragic consequence of stupidity. But he also knew how quickly a rumor can become reality. How quickly people spin tales and point fingers. How quickly a mob could form. How quickly a hangman's noose could be knotted.

Walter saw the typewriter on the dining room table. Out of an inability to suggest the consequences of the questioning townsfolk, he stared at the stack of pages. "Are you still going to write?"

"After what they told me, I don't see a need for that anymore. Hell, I can just tell her myself." Monroe spoke with healthy optimism, causing Walter to smile.

"Your work should go somewhere, since you spent so much time on it."

"Maybe one day it'll be put to good use." Monroe wrapped the bulky stack with wax paper. He removed a spool of red twine and secured it around the pages. "Damn, this is heavy." He dropped them in a drawer of the bookshelf. The loud thud sent particles of dust into the air. Monroe waved the dust away. "I should've hired a maid."

Walter laughed. "That's what Steven is for."

Monroe smiles at the mention of Steven, the little shit who broke into his house. His friend.

"Promise me one thing, Monroe." Walter kept his eyes to the floor. Any emotional display handicapped him. "Just go to New York, soon. Don't give anyone any time to fester on mysteries. Too many idiots think they're smart in this town. Too many think they're righteous."

Monroe was taken aback, as Walter was never one to be easily swayed by the gossip of the sewing circles. "The town has you spooked. Have another drink."

Walter drank the hot bourbon quick, allowing his stomach to adjust to the hit of illegal alcohol. "Call me whatever you want. Just hurry up. You don't need to linger here for anyone. Just go and get back to the city."

"I never liked paranoia, Walter." Monroe had a genuine sense of worry in his voice. "Coming from you makes it logical."

"That's what scares me. Look, send me a postcard when the surgery is done and then maybe in a few months, we'll drink like this again in Delaware with my sister, laughing at my paranoia." Walter held another glass out to Monroe to toast the idea.

"I'll drink to that." Monroe raised his glass with Walter for the last time.

* * *

It's hard to live life when a friend dies. Hope and condolences are the two words you hear the most: *I hope they get through this, my condolences: it's hard to lose a friend.* You just want to hit anyone who thinks talking sweetly will help you out. You walk around to the places you stood with them not a week ago, and they all seem different. As if the past was a dream and when you try to remember the moments of those days, they evaporate. When death comes fast, it clouds the memories you thought you would have for a lifetime. We only had ten years together, and half of them I barely remembered.

Marvin and I went to the fishing hole the day before the funeral to have our own little ceremony. We took his pole and broke it into pieces and tossed them into the stream. They floated in the current, never sinking. Within moments they were out of sight, making the two of us feel even more empty.

"I don't get why he did it," Marvin said, looking down at his shoes.

"He wanted to dive into the water; he always talked about it," I said, accepting it.

"But he would never do it without us."

"Well he did, dummy. He just did it, that's the way he was."

"Whatever you say, Steve." Marvin was quiet now. His timid nature took over, allowing him to silently mourn.

I was too angry to be silent. I shouted loudly at the water and threw stones and sticks, anything heavy into the current. Nothing made me feel better. It just added to the dizziness of losing a friend. It wasn't until I was quiet that I remembered something. The way

Billy looked at me when I left him in the driveway. He wanted to tell me something but couldn't do it. Something had a hold over him. I didn't see it at first, but now looking back I realized.

"Something was wrong with Billy."

"Yeah, he jumped off a cliff."

"No. He tried to tell me something before I left. Did he tell you anything?"

"No. He just tried to get me to go help out at the church with Brother Phillip."

"Did he seem weird?"

"A little, but I figured he was just tired. He was working long days. Why?"

"I don't know." I was telling the truth. I didn't know if there was anything suspicious to consider. When you're young, you don't think about the bad in people. You only see the broad strokes given to you.

"He just drowned, that's what happened," Marvin said, not questioning anything at all.

The block was too quiet when I got home, not even a barking dog or a puttering Model T. The whole town was in silent prayer over the death of yet another young citizen. You always question God in times like these, even if you don't believe in him. In the back of your head, you think God will finally make his presence known to you because you suffered the most. When nothing happens you just get bitter and cold. You stand in the dark waiting for an answer but never receive one. It leaves you apathetic with nothing inside left to get up for. Then I opened the door and saw Katie smile at me from the stairs.

"You want to play?" She made me smile for the first time in two days.

"Yeah, I want to play." I lifted her up over my shoulder, carrying her up to my room.

Dinner was as quiet as the town. There was nothing to say. My father and mother ate politely, and I played with my food, not feeling one iota of hunger. Katie ate heartily, blessed with indifference, as she was too young to understand grief. I was in the phase of mourning when you have stopped crying but feel remorse over doing so. Billy's funeral was in two days, and the town was teetering on the edge of hysteria. Two children lost in a span of one summer created anxiety in everyone. The townspeople kept a closer eye on their children, and those without children were being scrutinized. Questions were being raised about certain loners or old maids around town, all of them potential suspects for the so-called accidental deaths. There was no basis in fact and not one shred of evidence to prove guilt, but to the townspeople, that meant no shred of evidence to prove them innocent either. Someone was steering the people toward a mob mentality, and many of the fingers raised were pointed toward Monroe. Eventually, word got out about my work for Monroe. When I crossed the street, I heard the talking, the gasps, and the sudden change of subject anytime I walked into a room.

They were worried about me being the next victim, while at the same time, they wished I would die to prove their theories correct. None of them would ever admit to this, but human nature is one of those things you can figure out on your own, even at thirteen. The only thing I could do was ignore it and just let it pass without showing acknowledgment, hoping their whispers would vanish. Walter was not so interested in ignoring it. He kept me informed of his theories, all of which led to Brother Phillip.

"No way, he's a brother," I said, stocking shelves in the general store as a way to stop thinking about Billy. Walter was glad to have me work for free, not because he was a cheapskate, but because he wanted someone to talk to.

"Listen to me, boy, just because a guy says, Yes, Father, no,

Father, help them, Father, doesn't mean he knows Father." Walter pointed to the sky.

"He never tried anything on me, and I have seen him a couple of times."

"What did he do?" Walter whispered, noticing two old women enter the store.

"Nothing, just tried to get me to wear an altar boy robe."

Walter kneeled beside me, checking over his shoulder. "Were you two alone?"

"Until Reverend Thomas came in."

I could tell Walter's mind was racing. His eyes darted back and forth, trying to make logical connections for incriminating Brother Phillip. "Reverend Thomas went on holiday suddenly, you know that?"

"I heard."

Walter was ashen now. His mind was going too fast, with gears turning just as hard as any gossip queen, trying to remember the latest lies of the week. "I need to stop this. I'm starting to turn into old lady Vicky." He went back behind the counter, checking the stock in the glass cabinets.

"You don't think...?" I couldn't even bring myself to say anything remotely close to murder.

Walter raised his hand, shutting me down. "No, we need to just stop this and get back to work. I have more bags of beans in the back. Why don't you bring them out to the front so I can unload them before the weevils get to them." Walter threw me a pair of gloves as he headed for the old ladies looking at the dinnerware.

Billy's funeral was a small affair; most of the town was barred from the funeral. Billy's parents felt the sooner they buried him, the sooner they could move on, which meant a truncated service delivered by Brother Phillip, who managed to tear up giving his sermon. Marvin and I were the only children in the church, and both of us kept our eyes to the floor, afraid to burst into tears in front of the adults. Most of my energy was spent on my teeth chewing my inner cheek to keep my mind off the mood of the people crying around me.

It's hard to watch an adult cry when you're young. These people around you are your elders. They're supposed to be the teachers, the leaders, and the strong ones. To see them cry reveals their vulnerabilities and acknowledges their humanity to reveal their stoic attitudes were facades. Then I looked at my father, who never shed a tear in public. He gazed down on me with sad eyes and rubbed my head tenderly, then squeezed my shoulder. I was comforted immediately by his strength.

Brother Phillip came from behind after the service, grabbing my shoulders and leaving me with a chill through my spine. "Steven, have you considered spending some time with me yet?"

My mother smiled at Brother Phillip, as she did with every person connected to the cloth. "Are you offering any jobs in the fall, Brother Phillip?"

"Perhaps. Though by that time, I might be gone."

"No," my mother said with genuine disappointment, "you've done so much."

"The big city calls me back. It was nice to get away, but I'm a big-city guy. Once the call beckons, you have to answer. Which is why I wanted to scoop up young Steven here quickly. I feel I could use him for a few things and maybe impart some material to the next brother who comes to town."

"Or when Reverend Thomas comes back from holiday," I said, remembering Walter's suspicions. There was a definite change in his posture, like he had been punched in the stomach.

"Yes, when he comes back, of course." His smile returned quickly, but his eyes never left me.

"I don't know, Mom, I already have a summer job, and I don't think the church pays. You know, the whole Christian thing."

"Volunteering." Brother Phillip grabbed my shoulder again, squeezing it playfully.

"A few afternoons wouldn't kill you. It's for the Lord," Mother scolded.

"It wouldn't be for nothing, Steven. You could get first dibs on anything we have at the rummage sale coming up, my treat."

Brother Phillip knew exactly what to say. "Well, when you put it that way, I guess I can swing by."

"Billy was a hard worker. You have big shoes to fill."

"Yeah, I know."

He kneeled before me, putting both hands on my shoulders and bringing me eye to eye with him. "If you ever need to talk about it, my office door is always open to you."

In that moment, I saw something in Brother Phillip's eyes. A slight twitch that made me uneasy. Within moments, a smile flashed over his face, and his eyes flared back to life as if nothing happened. He walked away to comfort Billy's parents. My mother sat down on the church bench in front of the memorial wall; the heat was getting to her. I sat next to her, watching Brother Phillip calmly speak to Billy's parents as if this wasn't a funeral. It was odd, him being so nonchalant about everything. My mind went back to the twitch in his eye. For a moment I saw nothingness. The pale blue of his pupils vanished and were replaced by a gray void in a split second. Youth sometimes has a way of revealing truths in people. An adult would never look directly into his eyes because they had heard all the glories of God before. They would find something else to focus on while the good brother prattled on about morality, never gazing into the heart of the person speaking. If an adult actually looked in Brother Phillip's eyes when he spoke, they would notice a hollow soul. If an adult listened to the words Brother Phillip spoke, they would notice the tinge of sarcasm, as if he was telling the punch line of a joke. For the first time in my life, I saw what evil was.

That night, I stood in my room staring out the window to Cheryl's house. She was always on the porch now, all day and all night. No one ever bothered to speak to her; they all walked on. Even my mother hanging laundry in the front yard refused to look in her direction. It was as if Cheryl never had a child who died. A forgotten casualty from a summer accident. Her husband came out and said something to awaken her from the comfortable daze she was in. When she stood up, her eyes met mine. In them was all the hate and rage a mother could have over the injustice toward her. It was only her nature that forbade her true feelings from flowing out. In that moment, she revealed her pain and anguish through her stare toward me. As if she knew I was the one to do something about it. Before she could open her mouth to shout what I should do, her husband pulled her into the house and locked the door behind them.

My mother knocked on my door, then opened it. "Are you okay, Steven?" Her voice was warm, unraveling the knots in my stomach.

"I was just… I'm fine. How are you?"

She took my hand and kissed it. "I'm thankful nothing has happened to you. All of this loss puts things in perspective. What's important at the end of the day is what you have under your roof. For me, this is the only life I would want. You are the son I wanted, and your sister is the daughter I wanted. We're very lucky."

Her words didn't comfort me as well as she wanted them to, and she noticed. "What's wrong, Steven? You can tell me."

I didn't want to tell her what I really thought. Instead, I asked her a vague question.

"Mom, if you knew someone was bad but couldn't prove it, what are you supposed to do?"

"It's wrong to bear false witness, honey. No proof often means innocence, and when people spread gossip, it only makes them look bad. So ignore any suspicions against anyone because it's usually wrong."

"Yeah." Now I was far from comforted. "You're right, I just don't know what to do."

"Life is like that. You can't figure it all out even in a lifetime. Your dad doesn't know what he's doing half the time but manages to make it, God knows how. You just have to wait things out and hope they get better."

"Wait and hope."

"Sounds like life in a nutshell. Now it's late, and you should try to get some sleep." She led me to my bed and pulled the covers down. I got in and felt the chill that fresh sheets provide before the body warms them up.

"I love you, Steven."

"I love you, Mom," I said as she turned the light off, leaving me in the dark with my thoughts still churning around Brother Phillip. Only one person would be able to tell me what to do. This thought allowed me to drift into sleep, and for the first time in my life, I didn't dream at all.

Chapter 21

Monroe packed away his books as the sun went down. All his first editions were carefully placed in crates stamped with a New York City address. He had sent word to Samson that he would need a place to stay while he healed from the surgery. Samson was able to find him a modestly priced apartment near the hospital. He went through the drawers as a last-minute precaution, making sure nothing of value was left behind, and he came across the pages of his life wrapped in wax paper. He lifted them up, feeling the weight. His heart grew heavy recalling the last few pages he had typed.

```
When I returned from the war, your mother met me
at the train station. I could tell she was not
excited to see me. I made my way to her with the
stitched bag the army nurses made me over my head.
It was cotton, thick enough to hide my features
and light enough to allow me to breathe. The damn
thing never lasted through the winter, and I spent
it outside, hoping the cold would kill me. Lo and
behold, those nurses knew what they were doing.
```

Her face was stern, not bright. Her hands kept fidgeting from anxiety, so my eyes went to them almost immediately to discover the ring I bought her was gone. She put her hands behind her back as soon as she caught me looking.

"They said you were hit by a shell and almost died," she said, swallowing. I could tell she was frightened by my appearance as were many other onlookers.

"True." It was all I could say at that moment, feeling the eyes from fellow travelers staring.

"We should go." She moved across the station quickly, keeping a distance between us. It was hard maneuvering with the bag over my face, and I tripped over some man's luggage, spilling most of it onto the station floor. Your mother had to turn around to help me up. Her grip was tight and cold. No more love in it, no more tenderness. I knew at that moment she had found someone else.

The ride home was quiet. She kept her eyes on the road and never once gave me a second glance. I kept my gaze ahead to not give her an opportunity to look towards me.

"His name is David and I love him."

"You're my wife, and she is my daughter."

"She is more David's than yours. You left before she could remember you. And now you're back with a bag over your head to hide what the war did to you." She stopped herself, gaining strength I never saw in her before. "Tell me, Monroe, was that needed to save Europe? Was running away from us and becoming deformed worth the Treaty of Versailles?"

I slammed my fist into the car seat and screamed, "NO!" She recoiled, afraid that I would hit her. I almost did. "What do you want me to say? Do you want me to say you were right? Because you were. Do you want me to beg for forgiveness? Do you need me to love you like I did before? I can… I want to."

"It's too late. I love David, and he loves me."

"It's my house."

"You can have your house, the paintings, the books, the beds, the walls, and the goddamned cabin. It all reminds me of you too much. Take it from me, please." She was crying now.

"What would that leave you?"

"My freedom. David has business in California."

"You would go that far from me?"

"I would go that far for David."

"I love you," I pleaded.

She didn't respond.

"I love my daughter. She needs to know who her father is."

"She already does." She put her hand over her face, hating every moment near me. "You force me to tell you this." She exhaled and gained the strength needed to tell me the truth. "Mercedes called David 'daddy' when you were gone. For her sake, for my sake, let us go."

At that moment I took off my bag, revealing to your mother the face that war in Europe had given me. She screamed, slightly suppressing it with a hand to her mouth. "Let me see her just once then, so I know she wasn't just some dream I had. Maybe there is a chance she would remember me."

"Maybe just having her be a dream is the best thing you could do. If I let you see her, you'll scare her."

She was right. For the first time I saw my reflection in someone else's eyes. It was total shock and disgust. As if the man I was never existed. The memory of who he was is buried in the mud with the other young men who believed in the

romance of war, only to be left broken-hearted by
the truth. I lost your mother and myself forever
in that gaze. Any good memory I had was tarnished
by this one. This was the moment where my humanity
left me, and the monster gained life. I put the
bag over my head and left her, taking the backwood
roads to the cabin where I knew no one would be
waiting for me.

With a trepidation never felt before, Monroe put the pages in
the garbage can. No more need to write, no more need for catharsis.
It was just the future now, a concept coming to realization. Being
given a second chance created severe anxiety in Monroe. A rap at
the door brought him out of his daydreaming.

* * *

I stood on Monroe's porch for ten minutes, wondering if I should
ask his advice. This was not an easy thing to figure out alone. Hell,
even with another point of view, it was hard to figure out. If I was
right about Brother Phillip, I needed someone else's suspicions
to back me up. I needed permission. I needed an adult to give me
validation on the choice I had already made for myself. Monroe
opened the front door wide. The sun hit his face so that any pass-
erby could've seen him. It was good to see him smile, even if it was
crooked and mangled.

"Steven? What do you need?"

"Some advice."

"Always willing to dispense some."

Immediately, I realized Monroe was preparing to leave town.
The boxes and crates stacked in the den were awe-inspiring. I didn't
realize he had so many possessions. A part of me was glad he was

packing up, although I would be lying if I said I wanted him to leave. He had his reasons, but somewhere deep down, I had hoped he found what he lost with me.

"You're leaving?"

"No need to stay here anymore. The surgery will be next month, and I have found a place in New York for the duration."

I came upon the stack of pages in the garbage can. The first sentences of his memoirs were clearly visible through the ripped wax paper, forcing me to pick them up.

"Why did you throw this away?"

Monroe said nothing while checking the contents of each crate.

"You shouldn't get rid of this, especially since you spent so much time on it."

"A waste," Monroe said, slamming the crate lid shut.

I realized why he had thrown them away. "You're going to her, aren't you?"

"That's the plan." He sat down in the leather chair and exhaled. His face was a wreck, not from the drinking, but from a long night debating what the next course of action should be. Something else was on his mind too, I could tell. He kept shifting his gaze to the windows, as if someone might be looking in. I knew in that moment Walter had spoken to him. Hopefully, Monroe would be out of here before anything could boil over.

"Do you think it's crazy?" he asked me point-blank, assuming I had some tricks up my sleeve to talk him out of it. Still, I was amazed he asked me a question of this magnitude.

"Does it feel right?" I thought that was the best reply.

"It always felt right. I just couldn't do it before."

"You thought your face would scare her away?"

"Why wouldn't it?" he asked honestly. "Look at me, Steven." He lurched toward me, throwing his deformity directly into my face, but nothing stirred in me. I had known him long enough not to care about his looks. He turned away, feeling ashamed when I didn't avert my gaze.

"Maybe a girl would react differently." Monroe leaned against the crate, shaking his head at his lame reasoning.

"Wouldn't matter."

"What makes you say that?"

"A child just knows who their father is." It was the best thing I could come up with to cheer him up. Instead, he just smiled and shook his head.

"Sometimes that isn't the case." He started for the liquor, but it was long gone. "Damn it, I shouldn't have thrown all of it out yet… I will miss you, boy. It felt good to have a child in this house again."

"I'm not a child."

"Thirteen is a child to me. Don't rush it just yet."

"Other events rushed it." I slumped in the leather chair this time and was hit by the aroma of old earth. "If you knew someone was bad, but no one saw it, what should you do?"

"It depends how many people are behind him."

"A whole town."

"Best to leave it alone. Nothing good can come of it." Monroe was grave. He knew who I was talking about. Far from the answer I needed, but there was not much I could do but agree with him.

"You're right."

"Of course I'm right, I'm the elder." He smiled again. Twice in one afternoon was a revelation, and it forced me to smile back.

"Does it hurt your face to smile that big?"

"Don't be a smart-ass." He laughed, tossing my hair up. "Now since you're here, maybe you can help me pack up some more office stuff."

"It's always work with you."

"Builds character," he said as he licked the rim of the empty bourbon bottle.

After I helped Monroe, I took a shortcut without realizing where the trail was leading me. My mind was preoccupied with Monroe's behavior and packing when I came to the edge of the river where I saw Billy. For a moment, I almost thought I saw him playing in the stream with a fishing pole and smiling. As if all of this was a big joke he had pulled off. The sun hit my eyes through an exposed branch, and I lost sight of his ghost. Only the water greeted me, the cold rocks underneath, the fish swimming to the top, and the slight summer breeze whistling through the leaves.

This desolation reminded me of what I saw in Brother Phillip, his gray pupils returning to a pale blue just in time for any polite adult who may be looking him in the eyes. I grew dizzy, hot, and flustered at the images which kept repeating in my head. I remembered Cheryl's face and her eyes gazing at me through a shroud of mourning. Green eyes turned gray from her loss and injustice, as the one man who comforted her poured poison in her ear. The feeling wouldn't go away as I stared into the darkness of the shaded brook, reminding me of Brother Phillip's eyes. It was the way he cornered me, the way Billy acted after being with him, and the way the town was blinded by his charm. Walter was right, and my gut was right. I swore at that moment to do what was right. I no longer needed an adult voice to grant me permission.

No one was in the house when I pulled my cigar box from under my bed. The knife inside shone in the afternoon light as I flipped the blade out to examine it, making sure there were no dull edges or rust. It had to do the job of killing him or make him bleed enough to be incapacitated, just in case he got the upper hand. I wasn't nervous when I decided all of this, just excited. To avenge my friend, to put Brother Phillip in a trap, to catch him in a lie or a moment of weakness, allowing me to strike when his mind was freshly set on the crimes he perpetrated. He had to have his mind full of evil, so hell would gladly take him and spare me of my mortal sin.

I closed the knife quick, jolted from the snap it created. Second thoughts rolled through me, casting doubt on the whole endeavor. Thirteen years old was not an age to commit murder, but Billy's face kept entering my mind, pushing my need to do what no one else could. Brother Phillip had to die by the hands of someone innocent. It felt properly biblical. No guilt stemmed from the idea of murdering him. Usually I would sweat and my stomach would churn as a result of talking back to my parents or stealing from Walter's candy bowl in the front of the store. But here, there was no feeling, and it scared me. This had to be done for Billy and for Cheryl. Vengeance was not a sin against a man who perverts the pure. This was retribution for the innocence. This was the sacrifice of my soul, and I accepted it.

Chapter 22

Brother Phillip always had a plan. The years of being on the run taught him the ways of diffusing suspicion. In his experience, there was always someone else. Someone else to direct unanswered questions at, someone else to point blame at, someone else to hide behind when running became the next step. Brother Phillip always trusted small-town attitudes to offer up half-assed justice. In a small town like this, mob justice was a finger point away from reality. In this equation of shifted suspicion, he needed two factors: someone to pin it on and the elimination of doubt. Finding someone to pin it on was easy.

All he had to do was fish around town, usually with women who had nothing more to do than gossip. Every time he prodded for a patsy, one was delivered by the gossip small towns are known to cultivate. Monroe was the best thing to ever happen to Brother Phillip. All he had to do was mention his name and people frowned as if they had swallowed rotten food, and with the sudden departure of Sheriff Tate, he needn't worry about any doubters coming in between him and Monroe. Steven, the boy, could be a problem. He seemed to stare too hard on Brother Phillip at the funeral. Instinct was telling Brother Phillip the boy was a chink in the armor, a loose end. His plan could possibly fall by the wayside with this child running around, diffusing everything said about Monroe. People were already talking about his employment with Monroe, setting up a connection between them and providing a window of opportunity. A shame really, Brother Phillip truly liked this little town and its entire people. He could've fooled them for so much longer, taking pleasure in murdering so many more, but gluttony was one of the seven deadly sins that actually mattered to him.

He closed the door of his church office and sat down at the desk with the typewriter. It was time to spread the word more intensely. In times like these, all he had to do after working the crowd was to drop a bombshell. A note written by a concerned citizen trying to keep silent while his "wife" worries he may be another victim is always appreciated when no leads can be found. Local law enforcement is always a lazy joke. Maintaining the idea that law and order are being upheld is a tough job when most law officials nominated by the people finish less than three years of high school. Imagine their relief when a note arrives in the mail, detailing everything that occurred during an unsolved crime spree. Hell, these men became heroes overnight because they solved a crime that small-town folk only read about in big-city papers.

Of course, in the rush of sudden police activity there also needs to be a call to arms, usually the arms of the local deputized citizens who are itching for retribution. Sometimes, Brother Phillip would come across a lawman with brains who would just throw the note out and look for the man who wrote it. This time, however, he would have no trouble since the only brain in the sheriff's office, Sheriff Tate, was gone on holiday. This allowed Brother Phillip to drop his bombshell on the fool left in charge.

Deputy Peters was a weak man with too many problems. He had lived his life believing a uniform made a man. Respect would follow him if he had a badge on his chest: his father would love him more, his mother would acknowledge his success instead of his older brother's, and the women would finally lift their skirts.

Unfortunately, his father still hated him, his mother only talked about his brother, and the only girl who lifted her skirt was Beth—a thin, sickly girl with an overbite who volunteered at the library. He wanted people to need him. All they did was ask when Sheriff Tate was coming back.

On a hot morning in August 1928, a letter fell through the sheriff's office mail slot, cementing his inability to control anything or anyone.

Cheryl's husband's name was Marshall. He was a hardworking man with no big dreams or goals other than raising a family with the woman he loved. Simplicity was all he understood and all he wanted. The summer of '28 proved to be otherwise. Cheryl still hadn't snapped out of her depression, Dougie still cried in the corner for his brother, and booze was expensive and hard to find with prohibition in place. Alcohol to a simple man is the solution to problems he is unable to deal with. Without it, there is only the front porch smoke. Two packs a day was the count now. His lungs were filled with smoky phlegm and his coughs were frequent, but the calm warmth the cigarette smoke provided was enough to get him through the evening. Coming in after a smoke was hard. Cheryl would sit in her chair holding and smelling Sammy's clothes. Dougie would fall asleep in the corner every night, hoping he would be awoken by his brother the next day. Marshall lifted him up and took him to bed. In the corner was Sammy's still unmade bed from the last night he spent in it. Marshall put his face in it every time he put Dougie to bed. He too thought if he slept there, Sammy would wake him up the next day. When the daylight came through the window, there was only emptiness to wake him. The simple things were too hard to deal with now, until a letter fell through the mail slot.

Walter was walking down the street when he noticed the crowd gathering around the jail. Men with bats, chains, and other random bludgeoning tools were getting more and more aggressive. Deputy

Peters was enforcing the law as best he could, but the note in his hand was twisting his authority.

"There's no need to jump to any conclusions, we're just putting some facts together," Deputy Peters almost stuttered in front of this mob, prompting them to take a collective step forward and push him against the brick wall. "Now come on, guys, this isn't the way to act."

"Just hand out some badges, Peters," Marshall said in the center of the mob. His fist clenched around the note he'd received. "Let's get him now."

Walter made his way through the men, patting Marshall on the back. They all thought he would go with them.

"What the hell is going on here? Looks like a goddamned circus."

"Somebody sent Marshall a note telling him who killed his son," one of Walter's painters said.

"What? I thought it was an accident."

"Nope. Figured it wasn't when I pulled that kid out of the water. More than likely, little Billy was another victim."

"I can't believe that," Walter stammered.

"Believe it, because it's the truth. It says so in the note. Peters over there has another one that verifies the story."

"It's a note. Could've been written by anybody."

"Nope." He spit on the ground. "Just someone too afraid to talk. Makes sense when you really put your mind to it."

Walter had heard enough. He pushed his way to the front of the mob. Peters was beginning to relent. His cousin Merryl, a part-time deputy, brought out a wooden box filled with gold badges.

"All right, listen up. This is going to be law abiding. No need for mob rule bullshit." Peters was gaining some confidence now as the men took their badges under his command.

"What the hell is going on?" Walter yelled over the mutterings of the mob.

"Walter, listen, this may be difficult to accept, but we have reason to believe Monroe might be a suspect in the deaths of Sammy and Billy."

Walter was beyond shocked that anyone would believe, let alone form a posse over a note, accusing his friend of murder. "Are you out of your fucking mind?" Walter yanked the note from Peters' hand and read it. "This is all you have? A typed note? Did you think the person who wrote the note might be the one who did it?"

Peters was obviously struck with the notion that Walter could be right. "I understand. That's why I am making sure no one does anything rash."

"You're deputizing them right now! You got to stop this before it gets out of hand." Walter turned his head to the mob, catching the gleam of gun metal in the sun. "These men have guns, Deputy."

Peters swallowed hard, pouting more than commanding. "No guns, men! Come on now!" Peters began to frisk every man in the front line, removing pistol after pistol. Obviously, most of the men resisted Peters, since he demanded little respect. "Don't bitch, you'll get them back after we bring Monroe into custody."

"Custody? You don't have any bearings to arrest him on hearsay," Walter pleaded with Peters, incensing the mob around him.

"Get the hell out of here, Walter, this doesn't concern you," someone shouted.

"You don't have kids, Walter, you don't understand what we have to do!" another voice yelled.

"This is ridiculous. Most of you grew up with the man. You know him." Walter was pleading a case that wouldn't go far. "You're all out of your goddamned minds if you're actually buying this—"

A punch to the face ended Walter's appeal for sanity.

He launched into a fight, throwing both fists into the assailant's face and chest, knocking him to the ground. The mob ripped them away from each other.

"You need to cool off, Walter," Deputy Peters said.

"What about him?" Walter shouted, blood dripping from his lip and nose.

The man in question was knocked out on the ground. "You took care of him already." Peters pointed to the mob as they tried to wake up the knocked-out fool.

"Nothing's going to happen. I got things in control here. The law will prevail over this mob, I promise you." Deputy Peters seemed to be losing steam toward the end of the sentence. He knew there was no way to control a mob with vengeance on their mind. "I got it under control. It would be just like if Sheriff Tate was going after a lead, except now we got a lot more deputies behind us."

"He didn't do anything," Walter said, dabbing his bloodicd lip with his shirt. "Don't let anything happen to Monroe, Deputy. If they get their heads cleared and think, this will all blow over. But you got to break them up, damn it."

"Don't worry, nothing will happen while I am on duty."

Walter ran off towards Monroe's house, knowing full well the mob would go there first. He had to get Monroe out of town even if it meant getting thumped in the process. Walter just hoped he had enough time to do so.

* * *

The church office was empty—no Maybelle, no random kid working a summer job, and no janitor either. *Perfect timing*, I thought and made sure the knife was secure in my sock. I placed my pant leg over it, checking to see if any bulges would give it away. It was flat enough to conceal. Brother Phillip came through the back door, noticing me right away. His smile was unsettling.

"Steven? What are you doing here on a Wednesday? The weekends are when we need the most help."

"Well, I wanted to talk to you about that. My mom told me I should consider it for the fall when I'm in school." I stammered a little but kept it in check.

He moved around me like an animal smelling for fear, and his eyes never left me for a moment.

"Come into the office, and we'll look at the calendar for fall. See what the church has to offer you." He opened the door to his office, and his back was to me for a window of time. I didn't attack but walked into the office first, giving him my back to try and ease any suspicion he might have. He closed the door and walked to the corner of the office, allowing me to sit.

"I must say this is rather fast, you coming in here after you put up such a fuss," Brother Phillip said, looking out the window at the pond in the back. The path leading around the pond to the street was empty.

"The rummage sale put it in perspective." I laughed a little, trying to ease the situation with levity, but it wasn't taking.

"Yes, balanced reciprocity is a wonderful way of getting things done. Everyone wants something in return for services rendered." He kept his back to me, goading me to try something. I could see the corner of his lips curl into a smile. It was all a game to Brother Phillip, and he was ready for anything.

"It's quiet today. Is Maybelle out?"

"Yes, she often takes the afternoon off. Did you pass by the jail today? Did you notice anything happening?" He faced me finally with raised eyebrows.

"No, I didn't see anything happening."

"You're trying to play off what you know about me, but you're failing miserably." His hands gripped the sides of his desk like some professor casually speaking to a student. "My grandfather had a saying: your soul knows more than you. In your dreams it tells you what to do, what you should do. Being awake sometimes clouds the truth. It happens to most people in my experience. But unfortunately, you listened to it."

I never saw his hands move as he slammed my head against the oak desk. I blacked out immediately. Brother Phillip exhaled, cracking his knuckles as the blood from my head dripped to the floor.

* * *

Monroe opened *The Count of Monte Cristo,* smelling the aroma only an old novel can create: rain-drenched stones and a hint of leather. He fingered the typeface, feeling a slight indent, and checked his fingers to make sure no ink was on them. Steven had asked him why this book was so important, and he gave the best answer he knew. Secretly, the reason Monroe held the book in such high regard was because the Count was able to leave Mercedes behind. No forgiveness, no requited love, just a harsh justice. What Dantes did felt appropriate, even if she thought he was dead. When you love someone as much as she did, how could she allow an outside force to come and steal what she had made with Dantes? Monroe always questioned it, even as a boy. Love is the one undeniable force in the world that if shared between two people, absence is not an excuse to leave. Love can't be squashed simply because time passes. Time isn't supposed to be an enemy; it is supposed to be the ally of happiness. Monroe needed more time to love, and the time with Elizabeth was far from enough. He was reminded of the line Mercedes spoke to Dantes, *It often happens, that a first fault destroys the prospects of a whole life.* The truth of the world and the secret of life. One cannot forget the pain and the other cannot forgive it. As he put the book away with the rest, a crack from the wood floor interrupted the silence.

"Monroe!" Walter was screaming with frantic energy.

"Walter?" Monroe was at once startled at the sound of fear in

Walter's voice. He rushed to the windows to see if something was happening outside, but there was nothing.

Walter came through the kitchen, sweating profusely and heaving heavily. "You need to get out of here, now." Walter checked the windows this time.

"What are you talking about? I still have more packing to do." Monroe was scared. Seeing calm Walter in such a state unraveled his nerves. "Just calm down, sit down."

"We don't got time to do that shit. Somebody sent a letter to the sheriff, saying you were at the scene of Sammy's death. There's a mob coming for you."

"This is crazy. I didn't do anything. Who could've..." Monroe stopped, immediately knowing who sent it.

"There's only one person who would." Walter shook his head, realizing his mistake in ignoring his better judgment.

"Steven." Monroe was lost in thought. He felt something in his unconsciousness nagging at him. A sense of danger. Steven knew better and Monroe chose to ignore it. But now the worst-case scenario was playing out. "Have you seen Steven today?"

"No, I left the store to see what was going on." Walter froze, realizing something. "Steven suspected Brother Phillip too."

"What?" Monroe looked at Walter for a long moment. "What did you put in his head?" Monroe was angry.

"Nothing. We were just talking about what's been happening. Brother Phillip..." Walter stopped, feeling sick. "He wouldn't be capable of doing anything. He's a good boy, smart. He wouldn't." Walter knew full well Steven was going to attempt to get the jump on a crafty murderer. "He couldn't be able to do that."

"I gave him a knife, Walter," Monroe told him, falling into his chair, feeling the panic rise inside him. "He came to me and tried to tell me. I told him to let it go."

"We're all capable of doing something when our emotions are

getting the better of us. You're a prime fucking example." Walter kept going back and forth from the windows.

"It often happens that a first fault destroys the prospects of a whole life." Monroe repeated the line from *Monte Cristo* without a tinge of nostalgia, only the overpowering sensation of dread. "He would've gone to the church."

"And Phillip would've gotten the drop on him." Walter paced, trying to think clearly. "Or he went home, lost his nerve."

"No, Steven isn't like that. But it would be too dangerous for Phillip to hurt him now. Not in daylight, not with a mob roaming around."

Walter shook his head. "No, he would take him to the cabin. Your cabin."

"How do you know?" Monroe asked, lifting his pistol from an opened drawer.

"He wants you. He'll take him to the cabin. He wants the people to *know* you did it. Leaving his body there would prove it without a shadow of a doubt."

"I have to go."

"No, you don't."

Monroe couldn't believe Walter's attitude. "Why would you say that?"

"You have a chance to be free of what happened. Don't waste it on a brave rescue with no real way out." Walter didn't want to lose his only friend.

"I don't want to die either, Walter. Trust me. There may be some old combat left in me yet." Monroe was heading out the door. "Just keep the mob back. Give me a window of time, then we'll have drinks in Delaware with your sister."

"Only if you buy them, Monroe." Walter knew better as Monroe headed out the back door.

The summer heat was blistering as Monroe ran up the trail to the cabin on the hill. His gun at his side was heavy, dragging him down. It had been years since he had heard a gunshot. He hoped that he still was able to fire. He hoped he was able to save Steven in time. He hoped Walter's theory was correct. If it was, Monroe may have a chance at getting the drop on Phillip. Then again, if it was a frame-up, Phillip might be expecting him. Either way, Monroe had a loaded pistol and a mind to use it.

Monroe had run up the hill in record time. His back was soaked with sweat, his legs ached, and his vision was blurred by the dripping sweat rolling down his deformed face. It was the first time in seven years he had come up this trail without the bag over his head. On any other day, this could have been therapeutic. With the gun in his hand, Monroe scanned the tree line, hoping to see Brother Phillip.

There was nothing.

Suddenly, the sound of a hammer pulling back on a pistol cracked through the still calm of the forest. Monroe turned around, discovering Brother Phillip standing with a gun raised at him.

"I figured you'd come. Was it the boy? Or Walter?" Brother Phillip squinted in the sunlight. The gun was a Colt. If memory served Monroe, it was Reverend Thomas's Colt.

"Both." Monroe had his gun down to his side. He thought he could get a shot off quickly. But no man had ever walked away from a quick-draw showdown, especially when the other man had his gun aimed and cocked.

"Steven said you were in the Great War. Decorated like me, for bravery."

"I was there." Monroe took his finger off the trigger.

"You might as well drop that. You won't get a shot off." Brother Phillip smiled as Monroe dropped his gun into the dirt. "How long were you over there?"

"Almost a year and a half."

Brother Phillip came down to frisk Monroe quickly, keeping the gun raised the whole time. "We have much in common. Caught in the middle and forever changed by the romance of chaos. My eyes were opened to the bleak nature of all life and its shortcomings—the war showed me that. I heard all about you from those bitches down there. Their little minds festering with the illusion I created: Monroe, the monster, chasing children in the woods and killing them for pleasure only a man like me could understand." Brother Phillip smiled, delivering a sermon he deemed worthy of shouting from a rooftop. The many Bible stories lodged in his mind allowed him to maneuver around believers. His message was always cluttered with the teachings of Christ and the word of God. Now, no one was around to stop him from exalting. There was only a dead man with a mangled face and the trees. "Did you ever hear about Caligarism?"

"No."

"German word. Made up of course as a result of the world ending. Well, at the time, it felt like the world was ending. It was a belief devoted to hopelessness. Paradise for a man like me. I saw men kill priests and children just for standing in the way of a hot meal. Girls no older than eight, selling themselves to feed their dying parents or siblings. Raped and killed because a penny was too much for innocence. It was a world that didn't know what sin was. They had to call it something, so they just murmured, Caligarism."

"How many people did you kill out there?"

"So many. I came back to the States because I knew a man of war and a man of the cloth can be trusted. There is a sense of honor that exudes for those types of men in the eyes of the dull… How many people did you kill?"

Monroe was dumbfounded. All heinous acts began with bloodshed. He had spilt so much from others as well. He was no saint. At that moment he felt all the guilt of his soul. He saw the hurt in his wife's eyes. He saw his daughter cry when she looked upon his deformed visage from the crib. He saw his human face melt away from the fire and metal of the guns of war. "Many."

"And those that see you only remember what came back from Wilson's War. A monster. A monster who killed children. Who killed Reverend Thomas and his wife. A monster whispered about in the dark. As I sleep in my bed, with all their blood under my fingernails."

"They'll know it's a lie when all this is over." Monroe knew better. The act of defiance was to incense Phillip.

It only made him smile. "Those lies will become truth. Then they will be forgotten and only a legend will remain. In the meantime, I will be alive, warmed by a fire in the presence of children, who all trust me, who all like treats I give them." Brother Phillip's detour to fantasy made his hand flaccid. The weak wrist lowered, prompting Monroe to grab hold. But Phillip was too quick, and a pistol whip to Monroe's head stopped any course of action.

"Lost in thought for a moment?" Monroe felt the eye swelling quickly.

"When are you happiest? When you remember your wife's breasts in your hands? Or when you remember her scowl? Misery is much more compelling than love. Sorrow is always more potent because it lasts longer than love." Brother Phillip laughed as he thought out loud. "The Lord giveth and he taketh away just as fast. That's the way he is though. God, the deity better understood by the miserable."

"He who has felt the deepest grief is best able to experience supreme happiness. We must have felt what it is to die that we may appreciate the enjoyment of living." Monroe quoted the *Count*, smiling.

"Oh, the educated. Which idiot that all consider masterful for stringing sentences together said that?"

"Dumas."

"You should stop taking solace in words written by dead men.

Many try to put humanity into a category. Whether we were created by God or evolved from a tiny fluke in nature: humanity is capable of equal wonder and destruction. That much is an undisputed fact. We as people can be summed up in two words: war and renaissance. We've only had one Renaissance."

"How do I know he's still alive?"

"I do not kill without reason. There must always be reasons. Mine may be strange, but they suit me."

"You think these people will believe you?" Monroe was hoping the mob was en route to the cabin so they could see Brother Phillip with Reverend Thomas's gun jammed in his back. But there was no sign of anyone.

"They already do."

Chapter 23

The mob had made it to Monroe's house. Deputy Peters was leading the men as best he could, practically jogging ahead. The sweat had soaked his shirt as the August heat was growing thick. Marshall stayed in the center of the crowd, his eyes shifting to every window. He wanted to find Monroe alone. He wanted his time with him.

There was no other explanation for Sammy's death; the note made it clear. His mind was made up. Simple men find simple closure. Once Monroe was dead, Sammy could be free from him. Cheryl could wake up, knowing that justice had been served. His life would be changed because painful memories could be buried when it was needed. She could have another child. Maybe a girl. Marshall had always wanted a daughter and then he could be a grandfather. He could tell them the story of how he avenged the family. How he stopped a monster.

Walter opened the door, and the mob gave a collective moan of disappointment.

"Fellas." Walter leaned against the door. "Monroe isn't in today. Took the train to New York while you all were all measuring your dicks."

"Let us look for ourselves then!" Marshall shouted with a twitch.

"Just go home, Marshall. No one needs to dispense justice for a note written by a coward."

Marshall rushed Walter. He took him by the shirt collar and tossed him aside. His foot destroyed the front door in a single kick. The mob rushed in behind him, breaking any window in their wake. Walter was kicked as he lay on the ground. He tasted the blood in his mouth as Deputy Peters pulled him away from the men flowing into the house. They were the deluge of vengeance sent by the victims whose cries were not heard.

Walter saw the fire start in the bedroom. Marshall probably saw the leftover booze bottles and lit them with gusto. Walter watched the mob destroy the house he built with his friend. The house most of these men were paid to build when they were starting out. So many contractors came to Walter for work in the town. Now they all kicked him and spit on him as they rushed out carrying whatever item wasn't already shipped to New York. Anything of less value was thrown out the windows onto the lawn. Most of it shattered as it touched down.

Deputy Peters lost all control but managed to pull Walter across the street as the neighborhood came out of their homes to watch the flames. The mob hollered with laughter, leaving Marshall to the side of the road, holding the war medal belonging to Monroe. He was closer to the flames than anyone else, but no one feared for his safety. Marshall made sure it burnt to the ground.

Henry Twickens, a second grade teacher, approached Marshall with trepidation. The sweat pouring down his face matched that of Marshall's perspiration so near the fire.

"He had a cabin," Henry said, holding his hand to his face. The flames were too much for him to stand.

Marshall turned his head; the heat had created a rash on his face. "Then what are we doing here?"

* * *

Blood ran down my head, forming a puddle on the ground. The bandage Brother Phillip wrapped around my wound was seeping, and I drifted in and out of consciousness. The rope around my wrists cut into my flesh, and the burn from the fibers twisted against exposed bone kept me in agony. Brother Phillip had cut my skin against the ropes, keeping the pain intense. The worst part of all was that I could still feel the knife in my sock. It pissed me off that I never got a chance to use it.

The door of the cabin burst open, and Monroe rushed to me. In the process, he hit the table displaying his daughter's gifts and knocked them over, crushing the wrapped porcelain dolls with his feet. I wanted to shout, but couldn't.

"Steven! Come on, boy, wake up!" I could feel him slap me on the face, trying to get some sign of life.

"I wouldn't do that. The moment he wakes I'll kill him. The last thing I need is a boy shouting for his parents to the quiet of a summer evening."

Monroe was focused on me when Brother Phillip kicked him in the back. When he hit the floor, Brother Phillip didn't waste time. He kicked him in the ribs, the face, and the stomach. Monroe gasped for air.

"I've been rushed into this, Monroe, and I don't like that. This was supposed to be a year-long stay. I like this part of the country, and you two have really made it hard for me to enjoy it."

Monroe was inching toward my feet. He had noticed the knife protruding from my sock. Brother Phillip grabbed his hair and pulled him away.

"Put your hand on the table!" Brother Phillip screamed in Monroe's face as he dragged him over the broken porcelain pieces. Monroe refused to move even when Brother Phillip produced a knife from his belt. "Put your fucking hand on the table or I kill Steven and rape him."

Monroe's hand was shaking as he placed it on the table, fingers spread out.

"Good." Brother Phillip said with a grin. He jammed the blade down into Monroe's hand, connecting his flesh with the wood.

Monroe screamed loudly, making Brother Phillip even more angry. He took Monroe's deformed head by the hair and slammed it into the edge of the table.

"People need to understand that when a man has a duty to perform, they should just let him do it." He opened a cupboard drawer, removing another large knife. He traced a line with the tip along my stomach. "This is the intestinal tract, Monroe. I could cut into it and let them hang out for hours before he died. You ever see the inside of a human being? I'm sure you have on the Front. Nothing more fascinating than God's creation in the moonlight."

A rifle with a bayonet attached hung over the front door, catching Monroe's attention. He tried pulling the blade out of his hand, but it was too deep in the wood. Nothing was in reach around him to attack Brother Phillip. Tears filled his eyes and frustration started to get the better of him, until it appeared that he remembered the knife in my sock. Brother Phillip was checking for the mob from the window, back to both of us, giving Monroe time to pull the knife from the wood.

His gnashed teeth almost shattered as he strained every muscle to keep quiet while the pain rushed through him. It loosened enough to free him, and blood flowed from the wound. Reaching with his other hand for the concealed knife, he pulled it from my sock and flipped it open, lunging toward Brother Phillip's legs.

Connecting, they both hit the ground hard, forcing Brother Phillip to drop his knife. Monroe stabbed Phillip's armpit, making him scream louder than any of his victims ever did. Twisting it in deep, Monroe felt warm blood wash over his hand. Phillip managed to break free from the embrace, pushed Monroe's head into the wall, and brought him to his knees. Before Phillip could reach for the bayonet, Monroe stuck two fingers into the fresh wound he just created. Phillip screamed and grabbed Monroe by the throat. But Monroe wasted no time and used his head to bust Brother Phillip's nose. Blood shot out everywhere and forced Phillip to bring a quicker end to Monroe's life. He pulled out Reverend Thomas' gun from his waistband and fired a shot into Monroe's stomach. He took it at close range, then fell onto Phillip, sending them crashing through the front windows of the cabin.

* * *

The men landed on the front deck with a thud, and broken glass stabbed their palms and face as they rolled off each other. Monroe was sticky with blood as he held his stomach wound closed. He began to crawl down the steps toward an axe embedded in a tree stump. Brother Phillip's arm had a compound fracture. Using the rail as leverage, he yanked himself up with his good arm and limped toward Monroe as he crawled to the axe.

This display filled Brother Phillip with a glee befitting a child on his birthday. His laughter took his mind off the pain stemming from his break. Blood seeped through Monroe's shirt, slowing his crawl to the axe. Brother Phillip casually walked alongside the crawling Monroe. Brother Phillip gave a stifled giggle as Monroe's bloody hand kept slipping, preventing a grip on the axe handle. Brother Phillip pushed Monroe's hand away like a child playing with a weak cat.

"No more hope for this little creature. No more glimmer of light at the end of the tunnel. Only me, laughing at a bold attempt. I need to thank you. This makes me look better. The town will see my blood and embrace me like Christ on the fucking cross."

Monroe rolled over to face the full moon above. The night sky was brilliant, and the stars were clearly visible, displaying Orion's belt and the Big Dipper. On any other night he wouldn't have noticed.

With his good arm, Brother Phillip took the axe and tossed it into the forest. He left Monroe on the ground and headed back to the cabin. "Just lie there and bleed. They'll be here shortly to string you up for all the bad things you did."

A large stone with jagged edges was buried in the mud next to Monroe. The clear night allowed Monroe to see it sticking out of the ground. With his good hand, he lifted it up and stood tall to use all six feet of his bulky frame and fall on Brother Phillip, bringing the stone down on his spine. A crack erupted through the night air as the two men fell hard onto the wet ground. Monroe flipped Brother Phillip around and looked in his eyes as they went wide. Monroe slammed the stone deep into his face, breaking all his upper teeth in one strike. Brother Phillip's gargled last words were inaudible as teeth and blood shot out of his mouth. Another hit with the stone broke his lower jaw along with his collarbone. Another strike popped out his eyeball and another strike collapsed his forehead. The last strike popped his scalp, exposing brain tissue.

Monroe dropped the bloody stone next to a small stream that cascaded down the hill. Brother Phillip's blood mixed with the dirty water that rolled toward the approaching mob. He rose from the murdered man and headed for the cabin. "Just lie there and bleed." Monroe spat on Phillip's twitching body.

* * *

I was in and out of consciousness when Monroe came through the door looking battered. Blood soaked through his shirt, and mud covered most of his clothes as he knelt before me. I was still tied to the chair. After he cut me loose, I slumped into his arms. With his last ounce of strength, he laid me on the couch and put his deformed and bleeding face on my chest.

"End of the road, boy." He coughed up blood as the pain shot through his body at lightning speed. Monroe heard the sound of an approaching group coming up the hill. He had a few moments left. He thought about running, but when he stood up, the pain from his wound rippled through his body. He knew with a wound like this he had two hours left. Monroe sat back down next to me. I could feel him holding my hand. I wished I could speak, but I couldn't.

"I saw her once more when I was back home." He coughed up more blood and then continued. "Mercedes, my daughter. Playing in the window I sat at, to read to her when she was an infant. There she stood looking down on me, a monster with a bag over its head. I had frightened her away. I recoiled when she ran. I felt the guilt and the loss of all I had worked for. I lost her then. Lost everything. Every attempt to write her, all my hope in seeing her. I needed to just let her go. I couldn't let either of them go... My Elizabeth... I never got to write this down in my memoirs. I thought there was time for me to tell her myself. But looks like you've got to do it for me now." He trailed off as he held his stomach wound and felt the warm, dark blood leave his pierced liver. "Tell her about me, boy. I need you to tell her about me. Tell her, please." He leaned against me and kissed my forehead. "I love you, like I loved her. Remember me too."

"Monroe..."

"Promise me, boy."

"I promise..."

* * *

They stood before the body of Brother Phillip aghast and looked up at Monroe standing on the porch. He stood high, not showing

★ 228 ★

an inch of fear, which sent chills through the mob. All except for Marshall, who held the noose in his hands.

"Grab him," Marshall commanded.

They did it with brute force, throwing him down next to Brother Phillip's corpse. Marshall put the noose around his neck and pulled him up. Monroe was led to the White Lady Tree, and they hung him there. He never said anything; he didn't even scream out. He kept it in as they forced him onto the upturned apple box. Only his eyes burned with rage. It was enough to fill all those present with the sudden realization that this was no killer. Just a man with a mangled face, a perfect image of evil to a group of simpletons, led by unanswered questions no one bothered to ask. One by one, they walked away from the swinging body. In the years to come, I heard different accounts of what happened, but all of them ended the same: Monroe died, and Marshall was the last to leave.

Walter and my father raced to my aid shortly after the mob had taken Monroe. Walter went to my father first after the mob dispersed from Monroe's house. In a rushed attempt at explaining the situation, Walter had to be blunt. He told my father I was in danger, that I might even be dead already. My father told me, years later, that the run to Sunset Hill was eternal. His head was filled with images of my dead body, defiled and robbed of innocence. However, when he arrived, he saw me battered and bleeding, but pure.

"Steven, come on, we've got to get you home." My father lifted me up, his tears falling on my face like soft rain. It was the first time I ever saw him cry.

"Monroe... We need to help Monroe..." I was barely able to speak. I saw Brother Phillip's body on the cold dirt as my father carried me off, and satisfaction rolled through me so heavily that I forgot the taste of blood in my mouth.

"We can't help him. It's too late," my father told me before I passed out again.

Walter made sure my father found me, then went to the White Lady Tree. The mob had gone, as had Marshall. Walter cried coming upon the dead man who was his friend. Walter cut him down and buried him, knowing that a proper funeral was not in the cards. In the years to come, his grave would be vandalized every Halloween and August 23rd, the anniversary of his punishment. Walter wouldn't be around to see it though. As soon as Monroe was buried he left, handing my father a bundle of papers wrapped in wax paper and tied with a red string. It was for me. I never opened it. I put it under my bed next to my cigar box to keep it safe. Walter never contacted me again. He just disappeared from our lives despite the fact that we shared only good memories. To a man like Walter, new beginnings were in order to forget the past. He was like the town in an odd way, never able to grasp what really happened. He just ignored it and buried it deep down inside like the veteran he was. Walter was not a man to dwell on anything remotely philosophical, so he was forced into the realm of denial. Years later, my father ran into Walter and asked him how he was doing. Walter ignored him and kept walking down the street, as if he never saw him. My father didn't chase after him. He just let him go.

Days went by before I finally woke up fully. My physical wounds had healed. Everyone in town was talking about me, and all of them swore Monroe had his way with me before the chance came to kill me. It didn't matter that I repeatedly told Sheriff Tate the full story when he came to my bedside twice a week during my recovery. Tate listened to every detail and found evidence to corroborate my story. He even went so far as to connect the church ink type with the ink found in the letter. So many townies couldn't believe Tate's findings, and any evidence pointing at Brother Phillip gathered no support. Lies made far juicier gossip. Truth be told, it was a small town unwilling to admit they had been fooled. It would have made them all accomplices if they told the truth, so instead, they hid behind a lie created by hearsay and a finely typed note.

Brother Phillip's body was laid to rest in the church cemetery with the most expensive tombstone the town could buy, along with a memorial brick placed in the church wall. It read: *GOD'S CHOSEN BEACON, BROTHER PHILLIP, 1928.* Any time someone mentioned his name in church service, my family left. By the third straight month of leaving service early, we were asked not to return.

Reverend Thomas and his wife's bodies were found three months later, rotting at the bottom of a steep fissure in the most remote area of Sunset Hill. Their deaths were chalked up to Monroe and his killing spree. By the end of 1929, the murders were forgotten completely, but Monroe's legend grew on and on and spread to the towns around us. They called him "The Monster Monroe," a circus freak hung for the murder of two boys, a brother of the church, a minister and his wife. Eventually it would be ten children and a woman, then twenty children that he ate. Finally, he was forgotten altogether. His legend merged with the original White Lady story. Now, most say Monroe's ghost roams the hills during a full moon to look for children roaming in the forest at night. He'd cast an eerie white glow while wearing an onion bag over his deformed face.

Chapter 24

T he attic grew cold as I finished reading the memoirs. It had been two hours. A life read in two hours. I collected the pages and tied them together one last time. A leather satchel stood behind the trunk, I figured no one would miss it. I placed the pages with utmost reverence into the satchel and locked it. The memories of those days erupted in me and were silenced again. My past was over.

The nightmares ended.

When I told my mother about my enlistment, she cried. She laughed too. She knew I would do something foolish like that, because all boys are foolish when bravery is needed. My father shook my hand, then pulled me in for a hug. I saw him cry a second time in my life. Katie rolled her eyes, but I could see tears. My sister was progressive; she was preparing to work as the men were heading out. She told me to come back alive or not come back at all. She had an odd sense of humor.

I prayed that I would survive to see them again. I prayed that Monroe had saved me for a reason. I prayed it wasn't to die in Italy, Africa, the Pacific, or Berlin. I prayed because I had no idea what else to do. Basic training was in six weeks. I was running out of time.

Then like the nightmares, a name reappeared in my head.
Walter.

Walter had retired to Delaware, where he was born. My father was able to remember where he saw him, giving me a trajectory to jump from. He was twenty minutes from the edge of town. His name was in the phone book. I just hoped the old son of a bitch had a telephone.

Walter had aged. Hell, he was near 68 when I saw him sitting at the bar stool. He smiled at me as I approached. His hands were crippled with arthritis, the reward of years of manual labor. His limp made him look even more frail, and his kidneys flared with a sudden sting due to his developing stones, forcing him to wince and recoil his hand in mid-shake.

"Shit. I never thought it would hurt that bad." Walter took a shot of his cranberry juice in a whiskey glass. "Christ, that's even worse."

"I didn't think I would see you. Ever, for that matter."

"Years go by and you look at your own reflection and realize mortality isn't just a word. It is a fucking run-on sentence with a period. The period being death."

"I understood the point of the period." I smiled, helping him back to the stool.

"You look like a man ready to run off."

"I enlisted."

"I realize all men have to this time around. But it's still war. You still might be dead. You'll still lose friends. You'll still bring back unholy images, and you will see plenty. I went for Monroe, because I knew I could protect him. But I was wrong, wasn't I? Couldn't do shit for him then, couldn't do shit for him when they strung him up. But I sure as hell can do something now." Walter slid me a piece of paper. His crude writing produced an address.

"Mercedes?"

"Mercedes. You weren't lying when you said you had the pages?" Walter asked with fear in his voice.

"I have them. All of it."

"Then it wasn't for nothing. I never understood why he did that. Typing up his life for no one."

"It was never for no one," I said with a pang of guilt because it took me nearly twenty years to remember Monroe. I was glad he wrote the memoirs. I got to hear his voice again. I had a way to reflect on my life, which could end in six months.

"He hired the Pinkertons to find her, back in '24. I thought it was a waste of money. But they found them. He sent telegrams every other month, for a while. Elizabeth sent only one response. Stop."

"Did she ever find out what happened?"

"Yes. I told her. I also told her he died saving you. It gave her some solace. But that time together was a long-past memory. I doubt she reflected like Monroe. You'll learn that women can bury things better. Move on faster. Men are just fools."

"She's in California," I said out loud, reading the note. A long way to travel for someone with no money.

"Where do you ship off to train?"

"Louisiana. Then back up to New York Harbor."

Walter put a wad of cash onto the bar. "This should be enough for a round-trip ticket. And a little extra for you."

"I can't take that, Walter."

"He was my only friend." Walter drank his cranberry juice. "And I should be seeing him soon." Walter slapped my back and walked out, the money still there. I never saw him again.

My time was growing shorter. Finding Mercedes was taking longer than I hoped. Basic training came up fast. I had sent a letter to the address Walter provided, but hadn't heard back in weeks. If three more weeks were to pass I may never be able to live up to my promise. We were heading for Africa after basic. Most of the men I was with were young. Hell, younger than me, but they still had wives and girls they were leaving behind. Some had kids. Others were just trying to get away; things at home were worthless, and this seemed to be the only way out. I could feel time slipping. Every mail call I ached with hope. But Mercedes never sent word.

Monroe's memoirs were in my trunk at the base. Wrapped tight in wax paper. I hadn't read them since the day in the attic. I added to them as much as I could. Allowing Mercedes a better idea of what happened. She had to know he saved my life. She had to know what I saw. That the monster was a man. That he had a life even after his real one was gone. No one questioned my constant writing in notebooks. Everyone was writing to someone. And it was best left unspoken what all of us were leaving behind. Men can't face death knowing there is something better waiting around the corner. We would all turn and run.

It all changed the night before shore leave. Mercedes had finally replied to my letters. I had simply asked her for her address so that these pages could be mailed. I figured it was the only way to deliver them. But in her letter, she was insistent that we meet. She wanted to see me. She had to see if I was telling the truth. It was my eyes, she wrote, my eyes would be the deciding factor on whether or not to know her real father. She was on her way from California before she sent the letter. I saw her two days later.

Mercedes was beautiful. I was taken aback by her looks. She had brown eyes, a crooked nose that added to her exotic face, and raven hair. She was bronze, tanned from the West Coast sun, but not brown shoe leather. Her eyes were narrowed as she was looking for me. Most of the men at the train station were in uniform. I was no different. She locked eyes with me for a moment and gave a slight smile but retreated quickly when I looked back. Then I waved.

"Steven?" Mercedes asked, cautiously approaching as the hordes of people seemed to move out of her way out of sheer awe. She had a walk to her that illustrated confidence. She was a woman not mired in beauty but strength. It made her all the more sensual, all the more beautiful.

"Mercedes?" The smile breaking over her lips kept me looking away out of sheer fear that if she saw me sweating, she would flee.

"You can relax now. I am here." She laughed a little, and tapped my uniform with her bag. "Taking off too? All the good-looking men are. We're going to be left with the lepers and cowards. You going to buy me a drink?"

She flipped through the pages, her eyes tearing as she scanned all his words, all his handwritten notes, the tobacco-stained spots, the dried streaks where his tears fell. Mercedes smiled at me. Again, it made me uneasy. I didn't want to remember a smile like that where I was going.

"My mother, she told me about him a few years ago. My step-father, he was a good man, but cold to me. I knew I was never his. My brothers and sisters were always treated with more affection. I always thought it was my fault. But, my mother would always say, *You're my daughter, my love is enough.* And it was."

"He saved my life. I wrote about it, towards the back, there. I have too many pages written in my horrible chicken scratch."

"It's legible. My mother never told me what happened to him. But I figured it was too horrible to pry from her. I always left it alone. She did love him. I could tell when she spoke about him. The first love is never forgotten. Even if it goes to hell." Mercedes lit up a smoke. She grabbed my hand, causing me to blush horribly.

"He never stopped loving you or your mother. He couldn't let go."

"Men are different about love. They can say and do horrible things, yet will cry just the same when they're alone. They'll break up a good thing, only to pine for it rather than apologize. My mother was brave. Not many women leave. What made it easier for her was his deformity. But they fell out of love long before he left."

"He could be difficult."

"All men are." Mercedes smiled again, keeping her hand enclosed with mine.

"I wasn't expecting you." I said it with confidence, which surprised me.

"Were you expecting some old maid? I'm only twenty-six. Not married, granted, but too much life to live to settle down just yet. And with all the men taking off, what is a single girl to do?"

"Work."

"Of course. Now we can work like men. But when you get back, we'll be back in the yard stringing up laundry and cooking dinner. You're going to have another war at home when this is all over."

"I don't have to worry about that. I'm not married. I can deal with the new woman when I come back." I said *when,* not *if.* She was making me hope I would survive. I wanted to know her beyond this train station.

"Always say when."

"What?"

"Most men in your case would say *if,* not *when.* Men go to war to fight. In fighting people die. It's just the truth of it. But, I believe, if you say *when,* you fight to live harder. A man won't give up easily if there is something waiting for him on the other side."

"Hope."

"Wait and hope. The two greatest words in all of language."

"*The Count of Monte Cristo.*"

"I always loved that last line. I don't know why I liked that book so much. It's for boys. Everyone waits and hopes for something better. *Someone* better, I should say. I never met anyone who made me believe that those two words could mean anything."

"Monroe did. Your mother and you. I guess he was right to have that hope. Because here we are. What he wrote for you in your hands."

"What are you doing tonight?"

"This was my shore leave. I missed the bus to the dance."

"There's a carnival up the road, heard some kids talk about it on the train. Let's go." She pulled me out of the chair; we were closer together now. Face to face.

"You want to go up the road. To a carnival. With me?"

"Like I said, all the handsome ones are taking off. I need to get at least one of you guys to show me a good time before you send me back to doing laundry."

I lived life in that day. A single moment of time locked in my heart. We laughed. We kissed. We made love. All of this because of typed pages wrapped in wax paper. All of this due to one man, long dead from injustice.

Monroe.

I hope he is smiling.

I hope he saved my life to be with her.

I hope this war ends soon.

I hope I don't die without seeing her again.

I hope she waits for me if I live.

It's all we have, isn't it? We have to wait and hope to make life worth living. And in that fear, there is a light. In the oddest of ways, all the patience and all the hope make do. The promises are kept. The connections delivered. Love achieved. I just wondered if the fates liked to be ironic. Monroe was a good case for that. But whatever happened, I would be thankful for what I was able to have. And I would wait and hope it gets better.

www.ingramcontent.com/pod-product-compliance
Lightning Source LLC
Chambersburg PA
CBHW031227020726
47499CB00002B/668